A New Chapt
Bo

Kiley Dunbar is a Scot living over the border in Northern England where she teaches English and creative writing, devours romance novels, fusses over Amos the Bedlington Terrier, and loves two little Dunbars. She thinks making imaginary people find happiness and fall in hopelessly in love has to be the best job in the world.

Also by Kiley Dunbar

Christmas at Frozen Falls
The Gingerbread Christmas Village

Kelsey Anderson

One Summer's Night
One Winter's Night

Port Willow Bay

Summer at the Highland Coral Beach
Matchmaking at Port Willow

The Borrow a Bookshop

The Borrow a Bookshop Holiday
Christmas at the Borrow a Bookshop
Something New at the Borrow a Bookshop
Love Letters at the Borrow a Bookshop
A New Chapter at the Borrow a Bookshop

KILEY DUNBAR

A New Chapter
at the
Borrow *a*
Bookshop

hera

First published in the United Kingdom in 2025 by

Hera Books
Unit 9 (Canelo), 5th Floor
Cargo Works, 1–2 Hatfields
London SE1 9PG
United Kingdom

A CIP catalogue record for this book is available from the British Library.

Print ISBN 978 1 80436 465 9
Ebook ISBN 978 1 80436 464 2

Look for more great books at www.herabooks.com

Printed and bound in Great Britain by Clays Ltd, Elcograf S.p.A.

This book is for all the librarians

with love, gratitude and solidarity

Advertisement: A Novel Holiday Idea

Borrow-A-Bookshop invites you to live out your dreams of running your very own bookshop in a historic Devonshire harbour village… for a fortnight.

Spend your days talking about books with customers in your own charming bookshop and serving up delicious food in your cosy cafe nook. Get to know our wonderful volunteers (all locals), always ready to offer a helping hand.

After shutting up shop, climb the spiral staircase to your bedroom with picture window seat and settle down to admire the Atlantic views. When your holiday's over, simply hand the keys to the next holidaymaker-bookseller.

Request your booking early. Currently, there is a thirty-two-month waiting list.

Includes full use of cafe kitchen, courtyard seating, one double bedroom and bathroom upstairs, one single bedroom off the shop floor.

All bookshop and cafe takings retained by the Borrow-A-Bookshop Community Charity treasurer, Ms Jude Crawley, M.A.

Apply by email.

£400 charge per let for fourteen days.

Prologue

Evidence of the wildest party of the summer (if not in Wales's entire student history) was strewn everywhere. Champagne corks, crushed beer cans and cigarette ends dotted the lawns, while abandoned shoes, Claire's Accessories plastic tiaras and the ragged remains of feather boas decorated the bushes. The *CONGRATULATIONS CLASS OF 2016* banner hung squint over the doors of the halls of residence. Apart from the summer dawn sounds of birdsong, everything was silent. Harri Griffiths and Annie Luna were the only two people awake in the whole world.

At least, that's how it felt to Harri as they both sagged against the cabinet doors on the kitchen's vinyl floor, the onset of the most epic hangover of their lives still hours away. The blinding headache and queasiness would probably make their presence felt around about the time Annie was boarding her flight home.

For now, they were enjoying the boozy, sleepy stillness of the morning, but reality was dawning. Very soon Harri, in his soft Valley's accent, would be saying *wela'i di wedyn* to his closest friend since freshers' week. He wouldn't be able to say the word 'goodbye' in any language. That would feel far too final.

They'd tried not to think about this day all through their exams and their summer break spent bookselling together in Waterstones, but now that the sun was coming up on their last morning at Aberystwyth Uni (or 'Aber', as everyone called it) the sinking heaviness pressed hard on his chest.

Annie on the other hand, still in her graduation ball red dress, and swigging from a bottle of Co-op cava, knocked her booted feet together absently, looking like she could happily carry on the party.

At pre-drinks the day before, he'd watched her pinning those dirty-blonde plaits round her head in a coronet like any number of the Welsh medieval queens they'd encountered during their literature degree. Harri had held the pins for her as she worked. In the hours that followed, long strands had worked loose and were now hanging down around her face.

A prairie rose. That's what she'd always jokingly labelled herself, and it suited her perfectly. She was tough and wild, beautiful and intimidating like the Texan landscape she came from.

She'd often described to him – with eyes half closed and in the drawling voice she reserved for reminiscing about home – how her parents grew a garden where the desert met the Southern plains and where monster cacti reached for the sky alongside orchids and blousy English tea roses.

Harri realised he must have sighed out loud as Annie snapped her head towards him.

'What?' she asked, kicking her boot against his bare foot.

She'd opted for boots over heels for her walk across the graduation stage. Harri reckoned she'd probably never owned a pair of heels, but he'd never bet on it. Annie was the master of surprise, and he knew better than to make assumptions about her.

'What?' he echoed, giving her foot a softer nudge back.

'You've got that "miles away" look again.'

Harri sniffed a soft laugh. 'I was picturing you back in your mum and dad's garden, as it happens.'

Annie hugged the bottle. The cava must be horribly warm by now.

'*Hmm*,' she murmured, thinking, drawing her legs beneath her.

Mirroring her, Harri sat upright. 'Aren't you looking forward to seeing them?'

Annie's parents had flown over to visit their daughter that one time back in second year – around about the time the inseparable friends were slogging away in the big bookstore to pay their rent while everyone else had gone home for the summer break. Harri had only stayed in Aber to keep Annie company.

He thought back to that awkward meeting, when he'd smiled and reached out a hand, saying, 'Welcome to Aber, Mr Luna.'

Annie's father had stared him down, telling him it was 'Mr Luna, *sir*' like they were in the military (or the 1950s). A stickler for good manners, he'd nevertheless chosen not to shake Harri's outstretched hand. At the time, Harri had concluded Mr Luna was as chilly as the dark side of the moon and ultra-protective of his only child. Like Annie, Harri also had no siblings but his own dad hadn't shown anything like the same paternal protectiveness. Far from it, unfortunately.

Annie had been uncharacteristically quiet during those introductions, and for the whole duration of her parents' visit Harri had kept his distance at Annie's apologetic insistence. Harri would at least have expected her to laugh and gently correct her father's coldness, wrapping her old man around her finger like she could everyone she met;

instead she'd wilted in their presence, the only time he'd ever seen anything like that happen to Annie. It had only made her more relatable and drawn him closer to her.

'I'm hurtin' to see Mom again,' Annie was saying now. 'And it's gonna be hot and dry like you can't imagine.' Annie was smiling at the thought. It looked like genuine longing and excitement. Maybe things had thawed between her and Mr Luna too? He hoped so.

After throwing a quick glance at Harri, Annie added, 'And I'll Skype you, soon as I get there. And every other day after that.'

'Oh, only every *other* day, is it? I see how it is,' he tried to joke.

Silence fell again. Smiles faded. Annie looked around at the mess and the scattered sleeping bodies in their kitchen-lounge. The room appeared fuzzy to Harri since he'd taken his contacts out after they'd all stumbled home.

He guessed Annie was doing the same thing he was – running their 'highlights' reel in her memory – remembering all the pre-drinks and parties, all the stir-fries and burned toast, the movie nights and cramming sessions that had taken place here.

She wasn't likely to cry. She could be as serene as the desert night in moments like this, preferring to smile and dazzle away any pesky tears. But Harri? He was seconds away from bawling.

Annie exaggerated a wistful sigh and a stretch and looked to the window where the sun had been streaming in for a while now.

A little flicker of panic ignited in Harri. Were they about to start with the farewells? Maybe if he drew her into storytelling they could spin out their last morning just a little longer?

'How did you do it?' he said after a hard swallow.

Annie tipped her head.

'How'd you get the security guard to let us into the library last night?'

'Hah!' Her eyes lit up. 'I've been bringing Jim my mom's rocky road every Thanksgiving since I got here. He owed me.'

'You gave away your care package baking?'

'Totally worth it. Or it will be.' Annie waggled her light brows. Even in Welsh summers her cheeks grew freckled while her fair lashes and brows all but disappeared against her flushing skin. Harri always teased her about being secretly Welsh, and she always insisted Luna was hardly a Welsh surname.

Harri's name was Welsh through and through; the Welsh spelling of 'Harry' and the same surname as half his street in Neath, the market town where he'd grown up.

'Pity we won't be here to see everyone's reactions,' Harri said, still smiling but looking down at his hands clasped in his lap.

A sleepy groan from one of the flatmates set off a grumpy sound in another. Someone rolled over then all fell still again.

Just after two this morning, the five of them, Annie, Harri, Gregor, Ioan and Catherine, had crossed the bridge in the student village and watched from the bushes as Annie tapped on the window, summoning the library security guard. They'd watched on, giggling and shushing one another drunkenly, as she spoke with him, working her magic.

Jim had thrown his head back in a laugh and unlocked the turnstile. He'd been surprised when Annie motioned for the hidden gang to join her and they'd all spilled out onto the path, but he'd let them inside anyway telling them in his own American drawl to 'make it quick, five minutes max.'

Annie had saluted and told the group to 'roll out!'

Within minutes they'd scattered through the stacks, pulling out titles from the shelves, searching for any book with a full-face portrait on the cover and applying the googly eyes.

Only half an hour before, Annie had proudly presented her willing recruits with the sticky sheets, outlining the mission she'd been planning in secret for who knew how long.

It had been a professional hit. By the time the security guard let them out again, filing innocently into the dawn light, every biography from Aneurin Bevan to Waldo Williams, every serious study of Rembrandt, Vermeer and Shakespeare – anything with a face – was be-googled and carefully re-shelved for unsuspecting undergrads to stumble upon in the autumn, by which time the guilty occupants of flat 170 would be scattered across the face of the earth.

'Aber's not going to forget us any time soon,' Annie said as their smiles turned wistful.

'How could it?' Harri said, a new impulse of desperation blooming within him. He was going to have to say something, because if not now, moments before she put five thousand miles between them for Christ knows how long, then when? When would they next be together like this?

He'd tried to tell her how he felt umpteen times. The first time, when he simply fancied her like mad, way back in freshers' week at the foam party when they'd been slipping around on the dancefloor and his eyes were stinging with whatever the hell they put in that stuff, and his dazzling, exciting new acquaintance had been laughing raucously and gripping his bare arms with her slippery fingers, when there'd been so little space between them it had felt like they might be about to kiss. But then the lights had come up and there were blokes with mops sweeping the drunk first years off the floor and out into the night.

He'd tried again that first Valentine's Day when getting to know her better had only strengthened his interest in her, and he'd bought her those pathetic yellow roses in cellophane and she'd looked at them with unreadable tranquillity, saying, 'Yellow roses for friendship, right?' and he'd mentally kicked himself for being too slow to get to the supermarket before all the red ones sold out.

'Sure,' he'd said, shrugging the flowers off like they were little more than an afterthought while he'd picked up the ciders, and another big wedge lodged itself between them, even as their friendship took a giant leap forward.

They'd become devoted friends as their first year was drawing to an end, and so, by the time he finally plucked up the courage to confess that he liked her, 'no, a bit *more* than like, truth be told,' after an all-night study session that ended in them dozing against the headrest of his bed, most definitely too tired to even consider getting to their last nine o'clock lecture on Harold bloody Pinter, he had felt triumphant. But when he was done talking, his lips close against the top of her head, her arm resting across his stomach, all he'd got back was the soft sound of her breathing. She'd fallen asleep and missed the whole outpouring.

He'd been hit by frustration at first, and then relief that he hadn't spoiled things between them. After all, she'd never explicitly shown him she shared any of his heated feelings. There'd been moments where he'd suspected she had, but after closer analysis, he'd put it down to her friendly, bold Texan ways, and she was like that with everyone, pretty much.

It had never been the right time after that. Either she was seeing someone or she was in one of her swearing off dating phases (usually accompanied by her asking Harri to help her cut new bangs over the sink – he was *that* deep into the friend zone) and he'd started to take his bad luck as a sign that if they hadn't got it together by now, it was never going to happen.

By their second year, Annie's friendship, like the petals of the yellow roses she'd allowed to dry out and kept on the windowsill, had become a pure, perfect thing to him, far more precious than any risky student romance could ever have been.

But now they were graduates, both turned twenty-one. They would no longer be flatmates and study buddies or daring library raiders armed with googly-eye stickers. They were actual adults facing a whole new world and there was a possibility they could face it together – as well as a danger that things between them could dwindle away to nothing, what with them soon to be living an ocean apart.

'Heartburn?' came Annie's voice, cutting through his thoughts.

Harri snapped his palm away from his chest where he'd been rubbing at the ache inside.

'Nope, I'm good. Listen, Annwyl…' He shifted a little closer so their stirring flatmates couldn't possibly hear. 'You're leaving, and…'

Annie's eyes narrowed in concentration.

He always called her Annwyl when other people were out of earshot, and she'd never protested, assuming it was a Welsh form of Annie. Should he tell her now that it really meant 'my dear one', or rather, it meant so much more than that since the word was wrapped up in his pride for his Welsh heritage and his language? When he called her Annwyl it was a name somehow recalling hundreds of years of affection whispered between Welsh lovers. He really should stop using it.

Someone's alarm clock was going off in one of the flats around them. Harri cursed the paper-thin walls, and not for the first time.

Annie's eyes stayed fixed upon him. Her trademark smile was wavering a little.

'I don't know how to say this,' he began, with absolutely no idea what was going to come out of his mouth.

He watched her throat move softly as she swallowed.

He let words form, unsure where they were taking him, instinct taking over. 'You and me, we're special…'

Annie's head turned first.

There was a key in the door, shoes scuffing over the bristly mat, pizza menus and junk mail being scooped up, and all too suddenly, a figure in the kitchen with them.

'Paisley!' Annie said, staggering to her feet.

The woman was the same age as the flatmates, young and pretty. She was dressed for work in office gear and black sandals.

'God, is that the time?' Harri rubbed at his eyes and stood too, a little too quickly. Dizziness hit him and he steadied himself against the countertop.

'You stayed up all night?' Paisley asked, before turning to Annie. 'Aren't you supposed to be on your way to the airport?'

Annie took this as the dismissal it was. 'Yep. Taxi's coming in ten. I just need to grab my case.'

'You're going dressed like that?' Paisley said.

She'd never really warmed to Annie. And who could blame her? She was always there, stealing the limelight. But now the Texan was on her way out, there'd be nothing standing between her and Harri. They were, after all, boyfriend and girlfriend; had been all final year. Harri had dived in with both feet too. It had all been part of his making peace with the 'friend zone' thing.

'I'll change at the airport, or maybe I won't.' Annie shrugged and squeezed past the pair, heading for her bedroom, right next to Harri's.

'Aren't we getting coffee?' Paisley asked Harri. 'We're supposed to be job hunting, remember? If we're going to find positions close to each other.'

'Right.' Harri held a hand to the back of his neck. 'Of course. Sorry. I'll shower and we can go to the computer suite, see what's out there.'

His eyes travelled to Annie's door and the sound of trundling suitcase wheels. He wanted to howl like a wolf at the awful feelings inside him, but as Paisley stepped closer and drew his face down to hers with a finger at his chin, there was nothing he could do.

'*Eww*, morning breath!' she told him, but still lifted herself to kiss his lips.

'Sorry,' he said again. 'Last night got a bit out of hand.'

'And not for the first time,' Paisley said, softly scolding. 'It was a shame I had to work, but...' she took both his hands in hers, 'now we've graduated, there's nothing getting in our way.'

Harri knew perfectly well what his girlfriend was getting at, and the guilt stabbed at him. Annie emerged from her room in a faded denim jacket over her party dress, shouldering tote bags full of books.

Paisley went on, a little louder now. 'We have our whole lives ahead of us to be together, go on adventures, get our own place...'

'I'm heading out, then,' Annie interrupted.

Paisley was still gripping his hands. Was this how they were supposed to part after the most extraordinary three years of friendship? It was too awful.

Annie stepped nearer, struggling under the weight of her bags. Paisley had no choice but to drop Harri's hands because Annie was beaming her biggest smile at him, inches away.

'I'll be seeing you, my friend,' she said, holding out her arms.

Harri felt Paisley observing their hug, knowing it was going on too long for her liking. The book totes jutted into his sides but he didn't mind. He could have sworn he felt Annie's chest heave in a sob as they clung together, but when she stepped back, she was grinning the same as always.

He watched as Annie pulled the surprised Paisley in for a hug too, the first the women had ever shared. 'Take good care of him, okay?' Annie said, her voice like soft music to Harri's ears.

'I'll come see you when I've enough money saved,' he told her weakly.

'Me too,' Annie countered. 'I'll be on the first flight I can afford.'

'And remember, Annwy...' He stopped himself. '*Annie*. We've got our bookshop holiday to look forward to, if we ever get to the top of the waiting list.'

'Like I'd miss that.' Annie beamed, but seeing Paisley's face fall, she quickly hid her excitement. 'I should...' she hiked a thumb towards the doorway behind her.

Then weirdly, horribly, that's how it ended, with Annie shouldering her belongings and wheeling her cases away, her boots clomping across the floor.

Impossibly, the door clicked shut on the latch behind her and she was gone, leaving Harri with a sliver of himself missing.

Meanwhile Paisley breezily outlined their plans for the day and he really did try to force himself to listen as she reeled it off; packing, letting agents, the job centre, dinner at her family's home in Port Talbot when she'd finished her shift at the call centre, and then an early night...

He was nodding and wondering if he was managing to smile convincingly. He liked Paisley very much; he wouldn't have agreed to go out with her in the first place if he didn't. She was smart and caring, she knew what she wanted and was going to achieve it all, and he'd been drawn to her certainty and confidence. Even his dad loved her. Plus, she really was the prettiest girl in Wales, and she'd liked him right from the day they met. The perfect girlfriend.

He felt himself softening again, letting her talk him round, hoping she couldn't feel the awful tug within him that made him want to run after Annie's taxi.

The torn-in-two feeling would probably go away soon, and he'd be left in the glow of Paisley's warmth and good-ness. He'd eat at her parents' table tonight and they'd make plans for the rest of the summer and it would all be okay. He had to let Annie go and this was the next logical step.

Paisley kept talking as she gathered abandoned bottles and cans, pouring the dregs down the sink. The stretching, eye-rubbing, grunting figures under blankets and coats on the sofas and floor protested about keeping it down please, there were people dying in here.

Harri made his way into his bedroom, unbuttoning last night's tuxedo shirt that'd need to go back to the rental place by five.

Against the wall leaned the flattened cardboard boxes that would soon contain the last remnants of his student life in Aber.

Something caught his eye and he made his way to the stack of books on his bedside table where he found, upon closer inspection, every cover adorned with googly-eye stickers. He smiled at first, until the weird pain welled up again.

'What was she on about, anyway?' Paisley said suddenly from the doorway, making him jolt round, schooling his features into a look of placidity.

'Huh?'

'Something about a bookshop holiday? A waiting list?'

Harri knew she was trying to look unbothered. 'Oh, right, that,' he said with a coolness he didn't feel. 'It was just this thing we put our names down for ages ago.' By which he meant before he met Paisley. 'A working holiday kind of thing, down in Devon. It'll probably never happen.'

Paisley stared back, looking like a woman weighing up whether this was a potential threat of some kind. She cast her eyes into the now empty bedroom next to his and made her decision.

'Come on,' she said. 'Let's get some day-after-graduation pancakes before we start the job hunt. My treat.' She was already on the move, shooing groaning flatmates off the sofa so she could straighten the cushions.

'Okey-dokey,' he called back. 'I'm all yours,' and he made a silent promise to Paisley that this was true, and an even more solemn promise to himself that he'd take comfort in the fact that he had it all: a best friend in Annie Luna – even if she would be on the other side of the world pretty soon – and a loving, committed, super-smart girlfriend who he loved very much and had a future with right here in his beloved Wales. Given time to adjust to graduate life, he knew he'd come to believe it fully.

Chapter One

Clove Lore – eight years and seven months later

Devon, even in wintertime, is a mellow, bountiful county, a place where the dark water is alive with silver fishes, a place of sodden sands picked over by keen-eyed waders, a place of fern-dripping coves, mossy woodland and blustery promontories, no less beautiful in their austere winter livery. Come February, if you're lucky, the worst of the sea storms are over, the temperatures are sneaking towards double figures and the bulbs have pushed green shoots through spring-softening earth.

Folks up country say everything bursts back into life in the South West a good two weeks sooner than in their parts of the world, but the palm trees in the gardens are still wrapped in protective fleece, the greenhouses still require heating to spur on early seedlings, and every sleeping snail, spider and ladybird dare not rouse itself from its sequestered spot too soon because, even with the hedgerows awakening with birdsong, winter lingers on.

The chimneys all down the sloping village of Clove Lore still cough smoke right through February, and the tourists are only just beginning to think of spring minibreaks and rock-pooling in waterproofs. The dark still falls across the county as the school buses whisk kids home for dinner, and no one, but no one would dream of remarking how the light nights will soon be here for fear of tempting back the frosts or, worse, another terrifying flood, all too common at this time of year.

Harri had taken in the county with dull eyes as he made his way down towards the coast, passing shuttered arcades only open in the high season, giant plastic ice cream cones appended to roadside kiosks, signs pointlessly boasting, 'pick your own strawberries, June–August', and surf academy lock-ups which, come beach season, would be bustling from dawn to dusk with happy customers, salted and sun-bleached from the shore.

Thinking how this probably wasn't the *ideal* time for a seaside bookselling holiday, Harri stopped now in the middle of the fairy-lit, cobbled courtyard of the Borrow-A-Bookshop, flicking at his phone screen to find the bookings manager, Jude Crawley's, text with the keycode so he could get inside the darkened shop. It wasn't easy with his gloves on.

No messages from Paisley, he noted. It was simultaneously a sadness and a relief.

They'd never gone this long without talking. He hoped she was okay. He hoped she was beginning to forgive him.

Half-six in the evening on the first day of February, and the Devonshire sky was black. There was no point waiting out here. In the old days, Annie was always late. If she turned up at all.

Back at uni, Annie had been the kind of person who everyone hoped would come to their party, but nobody believed would actually turn up until she rolled in three hours late, bringing friends no one else knew, and she'd be the life and soul of the place, making everyone feel special and seen. But she'd also irritate a few and invoke jealousy in others, until she slipped out without saying anything, leaving everyone wondering why it suddenly felt like the party was over. Paisley put it down to rudeness; Annie making herself hard to pin down. Harri knew it was the result of being so in demand and having to spread herself thinly around her many friends. That, and the fact she was extroverted and she adored people, collected them, in fact.

He'd witnessed first-hand how she would become strangers' best friend on a night out, but the next day when they bumped into the same crowd on campus she'd struggle to remember their names. This turned some people off, while it made others her devoted followers.

Harri always thanked his stars he had something bigger than that with Annie. At least, he thought he had. Now they were about to see each other again for the first time in nearly a decade, he couldn't help worrying the magic they'd had was overhyped, all in his head. That's how Paisley had seen it, and she'd not held back letting him know.

'She was a user, babe. A here today, gone tomorrow kind of girl. If she was a real friend she'd have been here by now, wouldn't she?'

It was true, Annie had never come back to see him in Wales. She hadn't crossed the Atlantic at all since uni. Mind you, neither had he.

He'd lost touch with their other flatmates, Gregor, Ioan and Catherine, along the way, and hadn't made many new friends, other than his manager at work, and he wasn't strictly a friend. They only saw each other at the coffee shop.

For a long time it had just been Paisley and Harri, quietly taking care of each other and sticking to their routines of work, dinner, telly, turning in early, and

Toby Carvery Sundays with Paisley's two sisters and their husbands and kids.

Annie had orbited the pair of them from a distance, a comforting satellite presence for Harri, and his only enduring friendship outside of his relationship with Paisley.

All he knew for sure right now was that Annie's flight had left Houston on time yesterday. Then, ever since her last message, sent from the departure lounge, she'd been incommunicado.

She'd be fine, of course. Annie would be busy charming every person she encountered from Texas to Truro. He sniffed a laugh picturing this, and a plume of white vapour clouded the frigid air in front of him.

He should get inside. Yet, his feet seemed stuck to the cobbles at the foot of the bookshop steps.

He still knew her, right? Even though they hadn't actually met in the flesh in almost nine years? He should have tried to meet up before now, but how would that have worked?

Every time their place in the queue for the bookselling holiday had come up in the past, one or both of them had been stuck with work or study commitments. Then there'd been lockdowns and skyrocketing ticket prices to contend with. When it so happened they could both get away at the same time, it felt as though they'd pushed the friendly and accommodating Jowan's patience as far as they reasonably could. Jowan was the one who owned this whole borrowing a bookshop concept.

'Worst thing about February in Clove Lore is the cold,' Jowan had warned Harri when they spoke over the phone back in December when, due to a cancellation, the suggestion of a February escapade had first come up, 'and the dark, and the ice on the slope is trech'rous, and the shops are mostly closed over winter. Apart from that 'tis lovely.'

Harri had messaged Annie right away:

> The bookshop's ours from 1st February to the 15th. Are we doing this? What do I tell the guy?

There had followed one of Annie's characteristic two-day silences before she responded.

> Is Paisley joining?

He'd not waited two seconds before telling her she would be working. He'd held his breath for Annie's reply, which pinged back almost immediately.

> Do you reckon the Amarillo Westgate Mall sells thermal underwear?

Harri's heart had leapt with a relief he hadn't known he'd been waiting for, only for that relief to be struck through with panic moments later. He was going to have to tell Paisley that the bookselling holiday reunion really was happening this time.

It had not gone well.

In fact, he'd been sleeping on the sofa since Boxing Day when he'd finally had the courage to mention it, not having wanted to spoil Christmas for her, even though he'd been painfully aware of his nagging cowardice the whole time.

Now that he was here, staring at the sky-blue door of the Borrow-A-Bookshop, his feet frozen to the spot in the sheltered courtyard, he was realising Paisley had been right; he had no idea what he was letting himself in for and this was all very risky.

Even though he was proud of how well he and Annie had kept in touch over the years, two whole weeks of sleeping under the same roof, sharing meals, sharing a bathroom, living and working together twenty-four-seven could be their undoing. It was a lot to ask of their old acquaintance.

They'd Skyped when she first went back to Texas in 2016, not every other day like she'd promised, but once a week or thereabouts. Then, when Paisley had objected to surrendering those evenings to 'some girl on the other side of the world', they'd moved to regular messaging and exchanging occasional emails.

When work had inevitably taken over their lives, communication had reduced to holiday and birthday cards, the occasional meme or a quickly messaged update, usually sent when the time zones were against them and one of them was sleeping, so replies arrived feeling belated and their friendship out of sync.

Annie was a middle school library assistant these days while Harri had rebelled against the nine-to-five of the Port Talbot call centre (he hadn't racked up phenomenal amounts of student debt to sit in a cubicle under strip lights selling extended warranties *all* his life) and he'd gone back to uni for an English Masters. Yet he still didn't have the glittering career his dad might have hoped for him.

When he graduated the second time, Paisley told him she could get him back into his old job at the call centre, now that she was regional manager, but he'd have to interview like everyone else, and there was no guarantee he'd be the most suitable applicant.

Paisley hadn't understood what on earth he was thinking, sticking with his postgrad stopgap barista job in the coffee chain on the high street and she'd lectured him about how a bit of gratitude wouldn't go amiss.

He hadn't missed Paisley's lectures one bit since the break-up, when the touchy subject of the bookshop holiday had brought on another row and finally an ultimatum.

'If you really must run off to England for a reunion with an ex and leave me here to pay the bills on my own, then go!' she'd said, on the verge of tears, making him feel absolutely rotten.

'She's not my ex,' he'd protested. 'We were never together! I keep telling you. We're just friends. And it's only a fortnight. I'll be back before we even have time to miss each other.'

'*Will* you miss me?'

He'd faltered instead of answering right away, and that had been enough to bring on the crying fit and the plate throwing, followed by the silent treatment and the final, dreaded heart-to-heart where they'd faced the truth. He had a decision to make: he either stayed and they worked on their relationship or he ran off with *that Texan bint*. The choice was his.

Paisley had elected to take their bed, laying spare sheets out for Harri in the living room.

After five weeks of bad sleep, backache and icy-cold civility, he'd finally left his key on the kitchen table this morning, stepped out the door into the February frost, ready to catch a train to Cardiff, before a change at Bristol, and a delay at Barnstaple, before finally getting in a taxi for Clove Lore an hour ago.

He'd felt more sordid with every mile put between himself and Wales. Break-ups were supposed to be awful; goodness knows he'd had plenty of experience. Paisley had broken up with him before, many times, but it had only ever lasted a few hours at most and she'd reeled him back in, all apologies, blaming her hormones, making light of the argument when she'd picked over some small fault or other of Harri's. The last few years especially had been tumultuous ones, and now here he was in another country, barely able to process what was happening.

He had no girlfriend, no job, and no clue what the hell he was doing in Devon waiting for an old uni friend he wasn't even sure he'd get on with after all this time.

With a hazy vision circulating in his head of Annie Luna walking towards him out of the winter darkness and grappling him in a bearhug like she used to, he absently typed in the keycode and pushed open the bookshop door.

The dry, papery, chimney-soot scent of old bookshop reached his nostrils.

He hauled his cases up the stone steps, almost his entire life's belongings (far more than he needed for a holiday, but way too little to show for a life).

'Should have left all this stuff at Mam and Dad's or checked it at the station,' he complained to himself as he made the last few feet of his journey, the tiredness setting in.

Back in Cardiff, when he'd stood staring at the big lock boxes, he'd been prevented from unburdening himself of his belongings by the curious feeling that he needed them all. Not his best idea, he told himself, stepping through the door. He'd end up carting it all home to his parents' place in a fortnight's time. His mum had told him only yesterday that he'd always have his childhood bedroom waiting for him back in his beautiful, familiar Neath.

But now, here he was in a darkened shop, stamping the salt off his boots on the welcome mat, on the dream holiday he'd been waiting years for and it could only be a brief reprieve. Fourteen days of playing bookseller before facing the reality of his new, single barista life. Beyond the confines of the holiday there was nothing but a blank when he tried to imagine his future when before there'd been Paisley and all her certainty and her plans.

You can't grind coffee beans forever, he heard Paisley telling him now, as though he'd somehow conjured her up here in Devon. 'You should think of us and our future, like I do.' He'd heard her say it so often it played automatically in his brain like a voice memo he couldn't delete.

He shut the door sharply behind him, and its bell jangled above his head.

Standing still in the darkness, taking it all in, the brassy resonance faded away to silence.

At his feet sat the box of barista supplies he'd ordered days ago. His favourite coffee in compact bags of beans and blends, syrups, sugars, dusting spices and sauces, all addressed to him, care of Borrow-A-Bookshop. Just the idea of working with those familiar ingredients brought him a gentle sense of comfort, no matter what the disapproving spectral Paisley was telling him.

He hadn't realised how cold he'd been until he crouched and pulled the tape on the box, releasing the good, earthy aromas from his favourite artisan roastery.

The words on the small packages alone were enough to soothe him: Mysore, Monsooned Malabar, Brazilian Bourbon Santos.

The scent of coffee, books, sea salt, winter damp and the coal fire blended together. He breathed it all in with deepening satisfaction. The Borrow-A-Bookshop seemed to breathe too, waking from its winter's afternoon nap.

'Lights,' he said to himself in sudden awakening, like he'd downed a shot of espresso and kickstarted his brain. He couldn't crouch here all night, frozen like a crashed SatNav trying to reorientate itself.

The standby light from the till point and laptop guided him round the bulky cash desk to where a jumble of cables led to a floor lamp by the window. 'Bingo!'

The till area flooded with a soft orange glow.

'Okay, okay,' he nodded, taking in the spot where he'd be ringing up books and chatting with customers. His stomach turned loop-the-loop. Two tall stools behind the till reminded him Annie would soon be next to him there. He gulped hard and let his eyes roam towards the shadows where a fireplace blew a chilly draught from its spot beneath a cast iron spiral staircase, its black gloss shining.

He stooped to find the power socket on the wall and flicked both plugs on. Light filled the space beneath the stairs, revealing the children's book area where two patchwork beanbags slumped beside a green leather armchair.

Over the fireplace a sign read, 'Kids' Poetry Time with Austen Archer, Wednesdays, 4–4:30 p.m.'

He took this in, not knowing who this Austen Archer was, or how the whole volunteer-helpers thing was actually going to work, but he was glad the responsibility for this place didn't rest with just him and – if she showed up – Annie.

The book stacks loomed, a labyrinth of floor-to-ceiling shelving he'd have to familiarise himself with, but not before Annie arrived. She'd love leading the expedition.

He scanned the hand-painted signs at the head of each stack: *World Travel, Languages, Poetry, The House Beautiful, Gardening, Biography*, and there were others he couldn't quite make out from here, and over by the door, running along the far wall, there spread *General Fiction*.

He was hit by a vivid image of those long summer afternoons manning the Aber Waterstones with Annie. That was back before their manager realised that, combined, they were trouble and started scheduling them apart on the rota.

She'd say, 'Top three books about… snow?', or whatever it was she had in mind that day, and they'd deliberate and debate until they'd whittled down their lists.

'You must have read it for it to make the list,' she'd insist when Harri came up with niche titles or intimidatingly long works of European literature, and they'd bicker and laugh during stolen snatches of conversation while they crossed paths shelving and selling, tidying and stickering.

Annie had been a hit with the customers, of course. She was chatty and friendly, talking them into taking home all kinds of books they'd had zero intention of buying when they stepped inside. He'd be behind the till, keeping an eye on stock, signing people up for the loyalty card, and while both had worn the regulation black polos, Annie would style hers until it wasn't recognisable as uniform at all.

She'd singlehandedly increased the branch's sales by thirteen percent, purely because people dropped in to see her, hoping she'd be in, and she'd bewilder them into buying the absolute must-read of the month. She'd been in earnest too. Her enthusiasm for the latest books (combined with her sparkling eyes and American smile) set off a fervour in her customers. No staff get-together was complete without Annie being presented with yet another 'employee of the month' or sales target award.

Harri awoke from the memory with a start. If Annie Luna was really on her way, this place shouldn't be silent and lifeless when she turned up. He'd better get a move on.

Having never lit a coal fire, he wasn't confident he was doing it right (his miner great-uncles and the *Taid* who'd died before he'd formed any memories of him, would not have been impressed), but after making his way through half a box of matches and two firelighters he finally got a good, crackling blaze going in the grate.

Then he'd hooked up his phone to the shop's laptop and speakers, scrolling his Spotify playlists for something new that wouldn't leave Annie thinking his music tastes hadn't moved on in nine years (they hadn't, but she didn't need to know that; not when she'd been full of her Burning Man and Coachella exploits with her best girlfriend Cassidy, who went everywhere with her).

He'd gone for someone else's 'chilled bookshop' public playlist and its soft jazziness put him in the mood for wine, so he'd rummaged in his bag for the bottle of Côtes du Rhône he'd bought at the general store up at the top of Clove Lore village.

After locating two glasses in the little cafe kitchen just off the shop floor, he stood by the bookshop fire, unscrewing the cap, telling himself he'd only have the one glass to settle his nerves, which were crackling harder than the flames in the grate.

No sooner had the ruby liquid hit the bottom of his glass with a satisfying glug, the shop door burst open and there on the step stood a windblown Annie Luna, his Annwyl, in a long blanket coat and a ludicrously large felted hat, under which strands of her long hair hung wildly.

'I was gonna apologise for being late,' she said with a grin. 'But it looks like I got here right on time.'

Chapter Two

Old Friends

Harri could have sworn he was talking, welcoming her inside, being friendly and relaxed, but it was just possible that he was standing staring with his jaw hanging loose.

'You okay?' Annie was saying, making a cautious approach, dropping bags to the warped floorboards as she went, pulling off her hat and casting it aside onto the cash desk.

I'm okay now, Harri thought to himself, still not functioning well enough to say it out loud.

Annie was only an arm's length away from him now, stripping her long coat off her long body. The lamp lights caught her dangly copper earrings, making them shimmer.

In real life, as opposed to on his phone screen, her eyes really were that unusual Southern Comfort colour he'd half forgotten, half thought he must have imagined. Her mouth was just as beautiful as always, while something soft and life-worn had touched her at the corners of her eyes and between her brows.

He felt her hugging arms around him and found himself forgetting how to hug back. It had been so long since he'd held anyone, and he didn't want to squeeze her too hard or too limply with his one free arm – the other still shakily gripping the wine glass.

Annie smelled good, though not at all the same as he remembered. There was something sweet and almondy in her skin, a haze of sunshine and red sand in her hair, even here in damp, frosty England. Her presence felt miraculous.

'Is that for me?' she asked when she pulled back.

'Oh,' he said with a blink, realising she was reaching for the wine, which he surrendered with some relief. 'Hi,' he said at last, laughing at his own awkwardness, his hand reflexively lifting to the back of his head.

'There he is!' Annie joked. 'You're with me now.'

'God, sorry, I… it's been a long journey.'

That voice of hers was still vibrating through him, waking up a million old memories. His blood was flowing faster and he hadn't even taken a sip of wine. This is what it felt like to be standing next to Annie Luna. Now he remembered.

'Tell me about it,' she was saying, pouring him a drink like she'd already made herself at home, the metal bangles on her wrists jangling, their sound awakening him further.

He laughed, abashed, tapping his glass to hers. 'Sorry,' he said again. 'It's… amazing to see you.'

She didn't say anything, letting him settle down while they both took a drink. She kept her eyes fixed on him over the rim.

Harri remembered now that Mr Luna was something of a wine connoisseur. What would Annie think of this eight quid bottle from the convenience store? He hadn't even looked at the label, only scanning the price tags for the cheapest one.

'I needed that,' she gasped, holding out her empty glass. Clearly she didn't mind it at all.

There was soft laughter while he refilled her glass, just an inch or so, like Paisley had taught him. *Red wine is for savouring, and you only need a little.* He'd neck the entire bottle right now if he could; something in his brain was still going haywire.

'So, you're here,' he said, stupidly.

'Sure am,' Annie said, looking around the shop before snapping her eyes back to his. 'And so are you.'

It wasn't awkward, as such, just momentous. Nine years is a very long time not to stand together in the same room.

They took deep breaths as they scanned their new surroundings, as though evaluating exactly how this was going to work. Panic spiked in Harri that she might be regretting coming all this way.

'Is it okay?' he asked.

She didn't reply. She was staring in wonder at the shop. Something in Annie was blooming, bright and pulsing. He could feel it.

He'd forgotten this about her. Her body was like a transmitter. He'd always been able to, quite literally, feel her enthusiasm; it was shining out of her now like she'd absorbed the desert sunshine and had it on tap, an endless solar supply.

Lowering her glass to her side, Annie's foot knocked a wonky floorboard as she made for the shelves. She stopped herself stumbling and laughed brightly, her glow only growing.

'We got our own bookshop,' she said in that honeyed voice laced with wicked wryness. 'Our own *actual* bookshop,' she said again, flashing amber eyes towards him.

He folded his arms across his ribs, still gripping the stem of his glass. 'That we do,' he managed, shocked by how very Welsh his own voice sounded when it mingled in the room with Annie's drawl.

'It's just how I imagined it,' she said, stepping right inside the maze of shelves and disappearing. Harri's feet were stuck to the floor until she cried, 'Come on!' and he followed her like a shaky-limbed February lamb.

'You haven't changed a bit,' she told him from the deepest point in the book labyrinth, running her hands across the spines in the *Adventure Travel* section.

He knew that was a big lie. He was nearly thirty and kind of faded around the edges; at least that's what he thought when he looked in the mirror in the mornings. Maybe it wasn't showing itself physically, but it was there in his aura. He'd been fading away for years like an old Polaroid.

'You look great,' he blurted. 'Really great. Beautiful, like always.'

Annie laughed again, a touch of shyness in it. He made a mental note not to say anything like this again. She hadn't seemed to welcome it.

She did look beautiful though, better than beautiful. She was otherworldly somehow, in her long skirts and a jumper that managed to be both cosy-looking and somehow delicate like gossamer. He could see her skin through its woolly gaps all down her arms. She had a slight freckly tan even though it was only February.

'Do you want to go to bed?' she said, suddenly, and it drew Harri to a stop.

'What?'

'You look kinda...' She mimed someone looking lost and vague.

'Oh,' he tried to laugh it away. 'It's been a long day. A long year so far, actually. I'm not really...' He shrugged, not knowing how to finish his sentence. He hadn't told her about the break-up, thinking Annie might blame herself for not turning over her place on this trip to Paisley. *Not* something Harri had wanted. 'I'll be firing on all cylinders tomorrow.'

She nodded, letting her eyes move across his face. He couldn't tell what she was thinking. He only hoped she couldn't see how faded he was.

'I'm glad we're finally doing this,' he said, making a good show of suddenly admiring the books.

The distraction seemed to work, and Annie turned her attention to the shelves too. 'I know, right?' She plucked a title from the *Rural Living* section and showed it to him, reading aloud. '*Grow Your Own Beets for Fun and Profit* by Ifor Griffiths. Relative of yours?'

'Give over,' he said, laughing, before feigning seriousness and taking the book to examine it. 'Might be, actually.' He reshelved it. 'I preferred the sequel, though. *Cabbage Farming: How I Made My First Million.*'

He smiled goofily in response to her playful eye roll, and they passed along the shelves, inspecting them in increasingly loud silence.

'Have you eaten?' Harri asked eventually, remembering how he'd wanted to make Annie feel welcome and worrying he wasn't doing a great job so far.

'Not since the Amsterdam layover,' she replied.

'There's a kitchen,' he said, even though *of course* there's a kitchen. Why was he being like this?

They emerged from the stacks and passed through the low door at the farthest corner of the shop, entering into a room dotted with tables covered in red-and-white checked cloths overhung with red, retro diner lamps. Lace curtains hung at the windows and over the glass of the cafe's door. Everything in here was shiny and new but with the feel of a snug little hideaway.

They rifled through the white cabinets behind the counter.

'Ding, ding, ding, jackpot!' Annie cried, lifting the glass dome on a dish of fresh, fat scones in the walk-in pantry, just as Harri laid his hands on the clotted cream in the refrigerator. 'And there's a zillion jars of strawberry jam back here,' she added.

'Cream tea it is,' Harri said, grinning. 'Welcome to England!'

They paused before the espresso machine with a thick instruction manual by its side.

'That's intense,' observed Annie with a frown.

Harri filled a kettle from the tap. 'Hey, you're looking at the three-times winner of Port Talbot's "Best Cappuccino" award. Nothing could scare me less. But how about tea since it's getting late?'

While Annie extracted a promise that Harri would be the only one expected to brew speciality coffees for customers this vacation, they worked out how to use the grill and toasted two split scones and carried it all back to the fireplace in the bookshop.

Annie flicked the shop lights off, apart from the lamp closest to the hearth so the depths of the room fell dark. They flopped down on the beanbags in their warm, glowing spot. Annie pulled off her boots with a sigh while Harri poured milk into mugs.

Frosty designs were forming at the edges of the windows. Sleet pattered sharply in the courtyard outside where the strands of glowing light bulbs swung in the breeze, casting a shifting, twinkling light along the fireside wall.

Neither spoke while the tea was poured and the warm scones were spread with jam and thick cream.

Annie took bite after bite, smiling and ravenous.

'Happy?' Harri asked, watching her enjoying her food.

She didn't answer, only taking another bite. Her hunger made him wolf his food too. He'd forgotten how much they'd loved doing this. All those paper-wrapped fish and chip dinners devoured down on the water's edge watching Aber sunsets and drinking Coke, all those Red Velvets and milky teas in the Students' Union caff. Annie loved to eat and so did he, though recently he'd had no appetite at all. He smiled at the memories and filled his mouth again before a haunting voice spoke sharply in his mind.

Slow down, chew your food!

Paisley never seemed to take much pleasure in eating. He pictured her in their spotless little kitchen now, industriously making cheese and pickle sandwiches to take to work in the morning. He reminded himself sadly that if she was joyless, it was because he'd made her that way. There it was again: the guilt.

If only he'd been able to make her happy. He'd been in their relationship for years without fully being present. She'd deserved better all along.

'Harri?' Annie held the last bite of scone halfway to her lips. 'You okay?'

'Uh, well…' He glanced from Annie's face to the flames in the fireplace. It would be a shame to spoil the cosiness. 'I'm fabulous.' That sounded off. Definitely. 'So, tell me…' he tried, casually, 'how's life as a school librarian? Has Principal Johnson chilled out at all?'

Annie shoved in the last bite then spoke with a curled finger covering her mouth. 'He was still meaner than a junkyard dog last time I checked.'

'Sorry to hear that.'

She shrugged then asked him how his parents were. Harri got the impression she was trying to avoid discussing school, so he confessed guiltily he'd not seen his folks as much as he'd have liked, especially over Christmas, but they seemed fine. 'Same as always.'

He'd avoided telling his parents that things were increasingly rocky with Paisley – his dad thought she was the best thing to happen to Harri – and so he'd avoided seeing them at all after the Boxing Day break-up and he'd kept on avoiding them right up until yesterday when he'd popped in to his childhood home to deliver the bombshell news that he was heading to England for two weeks. He'd made sure his dad was out at work first.

His mum tended to worry about Harri, and his dad had a habit of gruffly urging him to do better, making comparisons between himself with his successful conservatory-installation business and the feckless Harri who hadn't made a go of anything yet, leaving Harri wondering if he'd somehow missed some mysterious lesson in manhood and now it was too late to catch up. Either way, it was hard to keep his parents from losing sleep over his wellbeing or his position in life.

He'd left his mum to break the news of his split with Paisley, and he hadn't heard anything from either of them since, though he'd texted his mum this morning to let her know he'd made his train.

'Mum sends her love,' Harri said, and it was true, she had. In fact, she'd told him with a wagging finger to make sure he didn't do anything to upset Annie while she was on her holidays.

'Tell her I said hi back.' Annie smiled, wiping the crumbs from her front.

Harri reached for his phone. 'Send her a picture?'

Annie shifted over, perching precariously on Harri's beanbag, squashed against his side, and he took a shot of them in the glow of the firelight. Annie looked beautiful. He looked like a ghost.

He quickly sent it, knowing for sure his mum would read into this. She'd always liked Annie; in contrast to her lukewarm, but always polite and welcoming, regard for Paisley.

An immediate love heart emoji shot back to them all the way from Wales. Annie smiled to see it. Instead of returning to her spot, she pulled her beanbag right up close to Harri's in front of the fire and settled herself again, cradling her mug, smiling into the firelight.

'Did you let your folks know you arrived safely?' Harri asked.

'Mom's tracking my movements,' Annie replied, nodding to one of the bags on the floor that presumably contained her phone. 'She got so sick of me forgetting to reply to messages she installed an app like my middle graders have.'

'Good thinking,' Harri teased. They both knew how she could go to ground. It was just her way and never malicious.

'I get wrapped up in my stuff,' she shrugged.

'How was Mr Luna about this trip?' Harri ventured with a grimace. There was no way her dad would approve.

'He sends you a great big snuggly hug.'

'I'll bet he does.'

The fire crackled as they settled into each other's company. It was easy, Harri was beginning to think, like no time had passed at all.

'I'm glad we kept this going,' Annie said, seemingly reading his mind. 'Nine years.'

'That's a lot of messages,' Harri said, shaking his head. 'I'm proud of us.'

'Who knew we'd be such good postcard writers?'

'Some of us were better than others,' he said through quirking lips.

Annie faked an indignant shove at his arm, making sure not to knock his mug.

'Hey!' he laughed. 'Here's to us. Class of 2016, eh?'

They clinked mugs before drinking.

'And how's Paisley?' Annie asked, inevitably.

'Uh…' Harri let a long moment pass. 'Well…'

'You broke up.'

'How did you know?'

Annie consulted an invisible watch. 'We've been here over an hour and she hasn't called once to check I'm not molesting you.'

Harri suppressed a smile. 'You got me.'

'Was it this vacation?'

'No. Well, not really. The holiday might have been the final straw, but it's been a long time coming. My fault, mostly.'

'*Hmmm.*'

His eyes snapped to Annie's.

'I'm sorry,' she protested, 'but it takes two, and you've been a perfect boyfriend.'

'Hardly,' he said, thinking he might cry and that would be hideous for both of them.

This time she really did shove his arm, but she seemed to be biting her lip too, reconsidering something that had been on the tip of her tongue. She composed herself and after a breath said she was 'real sorry' and asked if he was doing okay.

'I'm fine, honestly. Glad I had this trip to distract me. It's nice to be wanted somewhere.'

Annie nodded and looked away. There was a new caution in her that he wasn't used to. Annie usually spoke her mind. 'I'm sure you'll patch things up again,' she said, like that was all she had.

Harri peered at her. 'You reckon? I thought you might be glad.' Like, deep down, he was. Harri inwardly berated himself. What an awful thing to think.

'Uh-uh. I'm saying nothing. I've learned my lesson over break-ups.'

'What does that mean?'

Annie's face softened into a sad smile. He wasn't used to seeing her unsure of herself.

'What's the matter? Has something happened?' He searched his mind trying to recall if she'd mentioned seeing anyone lately but there hadn't been anybody since that thing with Billy the maths teacher had fizzled out last spring and she hadn't mentioned him since. 'Did I miss something?'

Annie let out a heavy sigh. 'You remember Cassidy?'

'Course I do.'

She was Annie's best friend back in Texas. They'd been joined at the hip as kids and after uni they'd picked up right back where they'd left off. Harri was always glad Annie had her in her life, a true friend amongst all the hangers-on and admirers.

'We haven't spoken since New Year's.' Annie's voice wavered. 'Remember I told you about her boyfriend?'

Harri set his mug on the floor. 'Deadbeat Dave?'

'That's the one.'

Of course Harri remembered him. Annie had hated him on sight back when he and Cassidy first got together. He'd been one great big red flag for two whole years, but Cassidy couldn't see it. It had killed Annie to see him breaking down her best friend, one undermining comment, barefaced lie or outright insult at a time. The women had been planning on moving in together, finally getting Annie away from her grumpy father, but Dave had put the mockers on that idea.

'He finally got caught cheating?' Harri asked.

'Yep, and they had a blazing row. Whole thing imploded and I can't say I was sorry. Fact is, I let it all out. I really thought he was gone for good, so I told her I'd had him figured for a skeeze since day one, and how she was a million times better off without him. Even told her he'd tried it on with me at happy hour on Christmas Eve! We did the whole break-up bit; revenge hair dye and cocktails, everything. We had a blast. It was like having the old Cassidy back.'

'What colour did she go?' Harri asked.

'Red.'

He nodded. 'Good choice.'

'*Right?* Anyway, Dave came crawling back at New Year's and they got back together.'

'No way!'

'I know! And I could *not* hold my tongue. I told her she was a fool and he'd only do it again, and it hurt me so bad standing by watching her slumming it with a two-bit man baby.'

'Ah!' Harri winced, realising what was coming. 'She didn't take it well?'

'She did not.' Annie's eyes flooded with tears, something Harri had never seen before.

'Oh my god, Annwyl!' he was reaching for her but she had already drawn her knees up and was hugging her legs, hunched over.

'She hasn't spoken to me since,' Annie said into the fabric of her skirts before turning her face to Harri's. 'And I've called and messaged, even went round her place...'

'How did that go?'

'Dave was there and he stood in the doorway with his arm around her neck like a chokehold, and she looked so mad at me. He told me to get off their property and I left. That was the last time I saw her.'

'Their property? I thought the house was hers?'

'It is. He knows when he has a good thing going.'

'*Hmm*. And now she won't talk to you?'

'Nope.' Annie sniffed. 'Feels worse than any break-up I ever had.'

Harri wished he could rub her back or something, but he kept his hands to himself. 'She'll come round, won't she? When he gets caught out again?'

'I have no clue. But if she does, I've learned my lesson. When friends break up, I keep my big mouth shut. Trashing their ex is *not* smart. How was I to know they'd get back together?' She hugged her legs tighter. 'I even told her we called him Deadbeat Dave.'

'Oh shit.'

'And now I've lost my best friend.'

'Hey, joint best friend, surely?' Harri tried to joke.

'I'm hurtin' for her,' Annie said, sitting upright.

Her sad eyes pained him. Annie usually laughed things off but this was like nothing he'd witnessed before.

'You'll make it up, I know you will,' he told her.

She shook her head, eyes glazing as she let them settle on the flames. 'You didn't see how she was set on hating me. I can't forget the way she looked, like she was so done with me. Even when it all happens again, and it will, he's got his hooks in her so deep she'll forgive him, and I'll stay cut off like this.' Tears tracked down her cheeks.

Nine years of distance and his arms were wanting to reach for her after just ninety minutes? He stopped himself pulling her close. 'I'm so sorry that happened to you,' he said instead. 'And I'm sorry for Cassidy too. Losing you won't be easy for her either.'

Annie's shoulders shook as she wept without a sound. This was new ground for both of them. What a way to start the holiday.

She slumped lower in the beanbag but had already seemed determined to stop feeling sorry for herself. 'Here's me breaking my heart and you've had a falling out with Paisley,' she said, swiping a hand over her wet cheek.

'What a pair of sad sacks we are,' said Harri, inwardly comparing his sadness over his break-up with Annie's heartbreak at losing her friend. Annie seemed to be taking things much harder.

When he really examined it, the strongest feeling in his heart was one of regret at having squandered a decade on a relationship that, if he'd been honest with himself, had been all but over for the last couple of years. He'd wasted Paisley's twenties. On cue, along came regret's companion, guilt.

'Don't go rebounding,' Annie was offering, wisely. 'It's never a good idea. I did it myself a couple of times at Aber, remember?'

Harri screwed up his face like he was thinking. 'Did you? Ah, it was all so long ago.'

Of course he remembered. Watching Annie hurling herself into another doomed fling with some rugby lad or bar crawl creep. It had felt rotten, but what could he do? He'd been on the sidelines while she'd been full steam ahead onto the next thing, and the next, never resting.

Annie seemed different now, though. She was calmer, if a little disillusioned and sad. Maybe they both were.

Sighing heavily, he hatched his fingers over his stomach. A stillness settled and for a while they said nothing, lost in their separate thoughts.

'I couldn't stand it if I lost you too,' Annie said eventually, as they stared into the dying fire.

'Luckily, you're not going to.'

Annie reached for his hand. He watched as his own travelled reflexively for hers. Her fingers were cool.

'Friends for life?' she said.

'Yep, friends for life,' he echoed, ignoring the unwelcome feelings this set off within him. 'And we're going to have the perfect bookselling holiday, okay? I promise. No more upsets.'

She nodded and squeezed his hand before letting go. She didn't seem to register the awkwardness of it. 'And you'll be back together with Paisley in no time,' she offered.

Harri knew that was never going to happen but there was no point pushing back against his friend who'd been burned so badly with Cassidy and Deadbeat Dave. How could she possibly know what to say for the best after all that?

'And you and Cassidy will be back on speaking terms very soon,' he insisted, even though he couldn't be sure about that. 'Just you wait.'

In the glow from the fire, not to mention the wine, the tea and the scones, and the feeling of having unburdened themselves after a long, long journey of nine years, Harri made a solemn, unspoken promise.

Annie's heart was already broken from losing one friend so there was no way he was going to risk all they'd built between them by following his inconvenient, and no doubt faulty, instincts that they could be more than friends one day – no matter how insistent those instincts were.

He was as alone in the world as Annie now was, and if *he* couldn't be fulfilled and carefree on this holiday, he'd damn well make sure Annie could. He'd pour his whole heart into making her feel safe and secure. That's what friends did for one another.

So, he sat by her side reminiscing about their uni days until the embers in the grate cooled to an ashy white, and they took themselves off to separate beds; Annie upstairs and Harri in the little bedroom just off the shopfloor, where he repeated his promise as he drifted off to sleep.

If Annie Luna ever suffered again, it would not be for the loss of their precious friendship.

Chapter Three

Annie's Secret

Annie woke shivering, long before her alarm, and quietly set about figuring out how the heating worked. She'd forgotten about the curiously British phenomenon of under-heating their buildings in winter and leaving them airless and stuffy in summer.

She wiped the pooled condensation away from the shop's window ledges with one of the cafe's tea towels. The sky was still dark and starless. She let her tired eyes rest on the rain-soaked cobbles in the little square outside. The cold was getting into her bones.

She'd thought about going back to bed and trying to read but she'd been carrying the same novel around with her for weeks and still hadn't brought herself to open it.

This was unusual for Annie whose Goodreads account charted a couple of hundred books finished every year since forever. She used to devour books like Valentine's candy. Now though, she couldn't get past the first page. So, she examined the contents of her suitcase instead.

Clothes always interested her, but dressing for this holiday was going to be a challenge.

She'd brought all her winter dresses, and picked out the warmest one this morning. It had a colourful book print against a black background of thick cotton. She'd worn it to work a hundred times and her sixth-grade girls had complimented her on it.

The thought of her library and her students so far away sent a pang of longing through her. It was mixed in with some anger too, reserved especially for that one parent who'd made the complaint about that one, perfectly innocent, book her kid had taken home.

She shook her head as she sharply knotted her belt. That complaint had snowballed into the whole awful thing that had sent her running to England.

This vacation could not have come at a better time.

She pulled her crocheted cardigan closed across her ribs and tried not to let the feelings of rage and shame overtake her.

This was her much-needed break; her first in years. She'd thought through her plan back at home. It would be her drawing-a-line-under-it-all trip. She'd left the past behind her and was set on beginning a new life when this excursion was done. Though how exactly her new life might look, she had no clue. If anyone had been born to be a school librarian, it was her, but how was that an option now?

No Cassidy. Possibly no job to go back to. Her community fractious and split. *Ugh!* She forced the thoughts away as her stomach churned and the bookshop reeled around her.

In the bedroom just off the shop floor Harri was stirring. She'd better pull herself together for his sake. She couldn't burden him with what was happening at school. Her parents' reactions, especially her dad's, had been bad enough, and she'd faced it all without Cassidy too. She hadn't reached out, even though there was no way she could have missed it on the local news stations.

She already knew what Harri would say about it anyway. He'd be indignant. He'd call that parent a 'moaner' and an 'arsehole'. He'd try to make her laugh about it, say it was a molehill not a mountain. He'd encourage her to go back and face it, or to find a new job in a new school. He couldn't understand what it's like, being publicly shamed and shut out.

Harri had enough to worry about. She was big enough and tough enough to get through this by herself. She *had* got through it.

One of the worst things to come out of it was that ever since the complaint, since she saw the shock on the faces of her colleagues and the consternation on Principal Johnson's face, she'd found she couldn't read. Not her favourite anime, not the lightest rom coms, nothing so much as a magazine article. The reading part of her brain was blocked off to her and as much as she couldn't understand why it was happening, she didn't dare try to investigate it. For now, her lifelong love of escapism and imagination was bundled up in the same airless, dark place as her motivation to fight back was hiding. No. She couldn't look at it any closer, in case it all started unravelling, taking the last of her happiness with it.

Decidedly, she jabbed at the power button on the shop's laptop, accidentally switching it on then immediately off again. Her hands had been shaky lately, but she was determined to ignore that too. She held a firm finger to the button and breathed.

The till display and Visa card reader blinked awake. Automatically the stock system appeared onscreen.

'All right,' she told herself. 'You got this.'

She set herself the challenge of mastering the whole system before Harri, who must have rolled over and fallen asleep again, appeared. Good. He needed to rest; he'd looked so worn out and pale last night.

She'd found the tech all pretty intuitive and a lot like the school library catalogue system back home. This one was designed to track sales and could be used to help any Borrower uninitiated with the shop's holdings locate books on the shelves if a customer turned up asking for specific titles.

By eight, she had moved on and tidied the already very tidy shelves and picked out a few favourites to display in the empty wall racks behind the till, pulling *Naughty Amelia Jane!*, *The Twins at St. Clare's* and *Swallows and Amazons*, just three of the beloved childhood books responsible for young Annie's budding Anglophilia.

She'd cultivated her love of British things as a tween reading Fay Weldon, Julia Donaldson and Anne Fine, before moving on to Jane Austen and Dylan Thomas at Aberystwyth, along with all the other canonical British and Irish authors of the uni English syllabus.

Now here she was in England, surrounded by books in an adorable, quirky, little building by the sea. She had to make the most of this opportunity; it would never be open to her again. If she worked hard enough to make these two weeks a success, she might be able to get back into her own good books. She wanted to feel proud of herself; something she hadn't felt since the 'temporary suspension' from library duties while her and her senior colleagues' 'conduct and suitability for school librarianship' was investigated.

She'd decided to steer clear of the coffee machine until Harri got up, instead pouring orange juice from a carton that read 'with orangey bits'. She'd smiled at the adorably English quaintness of it. Then she'd toasted the last two scones, assuming they'd been left for them by the previous Borrowers and not intended for selling in the cafe. Nobody would pay for day-old scones, surely? Not even in England. She carried it all through to the shop on a tray.

The smell had brought Harri stumbling out of his room in grey flannel pyjama trousers and an ancient Stereophonics t-shirt with a fluffy dark grey cardigan over it. She could have sworn he had the same one at Aber. He'd switched his lenses of last night for dark rimmed glasses. 'Did I sleep in?'

'You look so cute,' she blurted, not once thinking she shouldn't. He *did* look cute.

'I try,' he said, making a brief attempt at a sassy catwalk strut just to make Annie laugh.

'You've got a kind of Ryan Reynolds thing going on these days, especially with the eyeglasses.' A tiny part of her brain wanted to mention his jawline and his smile being similar too, and maybe the broadness in his shoulders, but she kept that to herself.

'He's at least a foot taller than I am,' said Harri.

'Well,' Annie shrugged, 'just don't stand beside him any time soon.'

'Got it. Hey, are these floorboards even more warped than they were last night?' He lifted a bare foot, rubbing the sole. 'What with the wonky beams and the wonky floors, a man could get seasick in here.'

'I thought the place had shrunk overnight,' joined Annie. 'Whole place is *topsy turvy*.' She overpronounced the words just to make him smile. He'd always been tickled by her accent.

She set his buttered scone and his juice on the desk by the till laptop, telling him to sit down, making sure to ruffle his bed-head hair which, she was remembering now, always stuck up in the mornings and couldn't be brought under control other than with a shower.

'You sleep okay?' she asked, aware she had circles under her own eyes.

'Better than I have in years,' he said, before seeming to think better of it. 'You know, after I got used to the sound of the sea.'

'Oh yeah, the sea! What a racket!' she mugged with a dismissive sweep of her hand, hoping Harri couldn't see through her bravado.

Annie had lain awake listening to the distant sounds of waves breaking and retreating for a long time, willing them to lull her to sleep and to feed her gentle dreams, a lullaby soundtrack keeping at bay memories of the mess she'd left back home. She'd had no such luck and lay ruminating in the strange moonless darkness for much of the night.

'Someone should do something about that noisy ocean,' Harri said. 'Shushing and splashing at all hours.' His brown eyes twinkled in the harsh shop lights. 'We should go for a walk later,' he said as he started upon demolishing the scone. 'Go see the beach for ourselves.'

'I'm not going anywhere 'til I've sold some books,' she told him, leaving her breakfast and busying herself at the circular display table by the door. It was set out with books on Perspex risers. 'Do you know what this is?' she asked him, knowingly.

'What do you mean?'

'Check out page two,' Annie told him, indicating the open binder in front of him on the cash desk.

Harri flipped to the front cover. 'Instructions for Borrowers,' he read.

'That's us,' she smiled. 'I've read the whole thing.'

'What time did you get up?' he remarked in what looked like genuine awe. She shrugged smugly with a laugh and he turned to page two and read aloud.

'The shop and cafe are yours to do with as you like. Any takings belong to the Borrow-A-Bookshop community charity, although you may avail yourselves of petty cash to cover modest cafe ingredients costs, special event expenses, etcetera…'

'Skip that bit,' she told him.

'Um, okay. Let's see…' He was scanning down the paragraphs. 'Keep your own opening hours as you see fit… There's a ramp over the doorstep into the cafe for better accessibility… Tie up all bin bags and cover with blanket provided to stop scavenging seabirds and wild-life… Our team of local volunteers will help out on a casual, drop-in basis… *Ah-hah!*' He pinned a fingertip to the page. 'The display table by the door is curated by Borrowers on the last day of their holiday and left in place for the duration of the next guests' stay. Please leave your own selection of books to reflect your reading tastes or any display on a theme close to your hearts on the day you leave. Previously, we've enjoyed displays on the themes of, for instance, foxes, favourite children's books, even original handwritten poetry.'

'Fun, right?' She was glad to see Harri seemed happier this morning than he'd been last night. Maybe the sea air was helping.

'Very fun. What did the people before us pick out, then?'

'Umm,' Annie looked at the titles. 'It's kinda random. Not sure what theme they were going for. There's a Chaucer, something called *The Parliament of Fowles*?; *A Life of Saint Dwynwen*, whoever that is; and, uh, this one looks really old…' She inspected an antiquarian volume, reading from the frontispiece. '*A Young Man's Valentine Writer*…' She shrugged, placing it gingerly back on display. 'That one's priced at fifty pounds.'

'Maybe it's all Valentine's themed?' said Harri, reaching for his orange juice. 'Saint Dwynwen's the Welsh answer to Saint Valentine, sort of.'

'Ah, okay. The rack of Valentine's cards should have been big enough of a clue.' She palmed her forehead.

Their two pairs of eyes fell upon the rack of red and pink greetings cards on the display table. They were of the hippiefied, handmade variety.

Harri's face had fallen, only a touch, but Annie noticed the change.

She shoved her hands in the pockets of her dress. 'Does Saint Dwynwen get a day of their own too?'

'Uh, yep,' Harri replied, his eyes still fixed on the cards. 'It's only just gone actually. Twenty-fifth of January.'

Harri seemed to be lost in a memory. She wished she hadn't asked now.

'Everyone in Port Talbot was celebrating,' he was saying. 'My manager let me bake some coffee cookies iced with daffodils and love hearts to sell in return for donations to the local hospice. All gone by lunchtime, they were. Didn't get so much as a taste.'

Annie watched him snap out of self-pity, trying to compose his face into an unbothered smile. It wasn't going to work on her. Her friend was sad and she wouldn't let him stay that way.

'There's always Valentine's Day coming up,' she suggested. 'There's no telling what Cupid's got in store for you before then.'

Not that she wanted Paisley back in his life with her judgy, grudging ways. She'd never say it, not now, but Paisley had been a pain in Harri's ass going way back. She'd have come to England for this bookshop holiday way sooner if she hadn't thought Paisley might decide to come too; she didn't want to make trouble for her friend in his relationship. But if it made Harri happy to get back together with her, she would be there for him, putting on the performance of her life in the role of Best Supporting Friend.

'I should go get ready so we can open up,' Harri said, hopping off the stool.

When he emerged after his shower he was in the same cardi but with a heather-grey henley underneath, and he was wearing dark cargos rolled at the ankles and thick socks showing over the same black hiking boots he'd clomped around the shop in last night. His hair had settled in damp choppy waves and he'd shaved too. In the winter morning light he didn't look like he'd changed all that much in nine years. There was still something boyish about him. She was glad he'd kept his eyeglasses on.

After he'd unbolted the side door that led into the cafe, he came back and approached her by the shop door, his phone at the ready to capture the moment she turned the sign so it read OPEN.

Annie grinned for the picture, and then they took a selfie together. Up close, Harri smelled of moisturiser and shampoo.

Swept up in the excitement of it all, Annie went so far as to swing the door open, peering out into the dull, rainy courtyard where a raggedy palm tree stood in a huge terracotta cauldron. There wasn't a soul out there. She immediately shut the door again and Harri caught one last picture of her grimacing as cold rain hit her face.

'Suppose we'd better bake something to serve the hordes of tourists?' she said, wiping the spots away with her sleeves pulled down over her chilled hands. She couldn't help her heart lifting. This felt absolutely right. They should have done it years ago.

–

'And this is the tulip,' Harri said proudly as he shook the frothed milk into the coffee cup and handed it to Annie. 'A latte art classic.'

Annie lifted the cup and took a considered sip. With a frothed lip she declared it a 'masterpiece'.

'Why, thank you!' Harri snickered, before drinking his espresso con panna, his coffee shop favourite, made with a single shot of strong coffee and a small dollop of lusciously thick whipped fresh dairy cream on top, served in one of the demitasse glasses he'd brought from home. It was strong enough to keep him going through his ten-hour barista shifts in Port Talbot, smooth enough to gulp down on busy days. He enjoyed making elaborate drinks for the customers, enjoyed even more making sneaky off-menu speciality drinks for his favourites, but his own tastes were simple.

Annie had asked him for a latte so that's what she got; only he knew he'd ground some of his best small batch beans for their drinks, and that it had to be up there with the best quality and freshest coffee on this side of the globe.

'You any warmer?' he asked.

'Much, thanks.'

Satisfied, he opened the notes app on his phone and typed a few words.

> Madagascan Robusta from the Mumbles Roastery:
> 2 Feb, Clove Lore. Toasty with tobacco notes, lifted
> by a sharp, berryish bite. Smoky and velvety smooth.
> Annie liked it, but I can tell it isn't 'the one' for her yet.

'What's that you're doing?' enquired Annie, hands wrapped around her mug.

'Just my coffee notes.'

She lifted a brow.

'If I try something new or come up with an idea, I write it in here. What? That's a normal thing to do. You keep notes about the books you read, right?'

Annie didn't say anything. She used to do that, yes. Nowadays, not so much.

'I just happen to want to remember the good coffees and keep track of things I could do better, or...'

'I'm not judging,' she cut in. 'I think it's adorable. Is the best coffee you ever tasted in there?'

'*Hmm,*' he considered this for a while. 'I've had my successes,' he conceded, 'and some failures...'

Annie tipped her head.

'My burned banana caramel latte didn't turn out anywhere near as good as it was in my head,' he laughed. 'And there was that time I tried toasting my own Kenyan peaberry beans at home in the kitchen.' He grimaced.

'Not good?'

'Tasted like charcoal. You could say I'm still searching for perfection.'

'Let me know when you find it,' she said, sipping her latte happily.

'You'll be the first person I tell.'

Annie gestured at all the stuff he'd unpacked from his delivery onto the glass shelves at the back of the food prep area. 'I knew you were into coffee, but this is a whole new level.'

'I suppose you pick it up, working in a coffee shop.' He lifted one shoulder, shrugging off the idea that this was anything other than a nerdy hobby, an extension of his day job. 'Paisley always complained that I came home from work smelling of coffee, like it was in my clothes and hair. I could never smell it.' He sniffed his sleeve now.

'That sounds nice to me.'

'Hmm.' He let this go. Paisley hadn't liked it one bit. It smelled of a lack of ambition.

Heat was radiating from the oven with its timer counting down its last few seconds. A good, sweet smell of creamed butter and sugar, eggs and self-raising flour had been blooming in the cafe for the last twenty-five minutes.

The sweetness, combined with the heady coffee aromas, and the sound of rain pelting against the cafe windows in the red lamp glow made Annie remark that the Borrow-A-Bookshop cafe must be in the running for the cosiest spot in the South West this morning.

As the timer bleeped, Harri set down his empty cup and opened the oven door to an 'Ooh!' of appreciation from Annie.

Twenty-three and a half simple sponge buns in paper cases (they'd run out of mixture on that last one) had turned golden brown while Harri had demonstrated his prowess with the espresso machine.

'Just like in Aber,' Annie said, watching him turn them out onto a cooling rack. 'Hangover buns.'

He smiled at the shared memory of whipping up his grandma's recipe in their flat that first time, way back during freshers' week, and how the whole gang had made him bake the buns regularly after that, since they were so easy to stomach after a late night in the Union bar.

Harri sniffed a laugh. 'They're not exactly coffee shop standard though, are they?'

'Folks like simple things, especially in winter when they can still remember their *new year; new me* resolutions. Half the little one with you? For taste testing purposes?'

'Obviously.' Harri was already tearing the bun to reveal its fluffy, golden, steaming insides, passing her half.

'Cheers,' Annie said, raising hers to Harri's.

The light in her eyes told him the taste was a time machine, transporting her right back to sleepy Sundays spent under duvets in the shared lounge, sprawled with their flatmates' feet across laps, heads on shoulders, taking tentative sips of what Harri taught her to call 'builder's tea', the TV showing *Friends* reruns.

'I've missed this,' Annie said, and Harri nodded his agreement. 'Maybe we can sass these up with a twist?'

'Such as?' Harri looked dubious.

'Something for Valentine's? Passion fruit filling?' she suggested.

'And pink frosting?'

She was laughing, white teeth gleaming. 'That oughta do it!'

Harri pretended to lose his enthusiasm. 'Where do you buy pink food colouring and passion fruit in Clove Lore in February?'

'Split another one?' She looked hungrily at their day's wares. 'Something tells me we won't get twenty-three cafe customers today anyways.'

As Harri peeled the paper case from another bun, she contentedly turned to watch the raindrops tracking down the cafe's glass door. He was making his friend happy. This was everything he could have hoped for from this trip.

–

'Text it to my mam as well,' Harri told Annie, after she sent their shop-opening pictures to her mother.

Annie didn't expect a reply any time soon. Her mom was kind of sick of her, but she hoped putting the Atlantic between them might soften her up a little.

'Okey-doke,' Annie said. She'd had Mrs Griffiths's number in her phone since uni and they always exchanged holiday greetings, so it didn't seem strange to send the photos now. Harri's mom was always nice to her.

She figured while she was in the messaging app she could try reaching Cassidy again. Harri was watching her, but if she was quick he wouldn't know she still persisted in trying every few days.

No response came, other than the 'heart eyes' emoji from Mrs Griffiths and a 'Have fun you 2.' Annie turned the screen to show Harri and he broke into a grin.

She loved his smile. A tiny thought nudged into her mind, something about how lucky Harri was to not only have tawny brown Welsh eyes but a really good mouth too, with full lips and a strong Cupid's bow.

It was then that the bookshop door opened.

The booksellers abandoned their cups on the cafe counter and bounded under the low door onto the shop floor, Annie whispering, 'I'm serving this one!' as she went.

'Hi!' she greeted the smiling woman, who was half inside the shop, shaking her umbrella into the courtyard.

She was about their age, Annie guessed, as well as small with dark hair and decked out in waterproofs like a mountaineer. Annie had her figured for a local before she even introduced herself as Jude Crawley, the bookings manager and treasurer for the Borrow-A-Bookshop community charity. She handed over a carry-container with a glossy brown cake inside.

'Chocolate ganache gateau. Figured you might need something to sell, since the weather's not great for nipping out to buy ingredients. I bake a wee bit.' Jude's accent was softly Scottish and her eyes genuinely smiling and bright.

'I bake *a wee bit* sounds like an understatement to me,' Annie cooed as she held the tub to her face like a kid examining the goldfish they'd just won at the fair. 'Thank you! Do we owe you money?'

'Nope.' Jude shook her head. 'It's all part of the volunteer scheme. You'll meet us all in the end, no doubt. Apologies in advance for that. Maybe you don't know about the phenomenon of the Great British Busybody? There's one behind every door in Clove Lore.'

This made Harri's eyes widen. 'Should we be worried?'

'They're a lovely lot, just a wee bit prone to getting overinvolved,' Jude replied, before diplomatically clamping her lips shut.

'I'll look forward to meeting them,' Annie said with conviction.

Harri didn't look quite so sure. 'Do the volunteers know anything about drumming up trade on a rainy day?' he asked. 'You're the first person through the door this morning.'

'Hmm.' Jude considered her answer. 'We're a pretty inventive lot in Clove Lore. In quiet times we tend to put on special events to bring folk into the village.'

'Special events?' echoed Annie, already liking the sound of this.

'Yeah, it's kind of our thing, having such a small population in the village. We rely on tourists and visitors from all along the coast.'

Jude evidently noticed Harri's brow furrowing at this, so she added quickly, 'Like the kids' poetry sessions every Wednesday. Austen Archer runs those, so you'll soon meet her. It used to be a storytelling session but now she's our resident poet, so…' Jude's shoulders bobbed. 'And towards the end of summer we have a book festival kind of thing, anything to sell tickets and get people into the village, supporting local businesses.'

'All right,' Annie said, perfectly happy with this. 'Should we be doing our own event?'

'There's nothing stopping you, if you want to. We can put word out through our channels. By which I mean Minty and Mrs Crocombe. They're better than any Facebook ads or billboards for spreading news, I'm telling you.'

'More volunteers?' Harri hazarded.

Jude drew a deep breath. 'Village matriarchs, more like, but yep, they run the whole show. You'll see.'

Annie was deep in thought.

'You know?' she began. 'Back at the middle school library where I used to… I mean, where I work…' she corrected herself. 'I hosted a silent reading club. Would local folks come to something like that?'

Jude nodded keenly. 'You mean people gathering to read, here in the shop?'

'Yep.' Annie gripped the cake tub closer as she mulled it over. 'Except in school we encouraged the older kids to come along, pick out a book and park themselves any place around the library. I'd make 'em turn off their cells.

There'd be plenty talk, but when the bell rang, they were all talked out and ready to read. Ah, it was so fun!' She knew she was getting swept away and tried to dampen it down. 'Then, after, they'd talk about their books some, before their folks'd bring them home.'

Jude was impressed. 'I wish I'd had a school librarian like you. I bet your Head loves you.'

'You'd think.' Without missing a beat, Annie shifted the focus away from her. 'So, what do you reckon? The Borrow-A-Bookshop silent reading club?' She spread a rainbow with a hand in front of her as though the words materialised in the air. 'For one night only. Bring your own book, or buy or borrow one of ours.'

'I'm in,' said Jude. 'And you could sell drinks.'

'Hot cocoa?' Annie enthused.

'Well, that and a few bottles of red.' Jude knew the Clove Lore crowd, evidently.

'So, we're doing this?' Annie glanced at Harri for the go-ahead, which she knew he'd never dream of with-holding. He knew it was best to let her run with her ideas.

'When's a good night to do it?' She looked to Jude.

'Sunday evenings can feel long in the winter round here, for some people,' Jude said after some thought. 'Week today would give us time to get the word out. You can charge for refreshments and keep the tickets free. That would be enough to cover your costs, since we're a not-for-profit kind of place. How's seven o'clock?'

'Sunday at seven it is!'

That was it, decided. And all in the space of ten minutes.

Jude was soon on her way again, leaving the friends alone with a huge cake under a glass dome next to the hangover buns on the cafe counter.

Now they had an event to organise.

They were mid-way through making a poster for the window with marker pens and a big sheet of card Annie found behind the till when the deluge outside tired itself out.

They didn't notice at first, since the sound of the rain was replaced by the sounds of the sea-swell down in the harbour, but all across the Clove Lore promontory, holidaymakers were clambering out of steamed-up cars and campervans, packing away Thermoses and pulling on hats and scarves, while the locals peered from tentatively opened doorways at the tiniest slices of watery blue sky through the cloud cover.

Soon the steep, cobbled slope that formed the spine running from the visitors' centre at the top of the village down to the Siren's Tail pub on the seawall was bustling with people making the most of this respite from the rain and determined to run errands and make memories before the short winter's afternoon drew to a close and darkness fell again.

Annie and Harri suddenly found the Borrow-A-Bookshop full of people, and Annie was in her element.

Chapter Four

Bookselling and a Summons

Harri had been awestruck as he watched her work. He'd kept a low profile, making the coffees and cutting the cake, mopping wet footprints from the floor, and generally being useful to Annie who he realised had assumed the role of bookseller-in-chief, just like in Aber.

Now the rush was over and the cafe was cleared of people, he brought Annie a sweet mint tea by the till.

'That'll be four pounds and forty-five pence, please,' she was saying, her grin broadening, as yet another customer counted coins into her hand over the counter.

'Nice to find a shop still 'cepts real money,' the older man said, before placing his new Bill Bryson and his biography of John Denver in his raincoat pockets.

Harri hadn't known how to respond but it was no problem to Annie, a natural at this kind of thing.

'Sure is,' she said, handing him one of the fiddly five-pence pieces she'd fished with some difficulty from the till drawer. 'My grandpa always said there's nothing realer than the cents in your pocket.'

With an approving tip of his waxed hat, the man went on his way.

'Mind you,' Annie said, turning to Harri with a cunning smile, 'he also used to shoot racoons from his porch and thought the Clintons were listening to him through his toaster oven, so, you know...' She shrugged her shoulders. 'Is that for me?' She cradled the mint tea in her hands. 'We got busy for a spot there,' she said, blinking like she was waking from a dream.

'A four-hour spot!' Harri told her. 'I sold the entire chocolate cake.'

'And the buns?'

'I think you were right about needing some passion fruit filling or something. They didn't do so well.'

'Never mind.' She shuffled closer to his side like she was seeking warmth.

'Are you still freezing? Why don't you wear my big jumper?'

He could hear her protesting, but he was already on his way to his suitcase to pull out his warmest jersey.

When he returned, he put it over Annie's shoulders and arranged the arms in a knot. She thanked him in a quiet way that made him step back again.

They surveyed the shop in silence. The stacks were messy where browsers hadn't reshelved books properly. Annie would love sorting that, Harri knew, while he'd empty the dishwasher, which was at that moment whirring noisily from the kitchen nook.

Annie sipped her tea. She looked contented, had been, in fact, since the arrival of their very first paying customers this morning. She'd greeted them like this had been her bookshop all along, without a hint of nerves or self-consciousness.

Within twenty minutes of those first arrivals stepping inside she'd rung up two titles on the till (for the grand total of six pounds), and had convinced them (a couple in their forties with a friendly black Labrador) that they'd better stay for coffee and one of Harri's grandma's buns.

They'd been unable to say no, of course, and Annie had chatted with them about their mission to walk the entire Devonshire coastal path in sections over the course of the winter. She'd discovered they were from Bristol, and that the dog, Bailey, was thirteen years old and going a little deaf, and all before Harri had ground their coffee beans.

By the time Harri had delivered up their cappuccinos they were already friends and Annie was looking at their recent wedding photos on the woman's phone.

'You were amazing today,' he said now.

She curtseyed a thank you.

'Daily totals?' she said, like they were back in Waterstones cashing up, where every night they'd take guesses at how much they'd taken through the tills and the person who came closest didn't have to pay for the post-work pints at the pub.

'Two *thousand* pounds,' Harri said, and Annie caught the joke. They'd easily make that on a Saturday's trading in the big bookstore.

'I'm saying a hundred,' she told him.

'All right... Sixty, no seventy-two,' he ventured.

Annie clicked the mouse with enthusiasm.

'Oh.' Her shoulders dropped. 'Forty-nine pounds, sixty-two pee.' She overdid the English pronunciation for laughs. 'How much did you take in the cafe?'

Harri pulled the printout from his pocket. 'Just shy of forty quid.'

'For a day's work?' Annie complained. 'I mean, I know I wasn't frantic, but we had a steady stream all day.'

Harri lifted *Swallows and Amazons* from the shelf behind him and opened the flyleaf, showing Annie the pencil marks inside. 'I guess since about half the stock is second-hand and they're pricing books like this at two quid a go, we're not talking Bezos amounts of profit.'

'I guess not,' Annie conceded.

'And since we're not getting paid anyway, it doesn't really matter,' he said, putting the book back. 'Anyway, wasn't I closest? Didn't I say seventy-two?'

'But with the cafe takings, I was closest, so I guess you're buying.'

'Hey!' Harri was ready to complain when the shop phone rang.

They both stared at it in alarm.

'You get it,' Harri urged.

After an exaggerated eye roll and a whispered 'grow up', Annie answered. 'Borrow-A-Bookshop?'

Harri watched as she listened and nodded, and made the occasional 'uh-huh?' sound. She widened her eyes comically at him as the call went on. 'Yes, we will… Okay… see you th…'

Whoever it was had hung up without letting Annie utter one full sentence. She set the phone back in its holder and turned ominously to Harri.

'Our presence is requested up at the Big House. That was *Lady* Araminta Clove-Congreve.'

'We're invited to dinner?' Harri said worriedly. He did not like the sound of this, not when he was so close to the promise of a pint of cider in the local pub. They'd probably have a blazing fire there too, and fish and chips, and any number of nice wintry puddings on the menu.

'Not dinner, no,' Annie tolled dramatically, clearly enjoying the absurdity of it all. 'We are summoned to a village meeting.'

Chapter Five

The Locals

'*Woah!*' Annie stopped dead on the threshold of the grand ballroom of Clove Lore Big House and every head in the room whipped round to face her. 'Sorry,' she said, shrinking a little and whispering to Harri, 'I forgot, this is England. You're not supposed to be impressed by a great big five-hundred-year-old manor house.'

Harri sniffed a laugh and led the way further inside.

A young blonde of about twenty-ish approached them with a drinks tray of wine and orange juice.

Annie was still looking all around her at the glowing candles burning in antique sconces along the wall. A great ball of mistletoe hung from the lofty ceiling. A grand piano stood under its cover beside a smoky fire in a very grand fireplace and in the centre of the room were chairs set out in a circle and a larger gathering of people than either of them had expected.

'I didn't know the meeting would be so fancy,' Annie said in a confiding tone to the blonde girl as she lifted a glass of juice and Harri took a wine.

'It's always like this,' the girl murmured back. 'Minty likes everything done proper.'

'Ah! There you are!' cried an imperious voice, both shrill and booming in the English country-house way. The woman attached to the voice was making her way towards them. She was a gracious figure in winter tweeds, green wellies and a silken scarf knotted at her throat.

'*Camilla Parker Bowles,*' Annie coughed.

Harri only just managed to hold in his laughter and a mouthful of wine. The girl with the tray scooted out of the path of the advancing woman.

'How nice of you to join us,' the woman was saying. 'I'm Araminta Clove-Congreve, proprietor of Clove Lore Big House Estate and Gardens. Friends call me Minty.'

This left Harri none the wiser as to whether she classed them as friends or not. She jabbed a hand out for the booksellers to shake.

Annie introduced herself and Harri knew she was fighting the urge to curtsey by the tiny smirk on her lips.

'And I'm Harri,' he said while the prim woman crushed his fingers.

'Did Minty mention she's also the manager of the Clove Lore Estate food pantry and community growers' association?' chimed an even more glamorous woman wearing an expensive-looking shimmery, belted kaftan and silvery ballet pumps.

'Co-manager,' Minty replied with an indulgent smile at the woman, who Harri noticed was alternately sipping from two glasses of white wine at the same time. She had no eyebrows to speak of and was extremely beautiful, in a slightly batty way.

'These are the new Borrowers, Estée,' the lady of the manor was telling her friend. 'Annie Luna and Harri Griffiths.'

Harri thought how they hadn't told Minty their surnames but she knew them anyway. *Interesting.* His mind flitted to Brenda Coxhead, the head of his and Paisley's street's residents' association who had her finger in every pie and somehow caught wind of everything going on in their area. Brenda was a menace, and if he wasn't mistaken there was something of the menace about Minty too.

His conjecture was interrupted by Annie exclaiming, 'I *know* you!' and almost sloshing her juice over the rim of her glass in her haste to shake hands with the woman in silver. She quickly realised the woman hadn't a hand free to shake and so gripped at her own elbow instead like she was trying to contain herself. 'You're Estée Gold! The TV star. I thought you lived in Hollywood?'

Estée smiled, delighted. 'Oh honey, I did, but one glimpse of Clove Lore and *poof*! I was transported! I never went back.'

That was her story and she was sticking to it, even though her very public divorce and bankruptcy had been splashed across every British tabloid a couple of years ago. Even Harri had a vague inkling of it somewhere at the very back of his brain.

'Vacationing with celebrities and royalty!' Annie continued, enjoying every second of this introduction to Big House life. 'It's *just* like *Downton Abbey*.'

Minty raised a brow at being identified as royal, but didn't correct her.

'Oh, 'tis just like it!' came another voice and the two glamazons parted to let a smaller, pink-cheeked, white-haired woman come between them.

'This is Mrs Crocombe, one of the volunteers,' said Minty in her clipped way.

'I thought I heard another American accent! Just like yours, Estée,' the elder woman said.

'Except Annie's accent isn't put on!' said a tall man as he slipped past trying to catch up to the girl with the drinks tray. Harri only just caught his wickedly purring Eastern European inflection.

'Don't be rude, Izaak!' chided Estée Gold in her strongest Scarborough accent, which surprised the newcomers. 'I'm *Transatlantic!*' she added, before sipping from one of her glasses, signalling that was an end to the discussion.

'And what do you two young'uns make of our bookshop, then?' said Mrs Crocombe, ignoring all the Big House nonsense like she was immune to it.

'We love it,' Harri said, quite genuinely.

Something about this made Mrs Crocombe snap her eyes between the two Borrowers. '*We* is it?' she said, her jaw jutting forward interrogatively. 'Jude said you was just friends?'

'Oh we are, just really good, long-term friends,' Harri said, aware he was labouring his point.

'So you won't be doing a Jude and Elliot, then?' Mrs Crocombe went on.

Annie cocked her head. 'A what?'

'Jude met 'er husband at the Bookshop when she was on 'oliday. Fell in love inside of two weeks. Now they both live 'ere. Elliot's our top vet. Jude's our resident baker.'

'Umm…' Harri began, clueless as to what to say next.

The man Estée had referred to as Izaak returned, now with a drink in his hand and a handsome man on his arm. They both looked to be in their thirties. Izaak introduced him as his husband, Leonid, before saying, 'You're not matchmaking already, are you Mrs C.?' He gave Annie and Harri an appraising look.

'Me?' said Mrs Crocombe innocently. 'I'm only telling them the story of Jude and Elliot.'

'And what about Austen and Patti?' Izaak said. Harri realised he talked with a softly Polish accent. 'They've been together for a while now, ever since Austen's bookshop holiday.'

'Woah!' Annie was enjoying this. 'Is this village some kind of hotbed for romantic liaisons?'

'There was the other ones as well.' Mrs Crocombe was clicking her fingers and circling her wrist, her eyes closed. 'The Icelander and the girl who washed ashore?'

'Magnus and Alexandra,' Minty put in.

'That was before my time here,' said Estée.

'All Borrowers,' Mrs Crocombe confirmed with enthusiasm. 'Then there was Joy and our Monty Bickleigh! Not one of them could resist the magic of Clove Lore.'

'Are you sure it didn't have something to do with your betting book?' Leonid added softly.

Harri didn't like the way Mrs Crocombe was looking between him and Annie like they were part of some new salacious project she was devising. She drew a book from her handbag.

'Annie and… Harri, isn't it?' Mrs Crocombe asked, her eyes narrowing. She produced a pencil from behind her ear. What was she up to?

'And what about you and Mr Bovis?' Izaak was saying with a look of cunning, directed right at Mrs Crocombe. 'Another big Clove Lore romance? Hmm?'

'Well, I reckon it's time to start the meeting, isn't it?' chirped Mrs Crocombe shiftily, hastily shoving her notebook and pencil away again.

'Ah, indeed!' cried Minty, checking a slender watch and turning towards the circle of chairs in the middle of the ballroom. 'Quick quick!'

Annie and Harri hung back with the waitress as the crowd obediently followed the lady of the manor.

'Why do I get the feeling we narrowly avoided getting involved in something…' said Harri, watching the villagers settling in the circle but speaking to the girl with the tray. 'Sorry, I don't know your name.'

'Samantha,' the girl replied. 'You want to watch Mrs Crocombe. She runs a betting book on all the incomers.'

'A betting book?' replied Annie.

Samantha's voice dropped lower. 'That lot are forever placing bets on who's going to get together next. And you Borrowers are fresh meat. She won't stop 'til she's won a tenner on you.'

'What do you mean?' Annie asked, incredulous, but not nearly as horrified as Harri.

'I mean, her and Izaak will either want the pair of you loved-up and together by the end of your holiday or they'll have you paired up with one of the village spares!'

Annie spluttered her juice as she laughed.

'*Spares* doesn't sound very nice,' said Harri.

'That's how she sees them. No single person is safe when Mrs C.'s around. And that nosy parker *boyfriend* of hers, Mr Bovis, is just as bad. Those two shacked up a while back and they're pretending to be just good pals, but the whole village knows the truth. Two peas in a pod, and forever up in everybody's business, pair of stickybeaks.'

'And what about you, Samantha? Has she paired you up?' Annie asked, laughing, like this was all just quaint, small-village custom and perfectly delightful.

At that moment, Minty called the last of the stragglers to order, and a young, handsome blond man went by, dressed from head to sneaker in black, designer streetwear.

'You okay, Sam?' he mouthed as he went, which made the girl smile back shyly. Annie had her answer.

The three of them watched on as he obediently took his seat next to Estée Gold.

'That's my Jasper,' Sam said.

'Another Clove Lore love match.' Annie was clearly enjoying this.

Sam didn't answer, only blushing pink all down her neck, and the three of them made their way to the circle to join the meeting, Harri feeling very much like an exhibit in a museum: a specimen of the single Welsh holiday-maker, and by the way Mrs Crocombe was scribbling frantically in her notebook and showing the page to a smirking Izaak, he guessed the villagers were determined he wouldn't stay single for long.

Well, more fool them, he thought smugly. Little did they know he was only here to make Annie happy. There'd be no matches made for these Borrowers, and they'd all know it, come Valentine's Day when they shipped out of Clove Lore once more and went their separate ways.

Suddenly, Harri didn't feel quite so smug. He finished his wine and hugged his arms around himself to quell the empty feeling.

–

Harri wondered if this was how all village meetings went around here. It had started off oddly with Minty's husband Jowan standing up to read the list of 'apologies' from people who couldn't be present, which included a regretful 'Aldous' who was 'hopefully not biting poor Anjali round about now', and this had descended into a long, involved discussion about how Aldous – who Harri

74

sincerely hoped was a dog – had grown so scruffy over winter he'd been sent to the vet for a tidy up; something, Harri gathered, Aldous was not keen on.

Jude the baker was sitting opposite Harri in the circle and beside her was a huge, dark-haired, ridiculously handsome fellow in green scrubs. They were holding hands. He must be the ex-Borrower the matchmakers had mentioned. Elliot, was it?

He'd chimed in to confirm his confidence in his colleague's abilities to handle the wrath of Jowan's elderly Bedlington Terrier, and then Minty had to call everyone to order because the circle fell to gossiping once again after Mrs Crocombe enquired after Anjali the vet and whether *she* was seeing anyone at the moment. She had pinned Harri with a meaningful look before writing something down in her book.

Annie witnessed the whole thing and didn't even try to hide her mirth until Harri threw her a scowl and she pretended to be chastened, clamping her lips.

The first item on the agenda came from the smart blond guy sitting next to Estée Gold, the one who had made Samantha blush. He got to his feet to address the room, speaking in a true Transatlantic accent with hints of a decidedly posh Chelsea twang.

'So, hey everybody, I'm Jasper Gold.' This was clearly for the benefit of Harri and Annie, the incomers, as Samantha had called them. 'As most of you know, my classic cinema afternoons begin on February fourteenth.'

This was met with a smattering of applause, and an exuberant little whoop from Sam.

'Tickets have been selling well for our first event and I think I've dealt with concerns about potential bad weather.'

'Don't want your first showin' to be rained off,' interrupted a very red-faced, stocky little man in green waterproofs sitting very close to Mrs Crocombe. 'I said it, didn't I? That sittin' outside watching a film in the middle of February won't be everyone's cup of tea.' He looked very proud of himself for making this observation.

'Yes, well, thank you, Mr Bovis,' Jasper continued, swishing sleek blond strands away from his eyes. 'There'll be one parasol to each pair of deckchairs in case of rain showers, and everyone has been told to wrap up warm and waterproof, and they can bring a blanket. There'll be hot drinks, not to mention Monty's grill for hotdogs.'

'I'm bringing my hot water bottle,' interrupted Mrs Crocombe.

'Yes, quite,' Jasper flustered. 'And if there's high winds, Minty has said we can move inside to the ballroom.'

'But it shan't rain,' Estée Gold added confidently, like she truly believed she had control over the Devonshire weather.

Harri could feel Annie's body radiating pure joy every time one of the barmy elder locals spoke. He was glad she was enjoying herself, but he was a little too worried about what Mrs C. might be planning to relax.

'Is it open to anyone? Your movie?' Annie piped up.

'Yup, I've got tickets with me, if you want some afterwards? It's *When Harry Met Sally*. Starts at sunset, four-thirty.'

'Oh, I love that movie,' Annie burst out.

Harri had never seen it. He figured that was about to change.

'Jasper's our local film buff,' Mr Bovis put in. 'Brilliant in the pub quiz, and so good for our young Sam Capstan.'

Poor Sam only looked down at her crossed ankles and pretended she wasn't blushing.

Mr Bovis and Mrs Crocombe are as thick as thieves, observed Harri, watching how close they were and how vehemently Mrs C. was agreeing with him.

'I'm mostly into avant-garde cinema,' Jasper Gold continued, 'but you have to show what the local people want, apparently.' This was said through a gritted-teeth smile, giving Harri the impression the film choice may have been a bone of contention at an earlier village meeting.

'First rule of box office,' said his mother, Estée. 'Give the people what they want.'

'Well, thank you very much, Jasper,' said Minty pointedly. 'We wish you lots of luck with your movie night venture, and of course we'll *all* be there to support you. Won't we?' She eyed the assembly sternly. That hadn't been an invitation but an instruction. 'Now, Estée has a report on the food bank project.'

This made Harri do a double take. Why was a local celebrity involved in the food bank?

'Food *pantry*, thank you,' said Estée rising to her feet. 'I'm pleased to report that after a visit to Sparing's Farm out on the promontory, I've managed to persuade the younger farmer Sparing to donate some of his early potato and kale harvest this year. He was also very forthcoming about delivering the produce himself, so long as I'm around to sign for it.'

'I'll bet he was,' snorted Mr Bovis under his breath, but still loud enough for the circle to hear. 'Daft lad 'ud be goggle-eyed at the sight of the *famous* Mrs Gold.'

'*Ms* Gold,' she corrected him.

'Amazing what a flash of those American chompers'll do,' Bovis said, paying her no heed, only to receive a jab of Mrs C.'s elbow.

'In fact,' Estée continued, ignoring him, 'the community has surprised us all with its generosity towards the pantry and, combined with the Clove Lore estate produce, masterfully grown by our own Leonid, we've enough donations coming in to get us through the winter and well into spring.'

'You're doin' a lovely job, Estée,' put in Jowan. 'And we're all proud of how you've made the food pantry take off, what with you having no experience of the real world or us normal folks' ways.'

Estée smiled at this and lowered herself to her chair in a floaty haze of voluminous silver fabric. 'Thank you,' she said graciously.

Harri couldn't help glancing at Annie to see if she thought the whole exchange as deranged as he did. He found she wasn't even trying to hide her delight.

'What's next?' said Minty, consulting her agenda. 'Oh yes, my husband reporting on the unhappy goings-on at Castle Lore.'

This made Harri sit up. 'Sounds like a novel,' he said, but the locals kept their eyes fixed on Jowan. 'I'll shut up then,' he whispered for Annie's ears only. She glowed beside him.

' 'Tis a sad business,' began Jowan, standing, his pearl drop earring bouncing at his jaw. Harri thought how like a pirate he looked as well as sounded. 'Seeing a once great castle up for sale and all its effects going to auction.'

'Not that any of us have set foot in the place!' tutted Mrs Crocombe, arms folded over her matronly bust.

'Not one amongst us but our Mint ever laid eyes on the mysterious late Lord Courtenay of Castle Lore,' Jowan said, turning to his wife.

'It's true,' Minty responded. 'My father included him in his hunting party when the young fellow first inherited the castle. He'd lived in France all his life, and came to England that winter. Gosh, it must be fifty years ago now. He rode over, drowning in his late father's hunting pinks, gulped down a sherry while astride, spoke to no one at all, and when the hunt moved off, he beat a hasty retreat back to his castle. I never saw him again. Sickly, he was, and ever so pale. I invited him to the Big House, of course, but he never responded and that was that. Some country folk can be a little strange,' she concluded sagely, leaning into the circle to address Annie.

Harri felt Annie's shoulders shaking by his side. He had to speak to stop himself blurting a laugh. 'And now they're selling off the castle, did you say?'

'Lock and stock,' said Jowan. 'There's no one to inherit; the entire line died out with him, title an' all. Auction's on Saturday.'

'We've all been agog at the auction catalogue, haven't we!' Mrs Crocombe said excitedly.

'Not everyone,' Elliot the vet put in dryly and with the look of a dutiful young husband dragged along to these things against his will.

'And that brings me to you two!' Jowan was saying, pointing his sandy-bristled chin at Harri and Annie.

'Us?' Annie grinned, totally lost as to what was going on, but having fun nonetheless.

'The bookshop always requires antiquarian stock. It sells well an' it looks good on display. The auction catalogue suggests Castle Lore's grand library has an impressive collection, much of it is goin' to be bundled in lots of unspecified titles, which suggests there's too much material to catalogue individually!'

'I smell treasure,' Mr Bovis butted in.

'An' that's where the Borrowers come in,' Jowan continued. 'We need representatives to attend the auction and bid on some of these lots. Suss them out, find the treasure.'

'It'll be goin' for pennies,' Bovis added knowingly.

'Will you go on our behalf?' Jowan was asking Harri. 'Auction's on all day and there's a drinks reception for buyers before the big lots in the evening. Collectors will be flyin' in from all over the world for a snoop.'

'Heck yes we will!' answered Annie. 'An auction in a spooky English castle, and with drinks thrown in?'

'Don't you want to go?' Harri asked Jowan. 'Since it's your bookshop, your stock?'

'We've an open house here for potential brides and grooms that day. It'll be all hands on deck. So, we've settled it then?'

Annie drummed happy feet on the floor.

'I can drive you over there,' added Jowan, 'and I'll give you the credit card before you go.'

As Jowan sat back amid satisfied murmurs of approval, Mrs Crocombe peered over her specs at Annie and made another note in her book.

'Do not make jokes about spooky castle,' came Leonid's serious Russian accent, silencing the room.

Jude smirked at Elliot, but Izaak weighed in, just as dolorous. 'It is true. Even I have heard the stories.'

Estée Gold, who Harri had mistaken for a reasonably sensible person added her two pennies' worth. 'The castle's unoccupied and has had no power for months now, but ever since Lord Courtenay's death, candlelight has been seen at night in the windows in the tallest tower.'

Annie was fit to burst with electric energy now. Harri didn't have to look at her to know she'd be beaming at the TV star in deeply amused admiration.

'Squatters,' asserted Elliot flatly.

'Haunted,' countered Mrs Crocombe adjusting her bosom between folded arms. 'Mark my words, there's trouble up at Castle Lore. You better keep your wits about you.'

'I'm sure they'll be fine, what with it being a public sale, and daytime, and everything,' Jasper Gold put in, looking right at Sam.

These two younger Clove Lore residents must hear this kind of garbage all the time, thought Harri.

'Any other business?' came Minty's cut glass voice.

'Actually, Annie had an idea for an event at the book-shop,' Jude put in. 'I suppose that counts as any other business.'

The whole assembly seemed pleased to hear this.

'Well, it's nothing really, just a silent reading group, for one Sunday night only,' said Annie.

Following an encouraging nod from Harri, she reached into her bag and pulled out the poster they'd made earlier that day, unrolling it to a fanfare tootled by Izaak.

'Silent reading group?' Mrs Crocombe read dubiously. 'As in…?'

Bovis completed her sentence. 'Sittin' around reading?'

'We already have a book club. Our murder mystery and thrillers club, at the Siren,' said Minty, perplexed.

'This is more of a cosy night in, but *out*, and together, reading, and it's for the whole community,' said Annie. 'And there'll be hot chocolate.'

'I'm in,' said Jude. 'That's right up our street.'

Elliot confirmed his attendance with an arm wrapped around his wife's shoulder and a kiss on her forehead.

'Sam? Come with me?' Jasper asked across the circle. Sam assented with another smiling blush.

The meeting rapidly descended into a loud cacophony of excited ideas for what books they might bring along.

Minty had clearly had enough and drew the whole thing to a close. 'That's decided then. A silent book club will take place for one night only on Sunday evening at the Borrow-A-Bookshop. You know what to do, people. Spread the word amongst your networks.'

Shortly, everyone was on their feet and chatting in groups. Sam did the rounds with her tray once more. Was there no end to this evening? All Harri wanted was a bit of dinner at the pub.

Annie had rolled up her poster and was interviewing Jude and Elliot about their meeting at the bookshop. He overheard Jude remarking, 'Hard to believe it was four years ago this summer.'

That was before he realised Jasper Gold was standing before him, flicking blond hair from his brow and holding a ticket book. 'Two, is it?' he said.

'Ah, of course, the Valentine's cinema night?' Harri dug in his pocket for his wallet, keeping his ears open to all those around him. He and Annie seemed to be the main topic of conversation.

'I reckon Anjali the young vet will do for him, and how about Kit at the pub for Annie?' Mrs Crocombe was saying to Izaak, Leonid, Minty and Jowan.

'We must let it happen naturally,' Minty hissed loudly. 'No point forcing things.'

Harri noticed Jowan reaching for Minty's be-ringed hand. He was making devoted eyes at her. Another recent Clove Lore love match, no doubt.

After having parted with twenty quid, he pocketed the movie tickets and scanned the room looking for Annie once more. They had to get out of here quick before they were married off against their will.

'And you and Harri aren't…?' Jude was asking.

'What, us? God no!' Annie said with a barking laugh. Harri knew she was overcompensating, trying to throw the community off their tails but still, she didn't have to be quite so emphatic about it. And then she said something that made his nerves jolt.

'There was a while, back in uni, where I had a crush on him, but…' Harri watched Annie swipe the idea away with a dismissive hand. 'We're just really good friends.'

Harri found he couldn't move. In fact, he felt like he was suddenly lit by a spotlight's beam, blindingly bright. Was everyone looking at him?

A crush? In uni? There was no way that could be true. He'd have known. If that was really the case they'd have…

'Ready to go?' Annie called to him.

The spotlight went out. Harri blinked.

Annie was smiling, forcedly now, and with a touch of tiredness around her eyes. She looked chilly. The thin silver and gold chains at her throat sparkled in the lights from the sconces. She'd worn his jumper the whole afternoon. It looked spectacular on her.

Now she was by his side and telling him in a low voice that all she wanted was to get out of here and have a hot bath and a long sleep.

'Right,' Harri faltered. 'Let's go.'

They picked their way gingerly back down the slippery cobbled slope towards the bookshop in the muted light of the village's Victorian streetlamps. It was sleeting sharply, right in their faces, preventing them from talking.

Harri collected his thoughts. *Had* a crush. Past tense. *We're just really good friends.* If she'd let on she liked him back then, they could have been together all this time, or it might have been the thing that destroyed them. It could have been just a fling or a short-term thing, and living so far apart she could well have become nothing but his ex. They might not even be in contact now. He shuddered at the idea.

They passed down the sheltered turning off the slope and made it to the shop door. As Annie punched in the keycode, he asked, 'We're doing all right, aren't we?'

'*Hmm?*' Annie swung the door open and practically dived into the warmth of the dark building. The heat from the radiators had at last built up to a decent temperature. 'How d'you mean *all right*?'

Harri shrugged. 'As pals? Here, on holiday? We're good, aren't we?'

Distractedly, Annie threw off her coat, and kissed him exuberantly on the cheek. 'We're the best.' She made for the staircase. 'We're the GOAT! Greatest of all time.'

Quietly astonished by the heat on his cheek where her lips had pressed, Harri locked the door.

Annie effervesced her way up the stairs, calling behind her. 'It says in the information binder there's only enough water for one bath per evening. Since you jumped in the shower this morning…'

'Go ahead. I'll hit the hay.' He pointed stupidly to his bedroom door. *Hit the hay?* When did he ever say *hit the hay*? He was being weird again and he hated it.

By the time Annie Luna emerged from the tub, the scent of her almond milk bath oil had spread throughout the whole place, Harri was under his covers with his pillow pulled firmly over his head, and on Annie's night-stand he'd left a bedtime snack of hot buttered toast and milky tea, made just the way she liked it. Beside it were the two tickets for *When Harry Met Sally* at the Big House outdoor cinema on Valentine's Day.

She stopped at the side of her big white bed, rubbing the towel over her damp hair, and thought herself very lucky indeed. Harri Griffiths really was the very best friend a woman could wish for.

The sleet had stopped around about the time Annie was drifting off to sleep, having made sure to check her phone for a reply from Cassidy. There had, of course, been none.

Chapter Six

A Visitor

The rain stayed away all that Monday morning, making for a decent day's book and bun selling. Harri had baked a fresh batch, adding a sugary lemon drizzle which he'd made with supplies from his dash to the convenience store up at the visitor centre first thing.

Annie could hear him in the cafe taking orders, clattering cups and banging out spent coffee grounds into the waste food bin. Now and again his soft Welsh accent broke through the chatter of the bookshop browsers and Annie's 'ironic Nineties college music playlist' over the speakers. Harri had popped his head round the cafe door to let her know he was, 'enjoying them unironically, by the way', at about half eleven when there'd been a momentary lull in visitors.

By that time Annie had sold a good few coastal path maps, a recipe pamphlet from the pile on the counter (which she noticed was attributed to Clove Lore's own Jude Crawley), plus a very fine 1950s edition of the field-notes of an obscure Italian botanist she'd no reason to have heard of. Altogether that had come to a little over seventeen pounds.

Harri had upped the price of his lemon drizzle buns in light of the fact the fruit and caster sugar had come to six-fifty and he'd grumbled for a good fifteen minutes about the rip-off prices of Clove Lore's only shop while he baked. Annie had balked too at the cost of ingredients for the meal she'd promised to cook tonight, but nothing could take the shine off her day's bookselling.

The morning brought three coach loads of visitors to Clove Lore, and they'd all been greeted by the sight of the sloping village glistening in the sheerest covering of frost.

Annie had been kept busy fielding questions from the coach tourers. *Did they detect an accent? Wasn't she feeling the cold terribly? Long way from home, aren't you? Assistant school librarian, indeed? What does that involve?*

She'd answered each one with her usual wholesome charm. *Yes, sir, she'd been told she had a strong accent everywhere but back home in Amarillo itself where folks found her words tinged with an Anglo-Welsh lilt* (which always delighted her when it was pointed out); *yes, ma'am, she'd been cold since she stepped onto the runway at Newquay; two planes – one big, one alarmingly tiny – and a bus journey she wasn't keen to do over in twelve days' time*; and she'd only smiled and said '*a lot of hard work*' in response to the enquiries about her real job back home.

If she'd told them the truth she'd have cried into their well-meaning faces. The truth was that she'd read for a degree in English, completed The School Librarian Certificate Programme, followed by the Educator Preparation Programme, and she was on her way to taking her State Examination of Educator Standards, all the while working for a tiny stipend, championing student wellbeing initiatives she rarely got credit for, and keeping up with reading trends and changes in state law and school rules, waiting for the day she'd take over as head librarian, which obviously was never going to happen now she was suspended.

Instead, she'd smiled and reminded the intrigued customers that the shop had a cafe too, if they – to echo Harri – 'fancied a brew'.

The shop had been bustling and cheerful, even if Annie was still nursing her woes, and she had barely batted an eyelid when the third set of coach trippers shuffled in and out at around noon leaving one of their number sitting by the fire napping gently, a tiny pair of copper-rimmed glasses over his generous nose and the shop's precious antiquarian copy of *A Young Man's Valentine Writer* closed on his lap.

Shortly before three, when the shop had emptied completely and a frosty darkness was descending over the village once more, Annie summoned Harri to come take a look at the old guy.

'You sure he was with one of the coach trips?' Harri whispered, standing by her side a good distance away from him.

Annie shrugged, observing him still. 'I didn't notice him come in. I think he arrived when it was super busy with the lunchtime rush.'

Harri peered closer. 'Is he…?' He turned ominous eyes to Annie.

'What? You don't mean…? Oh my lord! Go find out.' She shooed Harri towards the armchair.

'What do you want me to do?' Harri protested in a whisper.

'I don't know. Poke him?' she mouthed.

Harri rolled his eyes to cover the fact he was paling significantly. He edged forward. 'Excuse me, uh, Mr…'

There was no response.

Annie said a silent, slightly hysterical, prayer. *Please, please don't let him be dead.*

'Sir?' Harri tried, watching for the man's chest rising and falling.

She mimed a poking motion and nodded encouragingly, even while she was wincing.

Harri gently touched the man's arm through his coat. Getting no response, he shook his shoulder.

'*Agh!*' the man cried, jerking awake, arms flailing like he was falling through the air.

'Sorry, sorry! We thought you'd…' Harri recovered himself after jumping inches from the ground in fright. Annie bit her lips together. 'We think you've got separated from your coach party.'

The man's befuddled look fell from his face, and something crotchety and dark came over him instead. He looked accusingly between Annie and Harri before laboriously struggling to his feet. He seemed to sway for a moment before straightening his back (well, as straight as he could stand), and he shuffled towards the door.

Annie tried to stop him. 'Wait, sir, do you want us to call the coach company? Who are you travelling with?' The man pulled ineffectually at the doorhandle. After a glance at Harri, communicating her concern, Annie resignedly opened it for him. 'We can call them, see if they've left without you? Maybe the tour guide will come collect you?'

He raised a hand above his shoulder and wafted her words away as he shambled out into the courtyard.

'Can we at least get you a tea?' Harri tried, but he was well on his way up the dark passageway that led onto the slope.

'Maybe he's a local?' Harri said, watching him disappear.

'Maybe. He wasn't dressed like a tourist,' added Annie. The others had been wearing bright hiking gear, boots and bobble hats. The old man had worn a strangely old-fashioned coat, somewhere between a graduation robe and a caretaker's coverall, and there'd been little more than a brown rag tied round his neck by way of a scarf.

'Could he be homeless?' Harri said, beating Annie to her conclusion.

'We should have made him something to eat,' said Annie, pulling her cardigan closed across her body and coming back into the warmth of the shop. 'You scared him away.'

'You're the one who told me to poke him,' Harri complained, shutting the door once more. He looked at their empty, slightly dishevelled shop.

Annie replaced *The Young Man's Valentine Writer* back on the display table where it belonged. She wondered if the old man had read any of it before he nodded off. He'd been so deeply asleep, like he belonged in that armchair.

'What now?' Harri was saying.

Annie looked around. 'Five-minute fix-her-up?'

Harri smiled. 'What's that?'

'I did it at the library. Five minutes, reshelve as much as you can.'

'Then we call it a day?' Harri seemed to like this idea.

They'd only just set about tidying when the door jangled open. Annie plastered on a smile before turning to welcome the visitor. Only, it wasn't a customer. It was Mrs Crocombe, and she had her notebook open in her hands and a very determined look in her eyes.

Chapter Seven

Mrs Crocombe Being a Menace

'So, what do you say?' Mrs Crocombe tipped her head and blinked innocently.

'Blind dates?' Harri asked, incredulous.

'Double dates,' the old menace confirmed.

'And you've already asked this Anjali and… who was the other one?'

'Kit,' Annie said.

She'd obviously absorbed the details of the match-making plan better than he had, including the bit where Mrs Crocombe had unflinchingly announced that Anjali, Harri's date, 'is a vet and a She' and 'Kit's a chef and a They' and she'd wanted to know in a very direct way whether any of that was going to be a problem. Annie had shaken her head, untroubled.

Harri was less inclined to be set up with a stranger, even if she did love animals and is a 'lovely girl, from one of the best families on the promontory', whatever that was supposed to mean.

'I'm not really dating, at the moment,' Harri said as firmly as he could under Mrs C.'s wily grey-eyed gaze.

'One date can't hurt. Not when Anjali's been on my list for five years and said no to absolutely all my suggestions so far, but she said yes to you.'

'She did?' Harri wished he was above manipulation like this, but his heart had lifted a little in spite of himself.

'It's just dinner at the pub,' Annie said.

Of course she was up for meeting two random locals for a meal. She was the dictionary definition of an extrovert. Harri could be found indexed under 'homey, bordering on antisocial'.

'Go on, I'll be with you the whole time,' Annie cajoled. 'And you did say you were dying for some fish and chips and a cider.'

'Best cider in the county 'ere,' Mrs C. jumped in with a conspiratorial wink thrown at Annie.

'You're not going to hear the word *no*, are you?' Harri sighed, letting his shoulders drop.

Annie leaned closer to Harri's ear with a gritted-teeth smile, hissing, 'If we say yes now, the villagers will place their bets and we can get on with our vacation in peace.'

All it took was a nod of Harri's head and Mrs Crocombe slashed a pencil line under their names and hobbled right out the door, delighted with herself. 'Tomorrow, six-thirty at the Siren, table by the fire, booked in the name of Crocombe,' she said as she went.

Harri fixed Annie with a firm look. She only chuckled and set about her five-minute fix-her-up.

Harri, however, couldn't settle for the rest of the evening. Not even as Annie cooked and served up his favourite soft-shell tacos, using up the dregs of the red wine from their first evening here in the beef and black bean filling.

He hadn't had Annie's cooking in nine years and she'd seriously perfected her recipe in the interim. Everything was delicious, but still the thought circulated in his head; he was going on a real date with someone who wasn't

Paisley. It felt far too much like being *out there* again, and he really didn't know how people were supposed to act on a normal date, let alone a double blind date.

Annie had dabbled with Hinge back home and she had a large circle of festival-going friends who she could have her pick of. Harri had gathered they were all devoted to her. Then she'd had something semi-serious with that maths teacher last year, though she seemed to have forgotten about him.

Harri, on the other hand, had lived with one woman for nearly a decade, and before that there'd been a girl-friend who lasted pretty much all through sixth form, but she'd dumped him to go to uni in London, and that was it, the sum total of his romantic experience.

'I don't know anything about veterinarian sciences,' Harri mumbled into his third taco, while Annie topped up his Sprite.

'Just as well Anjali knows all about that, then,' she said. 'That'll be something you can ask her about.'

Harri observed Annie as she carried on devouring her food. 'You seem pretty relaxed about this.'

She fixed him with a simple smile. 'It gets the locals off our backs; we meet some people our age in Clove Lore. We get a dinner. What's the problem?' She took another big bite.

'Just dinner?' Harri said, a tiny part of him not relishing the idea of watching Annie inevitably charming this Kit person who Mrs Crocombe had described as 'an absolute looker'.

'Don't even have to do dessert,' she reassured. 'One and done.'

'Oh, I expect we'll want pudding.' Harri smiled, real-ising how silly he'd been acting. If he was going to have to start dating again, maybe this was as good a way as any to go about it, with Annie there to help with conversation if it turned awkward or if he ran out of things to say.

Annie seemed excited about the innocent prospect of going out and making two new friends, and since he wasn't exactly planning on a rebound holiday romance, maybe a friendly dinner was absolutely fine? It didn't signify a thing.

He raised his glass to Annie's. 'To double dates,' he said, and she smiled before toasting him back.

'To being each other's wingmen,' she said, and seeing his face fall, she laughed raucously. 'I'm kidding, I'm kidding!'

Chapter Eight

Wayfaring

Early the next morning, out on the cliff path, eighty-year-old William Sabine ambled slowly along, his head down, thin hair plastered to his crown. Frosty dewdrops hung diaphanous in the air, soaking through the clothing of anyone senseless enough to be out wandering. His only concession to the damp morning was a ragged brown muffler wrapped across his chest beneath his inadequate, shabby coat.

He'd have stuffed his hands into his pockets for warmth were they not already filled with treasures. Tiny leatherbound books, not one of them under a hundred years old, a fine compass, several stubby pencils, a vial of India ink and a tarnished fountain pen in its worn leather sleeve, all of which jostled in a jumble of rubber bands and crumpled handkerchiefs.

He pressed a hand to his chest pocket at regular intervals, struck with sudden worry, before sighing in relief. The keys – his own particular responsibility – were still there.

He had no idea how long he had been walking, but his feet were wet inside his leather slippers. He wondered vaguely where he'd left his shoes. He was glad he'd set a fire in the grate before he went out. Would it still be burning? He couldn't quite remember when he'd set off or, for that matter, where he was off to.

Nicholas had wanted that *Baedeker*; he knew that much. Was that where he was going? Did he have an appointment with a dealer today?

'Oh dear,' he said through a ragged breath that sent white fog floating in clouds across his vision.

He'd stopped to wipe his cold, clammy forehead with a handkerchief when all his attention was stolen by the sound of a robin singing its hardest from the tall wall that lined the path on his left.

The robin hopped into view in a mossy recess in the stones, which were dotted all over with fuzzy orange lichen and the first curled fern fronds waking up at the end of winter. Even through Mr Sabine's filmy eyes, the red of the robin's breast against the orange and green made a lovely sight.

'Hallo, tiny fellow,' he croaked hoarsely. 'Where's your lady friend?'

The robin sang again, and, to the man's delight, it was met with an answering call from the scrubby gorse that lined the cliff edge to his right.

A second robin appeared, singing brightly.

Mr Sabine observed them with childlike wonder, his eyes wet, as the birds set off together in chirruping, tumbling flight along the path.

'Sing your hearts out!' the man told them, his reedy voice swept away in the swirling wet air. He shivered as they disappeared and his brows fell, dismayed.

He looked about the spot where he stood like he'd been suddenly placed there.

'Nicholas will wonder where I am,' he muttered. 'Oh dear, oh dear.' His soft slippers scuffed the loose stones of the path as he moved off again and the grey wintry weather set in around him.

Far along the path ahead, the lights of Clove Lore glowed through the low cloud. A flag flew on the turret of the Big House, and the chimneys smoked thickly from the higgledy-piggledy collection of slate roofs dotting down the sloping spine of the village. Had Mr Sabine been thinking clearly, like he had until recently, he'd have thought how like heaven it all looked.

The robins kept singing, concerned only with their courtship and answering the impulse of the turning wheel of the year. William Sabine tried to whistle in imitation of their song as he walked slowly towards the village, the hazy memory of an armchair, a warm fire and floor-to-ceiling books somewhere down there in amongst the tumbledown cottages calling him on.

Chapter Nine

The Wanderer Returns

There was no getting away from it: Harri was nervous that Tuesday morning. He made up for it by keeping busy. He'd baked a batch of glacé cherry buns, icing them and letting Annie put the half cherry on top for decoration. Then he'd swept and mopped the floors, all while Annie dealt with the scattered arrivals throughout the morning. Nobody could be induced into buying anything, no matter how chatty Annie was.

By twelve, the drizzle had chased away most of the visitors and Harri had fallen to entertaining Annie by reading aloud from one of the Valentine's display books.

'The Roman festival of Lupercalia fell in February and is closely linked to our modern Valentine rituals. Lupercalia, a festival of fertility, saw the pairing up of the unbetrothed by means of a lottery system which varied across regions.'

'*Pfft*, no one tell Mrs Crocombe she could be running a love lottery as well as a betting book!' Annie cut in.

The mention of the old matchmaker quietened Harri and he returned the book to the display.

'How um, do I go about it then?'

'Hmm?' said Annie absently sorting the postcards in the rack by the till.

'Uh, dating again?'

This drew Annie to a stop. 'You've been on dates,' she shrugged.

'Not for a decade. I mean, me and Paisley would go out and stuff, but it's different when it's your girlfriend.'

'Are you asking me for first date tips?'

'You've been on more dates than I have, not that that'd be hard.'

'I haven't been on as many as you think, honestly. Look, where did you take Paisley on your first proper date?'

'She took me to her debating society meeting,' he said, a slow smile forming.

'Geez, what was the topic?'

Harri pretended for a moment like he couldn't quite remember but it was in fact burned in his brain.

'Romantic attachment is a capitalist construct designed to dupe women into forfeiting their economic and bodily freedoms and submit to the patriarchy,' he said. 'Or something like that. Paisley was leading the debate.'

'For or against?'

'For.'

'*Ach*, you guys were pretty romantic, I seem to recall.'

She wasn't wrong. In the beginning they'd been magnificent. Harri had been completely overwhelmed by his date that night, watching Paisley on the stand, stating her case, point after point. She was nineteen and fearless. He was nineteen and smitten. She'd been so full of fire and energy.

He'd curtailed her ambitions, surely? Living with him had dampened her spark. The realisation hit him like rockfall.

'Hey?' Annie was before him now, her head tipped, assessing his face. 'You were gone again. Listen,' she sighed. 'If you insist, I can teach you, okay? Just don't go getting all sad again. Here.' She crossed the room so she could pull on her coat. 'I'll be Anjali the eligible vet from the very nice British family.'

Harri watched her, bemused. 'We're acting?'

'Role playing. Okay?' She fixed two chairs in front of a tiny bookshop table with its vase of dried flowers. 'You introduce yourself.'

Annie transformed into an adorably unsure person, pretending to scan the room looking for her date.

'Uh, I don't know about this…' said Harri.

'*You must be Anjali,*' Annie hissed, breaking character for a second.

Harri jolted towards her. 'You must be Anjali?'

Annie simpered a smile and nodded shyly.

'That's not how English girls act,' he said, laughing.

'The ones in books do.'

'From a hundred years ago. Start over.' He wasn't quite so shy now he was smiling into Annie's wickedly gleaming eyes.

'Hi, I'm Anjali,' she said, sticking out a hand.

He looked at it. 'Bit formal, no?'

'If she offers her hand, you shake it.'

Harri obeyed, taking hold of Annie's hand. 'I'm Harri Griffiths. It's…' He paused, searching for the right words, but finding his brain circuitry was having trouble making connections. It had everything to do with Annie clasping his hand the way she was. She was looking at him with curiosity, really playing her part, like they were strangers. '…so nice to meet you… uh… like this.'

'*You can offer to take my coat,*' she whispered. It took him a moment to register.

'Oh! Uh, of course. Allow me…' He'd moved behind her and was cupping her shoulders with his palms, peeling her coat from her. A wave of her perfume reached him. Almond milk, sunshine and summer. Time seemed to be running slowly.

He didn't know he'd messed up until she turned, a strange look on her face. Was she still playing the part of Anjali? He couldn't figure out what was going on.

'You know, maybe she should take off her own coat?' said Annie, finishing the job of removing it and putting it over the back of the chair.

Had she picked up on him being weird again? This was excruciating.

Whatever it was, it had awakened Harri from the faltering feelings that were interrupting his brain signals. 'Right, sure, but… I'll get your chair, right?'

'Why, thank you!' Annie had never sounded more Texan. They both smiled. Annie seated herself and Harri tried to shove her chair closer to the table, but it didn't budge.

'Why do we do this?' said Annie. 'Hoofing someone's chair when they're on it? It's weird. Won't she think it's weird?'

'Who? Oh, Anjali! Yeah, it is kind of a strange thing to do. It's supposed to be gentlemanly.' He hurried into his seat across the little table. He mimed picking up a menu and handed it to Annie. 'You can choose the wine.'

'What if I order the hundred bucks bottle of Champagne?'

'Who said *I* was paying?'

'Touché. I'll have a lemonade.' Annie was back in English girl mode and her body blazed with enjoyment.

Harri couldn't help getting carried along. 'May I say you look very pretty tonight?'

If she hesitated, it was only for the tiniest beat. 'You may.' She fanned herself with the invisible menu. 'What are you looking for in a woman?'

'Ooh!' Harri drew back his jaw. 'Bit direct!'

'Dates have to be direct. Pussy-footin' around gets you nowhere.'

'Oh, okay.' He thought for a bit, and Annie kept her eyes laser-focused on his. She was having fun. So was he. 'Let's see. Umm. She'd have to read, and like food. I'm a big foodie. And uh, I uh…' He felt himself getting coy. 'I like snuggling, I suppose.'

'Snuggling,' Annie echoed in his accent. 'You're too cute.'

They were beaming now. 'And I want someone I can just be myself with,' he continued. 'Someone who'll drink their morning coffee with me, and tell me about their day at night, and someone I can just *be* with.'

'Are you going to ask your date any questions?' Annie put in, that eyebrow quirking again.

'I was just about to! Same question to you. What are you looking for in a date?'

Annie assumed a brash coolness. 'Obviously,' she held down one finger, counting. 'Hotness.'

'Of course.'

On her second finger she counted, more seriously, 'Kindness.' Then, 'Nerdiness.'

'I'm currently three for three,' Harri joked.

'Four, good teeth.'

'This *is* England, you know?'

Their laughter took their little game to a new place, and when Annie pulled her hands to her lap under the table and leaned a little closer, Harri felt she was looking right into him.

'Five, nice brown eyes.'

No one was laughing now. Silence held them fixed across the table, smiles growing wistful.

'Did I say you look really pretty tonight?' Harri's voice came out gruffer than usual. He wasn't aware.

'You already said that.' He could swear Annie (or was she lost in the role of Anjali?) was looking a little peaky.

The fear of making her uncomfortable sent a little current of common sense to Harri's brain, and he became aware of the bookshop around them once more. He broke eye contact and leaned back in the chair.

'Was that okay? Will I do?'

Annie scrunched her eyelids closed then opened them again. He caught the deep whisky-coloured flashes of amber in her irises before she drew back her chair and stood. The dream of the fake date disappeared entirely.

'*Hoo-ee!* Anjali better watch out!' she hooted. 'There's a new wolf in town. And he's come down from them mountains hungry.' She was mugging again, brash Southern accent and all. There was nothing to do but join in and hope the strange sensations of having got lost in their game were one-sided.

'A wild Welsh wolf,' he joked, returning the chairs to their spots, still dazed from whatever it was that just happened.

He couldn't help thinking of meeting the teenage Annie for the first time. She'd arrived at their flat with little more than a stuffed backpack and an incandescent light shining through her skin. She'd made all the flatmates a grilled cheese and talked them into going out that night to the freshers' meet and greet drinks.

He'd arrived in Aber shy and sheltered, having avoided social stuff and sports all through school, preferring to read at home, much to his dad's bewilderment.

Annie had been delighted to meet him. She thought he was interesting, right from the off. Miraculously, he found he could make her laugh. When she spoke to him, she seemed to see right inside him, even when he'd been a stuttering, shy kid with nothing very interesting to say. She'd stuck by him while he came out of his shell, had encouraged it, in fact. He'd never made a friend as easily before or since. In fact, he hadn't made any proper friends since. Now he was taking dating advice from her. He'd brought about the end of his long-term relationship just to be here with her for two weeks. If this wasn't serious, unshakeable friendship, he didn't know what was.

The door opening ended deeper introspection on Harri's part, and Annie was putting her coat away, seemingly happily oblivious to Harri's ruminations, thank goodness.

A bony, beige dog had trotted through the open door and was shaking himself so vigorously on the mat he overbalanced and had to sit down on his skinny question-mark tail.

Jowan followed behind his beloved mutt, giving him a gentle shove further inside so he could shut the door. 'Go on, sit by the fire, Aldous,' he told the creature.

He eyed first Harri, then Annie. 'Not interruptin' anything?' he asked warily.

Annie clearly didn't hear him. '*Aww*, is this the famous Aldous?' she asked, following the mutt to the fire.

Aldous circled once on the hearthrug before plopping himself down and generously offering Annie the chance of scratching his bald pink tummy.

'Scourge of the county vets?' Harri added, grateful for the reprieve. 'He got his haircut then?'

'Certainly did,' Jowan said fondly. 'And there was no biting whatsoever. Anjali found he has not a tooth left in his head, poor old boy.'

Harri looked at the little curly-coated terrier, wondering how old it could possibly be.

'Live forever, Bedlingtons,' Jowan told him, as if reading his mind. 'At least, I hopes they can.' The old pirate turned pensive.

'You're just in time for a cherry bun and tea, if you like?' Annie offered.

Aldous watched her through sleepy eyes as she made for the kitchen. He'd have been offended at the lacklustre petting he'd received if he wasn't so cosy by the fire.

Jowan followed her through the low door and Harri went behind him, his eye on the two shopping bags in Jowan's grip.

'Quiet on the slope today,' Jowan confirmed, while Annie told him they hadn't taken a penny all morning.

'Some days is like that,' he said, his accent as thick as Devonshire clotted cream.

Harri hung back by the cafe entrance while Annie poured out three mugs of tea and lifted the glass dome off the buns.

'There we are,' she said.

Before Jowan sat, he offered up the bags onto the cafe counter. 'Minty sent these, for the shop. They were left over from a Big House wedding last Valentine's. Thought you could brighten up the place.'

Harri took his tea and watched Annie unpack the love heart bunting, blush balloons, baby-pink tealights and scarlet tablecloths.

'I can definitely use these!' she said. 'Tell Minty thank you from us.'

Jowan took a long slurp of tea. 'You're welcome,' he said. 'Oh, and there's been a deal of interest in your silent reading club; half the village is plannin' on coming. It might pay to make it a potluck with the baking. Reckon you'd run short on buns, knowing this lot.'

'Got it,' said Annie, happily.

'I hear you've fallen into Mrs Crocombe's clutches,' Jowan went on, smile-lines radiating from the corners of his eyes.

'Does everyone know?' said Harri, dismayed.

Annie was setting about hanging some crocheted heart bunting along the shelves behind the cafe counter.

'I should say so,' said Jowan, gently. 'There's a pretty penny riding on young Annie here and our Kit.'

Annie laughed hard.

'What about me?' Harri acted affronted, folding his arms, all to cover the very real pang of offence he felt.

'My money's on you,' Jowan twinkled.

Annie turned, an enquiring look on her face. 'Who?'

'The two of you,' Jowan said, and Harri's opinion of the bookish old pirate plummeted. He'd thought he was above Mrs C.'s betting book. Obviously not.

Jowan tried to cheer him up. 'There's no harm in it, not really. We need sommit to get us through the long winters.'

Annie set a cherry bun before him on a plate. 'Harri's nervous about tonight,' she told Jowan, like Harri wasn't standing right there.

'Anjali's the gentlest soul,' Jowan replied. 'Pretty as a picture an' all. Nothing to be nervous about.'

Harri was about to grumble that it wasn't Anjali he was worried about, but all the Clove Lore eyes upon him, when the door tinged open in the shop.

'I'll go!' Annie swept out, leaving Jowan and Harri alone with the jumble of Valentine's décor.

'That one's a firecracker,' Jowan observed.

'Yes she is.'

'Delicate though, I reckon, underneath it all.'

Harri cocked his head, but he couldn't say anything as Annie had her head around the door again.

'Jowan?' she was whispering. 'Can you come through?'

When Harri passed into the shop behind Jowan he found the old man from the day before panting and dripping wet, fit to fall to his knees.

Jowan was dragging the armchair closer to the fire, sending Aldous scurrying for cover into Annie's arms.

'Sit, please. Let's get you dry,' Jowan said and the man obeyed, shuffling to the chair.

'I'll get a blanket,' Harri said, running for the linen cupboard in his room.

'I'm gonna bring you some tea,' Annie told the man loudly. 'And cake. Stay there.'

The man said nothing, only accepting their help.

Jowan went so far as removing the man's sodden slippers, setting them on the hearth to steam. He wrapped the old man's bare feet in a towel.

'Are you on 'olday?' Jowan asked him. 'Visiting someone in Clove Lore?'

The man shook his head. His tiny spectacles were spotted with rain but he didn't draw them off.

Annie, still gripping the unimpressed Aldous under one arm, set the tea and bun on the table by the man's side.

The man set about feeding himself with a deliberate restraint, placing the paper napkin across his damp lap like this was the Ritz.

The three stood back and observed him, Aldous wriggling until he was comfortably curled up against Annie's chest, totally disinterested in the stranger.

'You don't recognise him?' Harri whispered. 'We thought he must be a local.'

'Never seen him before,' Jowan said. 'And I've lived 'ere all my life.'

'What should we do? He seems lost,' Annie said, rocking the little dog and hugging him close.

'Do?' Jowan said, perplexed. 'Dunno. Might just be passing through.'

'But he was here yesterday. He slept right there for a long time,' said Annie.

Harri started at this. 'You don't think he's been outdoors all night, do you?'

'I hope not,' Annie replied in a low voice, approaching the man again. 'Is there anyone we can call for you? To pick you up? Any children? A carer?'

The man looked at her with an air of irritation. Harri saw the sharpness in his eye. It was the same look he'd given them yesterday when they'd suggested he'd been left behind by a coach group.

'Reckon I'll call Mint,' Jowan said. 'She'll know what to do.'

–

Within the hour, the bookshop was full of whispering locals, and the old man was fast asleep, his cup drained and the cherry bun delicately nibbled away. Aldous had, unnoticed, crept up onto his lap and was also sleeping soundly in the warmth from the fire, happy to share the best seat in the place with the old stranger who, to the little dog's expert nose, smelled of mothballs, Murray Mints, and conservators' resin, not that anybody ever asked Aldous's opinion about anything.

As they dozed, oblivious, the village elders, Minty, Mrs Crocombe and Mr Bovis, agreed he was no Clove Lore local; they'd recognise him if he was.

Two brothers, Monty and Tom, definitely identical twins, Harri concluded, had called in too, and confirmed he hadn't been a fisherman pal of their late father's, and they'd left again, but not before a friend of the twins, a young police officer by the name of Zoë arrived. She was in running gear, evidently not on duty today.

Minty spoke to her with discretion. 'If he's here; he's in our care. No need to involve Social Services just yet,' she said, and Harri had been surprised to see Zoë deferring to the lady of the manor.

Zoë made a few phone calls on her mobile and came back to let everyone know there were no active missing persons reports for anyone meeting the man's description. 'Not in the county, not in the country,' she elaborated.

Minty's eyebrows raised. 'Check his pockets?' she said.

Zoë did as she was told, deftly lifting the strange objects out one by one.

Harri tried to piece it all together. 'A pocket watch, and are they matchboxes?'

'Miniature books,' Jowan corrected him. 'Fine ones too. And that's a mariner's compass, not a watch.'

'Has he come from the sea?' Mrs Crocombe wondered aloud.

'Wearing slippers?' Bovis screwed up his face at the suggestion. 'He's a landlubber, if ever there was one. A grockel?'

Annie wanted to know what the heck a grockel was.

'An outsider,' Jowan confirmed, as Zoë reached into the sleeping man's chest pocket and revealed the bow of an antique key. The man's hand flew to hers and held the key fast as he jolted awake.

Zoë yelped in surprise. 'I'm sorry, sir,' she told him once she'd collected herself. 'I'm just looking for ID. Do you have any?'

The man fixed his eyes upon her. He didn't look cross now; he looked afraid. Zoë stepped back.

'I have to let the chief inspector know; in case a report comes in.'

'Of a vagrant?' Minty asked.

'Of a missing vulnerable person. But there's nothing out from any of the care homes nearby.'

'Check them again,' Minty instructed. 'In the meantime, he ought to stay here.'

The man was struggling to reach his slippers on the hearth, rocking like a turtle on its back to get himself upright.

Harri knelt at the man's feet. 'It's okay,' he told him. 'You can stay here and rest. We'll look after you until we find your family.'

'I can call a car to take him into custody, until Social Services can find him somewhere to stay,' Zoë said. 'That's the proper procedure for an unidentified absconder from any institution.'

'Custody? We don't know he's absconded. He could be a holidaymaker. And how long would all that take anyway?' Minty said dismissively. 'No, young Harri is right. He should stay here until his people come looking for him. Harri, go get him a pair of your socks, if you don't mind.' It was not a question. Harri went to his suitcase immediately.

Zoë admitted that there were only the cells at the police station to house him if she took him in. 'But the chief would probably have him admitted to hospital right away anyway.'

Minty was even less keen on this idea. 'Call the surgery. Dr Mateeva will come out to see him here. Jowan, ring the Siren's Tail, have Bella send up a dish of her winter stew and a brandy.'

Harri was back and fitting his socks on the old man's feet. He couldn't believe he was hearing this; Minty ordering everyone around like she was queen of the whole village. Nevertheless, the flurry of obedient activity proved she as-near-as-dammit was.

'What's your name?' Harri asked him softly under all the hubbub.

The man seemed to look around for something, struck by an idea, but it died away and his eyes fell dim again. He shook his head.

'It's okay,' Harri told him.

He became aware of Annie's soft eyes on him from behind the old man's back. She smiled affectionately when he looked to her as the rest of the villagers dashed here and there: Mr Bovis to fetch one of his jumpers, Mrs Crocombe taking the man's damp coat away to her washer-dryer behind her ice cream shop down the slope, and Zoë continuing to make phone calls, all while Minty held court.

Harri had time to register amongst the chaos how warm and how like a community this little corner of

Devon felt suddenly. He was, at least for today, a part of something bigger than just him and Paisley and his barista job and his circumscribed little life split between what was now Paisley's flat in Port Talbot and his parents' place in Neath. It felt oddly reassuring.

Annie came to sit at the other side of the old man and the sleeping dog, and she patted the back of Harri's hand, just for a second, letting him know without words that she felt the same about the funny little bookshop and all its drama, while the lost stranger nodded off once more.

Chapter Ten

Accidentally Annwyl

A handful of booklovers called in through the rest of the afternoon and Annie had seen to them but only rung up one title (a new children's picture book), making today's total sales a meagre six pounds ninety-nine.

By five, the old man had napped, picked at a really delicious-smelling stew from the Siren's Tail and been examined by the doctor, who'd taken one look at the brandy Minty had ordered for him and pushed the glass away saying it could do more harm than good. Minty ended up downing it herself to settle her agitation.

The old man had fiercely refused the blood and urine samples, upsetting everyone, uttering over and over again, 'NO!' The doctor had insisted it was that or an ambulance, and he'd finally agreed with a lot of consternation. When asked if he took any medication, he insisted he did not but then conceded that perhaps he did, he wasn't sure.

Zoë had set off for the police station along the main road to file her report having photographed the old man with her phone.

Minty maintained a possessive protectiveness over him, using the shop landline to call around all her contacts on every committee she sat on to ask if any elderly person amongst their number had disappeared.

Mrs Crocombe was on her mobile doing the same thing, sequestered amongst the stacks, trying to be discreet, but falling into lascivious gossiping on almost every call and forgetting her mission for minutes at a time.

Mr Bovis had long since turned up the collar on his ancient Barbour, obviously feeling every inch the TV detective, and stalked off into the drizzle, intent on knocking on every door in the village looking for leads.

The doctor concluded the man had a bladder infection that might be contributing to his confusion and antibiotics were sent for from the pharmacy along the promontory. Jowan had taken care of collecting them.

Annie had been impressed at Minty's commitment to keeping the man comfortably installed in the village as opposed to being carted off to a hospital ward where he'd be exposed to, in her words, 'goodness knows what infections and indignities' and she wouldn't hear of him 'slumbering in a cell like a convict'. He was a guest in her village, as far as she was concerned.

Harri had kept the kettle boiling all afternoon and the man had steadily drunk two cups of tea with milk and sugar that he added himself. His cheeks had pinked up a little in the hearth light and, observing him, the doctor concluded it would be difficult to force the man's admission into hospital, what with all the men's respite wards being full to capacity and there being no passenger ambulances in the vicinity to take him on the hour's drive anyway.

The doctor left with instructions to keep him topped up with antibiotics, hydrated, rested and warm until his family was found and, 'under no circumstances is he to go wandering in this weather'.

As darkness fell, talk in the shop turned to what exactly they were going to do next.

'The report will be circulating all across Devon by now,' Minty insisted. 'If someone's looking for him, or if they recognise him, we'll hear soon enough.'

'And if they don't?' Harri asked in a low voice. 'Where will he stay?'

Jowan and Minty exchanged glances.

'You've got the whole of the Big House, don't you?' Annie said, not understanding why, after being so keen to keep their foundling, Minty wasn't positively bursting to put him up for the night.

'The estate is ours, yes, the gardens and such,' Jowan explained in his soft way while Minty looked pained. 'But the house was sold to developers, and split into apartments, which are privately owned now. There's only one still on the market. An' we've only our one-bed behind the original kitchens on the ground floor.'

So the *Downton Abbey* dream wasn't quite what Annie had imagined. What a pity.

'We'll sit here with him, until word comes,' Jowan said.

'Mark my words, Clove Lore is a whispering place. He'll be reunited with his loved ones within the hour,' Minty proclaimed confidently.

Annie looked at her phone. It was almost five-thirty. In the commotion she'd forgotten about the double date. A glance at Harri, who was lurking by the stairs, told her it hadn't slipped his mind for a second.

'Maybe we should… knock tonight on the head, given the circumstances,' Harri said, furtively.

This made everyone in the shop, apart from the insensible man, snap their heads to him.

'*What?* No!' This came from Mrs Crocombe emerging from the stacks, her phone lowered momentarily. 'It's all arranged. You two young ones go and get yourselves ready. We've everything under control.'

Annie wanted to go to the pub. Anything to get out of the strange atmosphere of suspense that was falling over the shop. She approached Harri on the stairs. 'You heard the lady. They've got this under control,' she said, and he let her pass. 'And I was promised cider and chips.'

Harri folded, just as she knew he would, and he sloped off to get changed.

Within half an hour Annie was showered, made-up, and in a dress she'd originally bought to wear to her school's Christmas pageant, in a clingy, pale olive velvet. She'd been desperate to wear it again and paired it with her long blanket coat, her chains and rings, and her brown boots. She felt pretty good as she made her way gingerly down the clanking spiral stairs.

'*Annwyl!*' Harri gasped when he saw her, which didn't go unobserved by the Clove Lore cronies. Even the old man turned laboriously to look.

Harri was in a proper shirt with his thick woollen jumper, black jeans and boots (not his walking boots, for once). He'd even scrunched his hair with some product and put his contacts in. And he was blushing right to the tips of his ears.

Annie was about to tell him how cute he looked but everyone's attention was on the lost old man who was trying to get to his feet. The whole shop fussed at once, and Jowan offered him his arm. He seemed intent on coming close to inspect Annie.

As he drew near, Annie smiled broadly for him. 'Will I do?' she asked, suddenly struck by the memory of twirling in her party dress for her grandpa.

He was going to say something. Everyone waited. The only sound was his socks shuffling across the floorboards.

'Annwyl?' the man said, reaching for her hand, which she took.

'That's what Harri's always called me. It's Welsh for Annie.'

The man's face fell. 'No,' he said weakly, before clearing his throat and trying again. 'It's old Welsh. It means *beloved* or rather, *my loved one*.'

The silence in the shop fell another notch, just as the warmth swelled in Annie's chest. 'It does?' Annie asked, her eyes darting to Harri, who was already shrugging it off and making to protest.

Mrs Crocombe was fit to combust with excitement, and Jowan staged a one-man rescue attempt by leaving the old man's side and hurriedly freeing some notes from the till before presenting them to Harri. 'For drinks, on us,' he said, shoving them into Harri's hand.

Annie however, seeing the sudden clarity in the old man's eyes, determined to make the most of it. 'I'm Annie Luna, from Texas,' she said, giving his hand a little squeeze. 'Pleased to meet you, Mr…?'

The man's face changed. She saw decades of politeness and social training clicking into place, his mouth opened out of habit, as his head lowered in a bow. 'Mr William Sabine,' he said calmly. 'Pleased to make your acquaintance.'

Then in a blink, the spark was gone again. Jowan gently led the man back to the fireplace.

The matriarchs took to their phones once more, armed with this new information, and Harri pulled on his coat and made for the door, looking like a man still very much thinking of the way he'd stupidly yelped 'Annwyl' and been exposed by Mr Sabine as some sort of secret admirer when he was supposed to be a friend. He seemed only too glad to get out of the shop for the evening.

Annie followed into the darkness after him, tucking the lengths of her hair into her coat, smiling and promising the chattering women they wouldn't be gone long but getting no reply. She pulled the door closed behind her.

'Beloved?' she said under her breath as she followed Harri across the courtyard and through the passageway onto the dark, glistening cobbles.

'*Hmm?*' Harri answered, the wind whipping his hair and making him squint.

'Nothing,' she said, determined not to embarrass him further, her mind racing back into the past, trying to recall the first time he'd used the name for her.

When had he christened her Annwyl?

She'd taken it for an endearing affectation, like how he called Paisley 'Cariad' when they first got together. She was struck by the memory of that sweet nickname bugging her. She knew what Cariad meant. It meant he loved Paisley.

Now she was thinking it through, Harri never called her Annwyl in company, only when they were alone together. He'd definitely never said it in Paisley's hearing. That she was sure of.

A tiny part of her registered how much she'd liked the way he said it this evening as she came down the spiral stairs, even when she thought it was simply her name in his language. She hoped he wasn't going to stop using it now. From the way the tips of his ears had turned pink at Mr Sabine's words, she feared maybe he would.

Harri had stopped to wait for her on the slope. 'Let's get this over with, yeah?'

'Sure,' she said, and then neither of them spoke all the way down the path, past soggy gardens with their fleece-wrapped palm trees, finally making their way past the lifeboat house and onto the seawall where the dark beach and black waves spread out before them and the jolly lights from every window of the old white pub hastened them into the warmth.

Chapter Eleven

The Double Date

Harri was too agitated to feel the full benefit of the Siren's Tail's warm welcome, where the fire glowed strong in the hearth, mouth-watering food and beery smells filled the air, and the room buzzed with good humour and community.

He scanned the room for his date. Bovis, no longer on detective duty, was already installed at the bar nursing an orange juice, no doubt Mrs C.'s informer on how the evening was panning out. He was pretending not to notice their arrival, but Harri could see his beady eyes following him in the bar mirrors. Daft old crow.

The women seated at tables around the room were all much older than Harri: coastal-path walkers in pastel raincoats with ski poles and bobble hats. No sign of Anjali amongst them.

'Are we the first to arrive?' Annie asked cheerfully from close behind him. She was looking around too.

That's when a figure emerged from the kitchen doors behind the bar, unbuttoning a chef's jacket to reveal a beatnik stripe t-shirt and lean muscle. They too were casting a furtive glance around.

When Kit's eyes met Annie's, Harri noticed their look of relief and he positively *felt* the swell of excitement in Annie.

Kit was gorgeous. Smooth cheekbones and sharp brows, full lips, and surfers' sun-bleached hair pushed back and buzzed at the sides where it was darker.

'Well, I'll be!' Harri heard Annie mutter through her smile before she launched herself towards them asking if they were a hugger.

Kit looked like they'd usually demur, but they said yes, no doubt melted by Annie's enthusiasm. Harri stood by as they shared a hug. So far, so much like a real date.

'Mrs C. said you were pretty,' Kit was saying shyly, their hands now shoved in baggy black pants pockets, a full four inches shorter than the towering Annie. Neither of them seemed to mind this one bit.

Harri was hit by the anxious thought that his own date might not show up. He hadn't even considered that as an option until now, but what if he had to watch these two being adorable together all night? As much as he hadn't wanted to come on this date, he didn't relish the thought of going back to the bookshop by himself and explaining to the gossips how he'd left Annie and Kit to their evening.

Kit and Annie were admiring one another's accents. Kit was calling themself a 'Cockney Sparra' and making Annie laugh.

'Drinks?' Harri said, interrupting.

They decided on ciders and Harri was putting in their order with the barman – who clearly knew all about their date, judging by the amount of smirking he was doing – when someone appeared tentatively by his side.

'Are you Harri?'

Anjali was small, dark-haired and beyond pretty in a midnight blue sweater and jeans with strappy black boots up to her calves. Tiny gold studs traced the shell of her left ear. Harri gulped away his nerves and tried to shake her hand, managing to knock one of the ciders so it spilled on the bar.

'Oh god, sorry.' He took her hand, realised too late that his was wet with cider suds, apologised yet again, and would have prayed for the ground to open up and swallow him if it wasn't for Anjali's reassuring laugh. She shook his hand in spite of the wetness and told him it was nice to meet him.

The barman mopped up the mess while Harri suffered.

'You want a cider?' he said, aware that Annie and Kit were already taking their seats at an elaborately set table by the fire. None of the other tables had white cloths and fresh cut flowers. The work of Mrs C., no doubt.

'Coke's fine, thanks,' said Anjali.

'So, you're the vet who tackled Aldous, the ungroom-able beast?'

She laughed again at this, thank goodness. 'It was a piece of cake now he's used to me. When he first came to us, I had to shave him under sedation.'

'You or the dog?' Harri blurted, then wished he hadn't when Anjali didn't laugh quite as much as before.

'You take a seat, I'll bring these over,' Harri said. 'That's Annie Luna over there with Kit.'

Anjali walked away, leaving Harri alone to have a stern word with himself. *Stop fumbling! It's not an audition. It's a date. And not even a real date. This is just to get the villagers off our backs.* Only, the way Annie was laughing sure sounded like this was a great big, very real, double date.

When he'd paid for the drinks and turned to face the room, Annie was sitting right next to Kit and telling them she loved their t-shirt. *It's just a plain old striped t-shirt*, Harri thought, grudgingly.

'How long have you and Kit known each other,' he asked as he set down Anjali's Coke and took a sip of his cider. He hadn't known how dry his mouth was until the bitter apple tang hit his tastebuds and he wanted to down it on the spot.

'We don't,' they both said at the same time.

'I don't come into the pub much,' Anjali explained.

'And I've only been chef here for a year or so,' Kit added.

'You're an incomer like us,' Annie said, and Kit agreed they sure were.

There came a moment of awkwardness when Harri settled on the chair next to Anjali, directly facing Kit, and the barman appeared with the menu, which listed a few simple, wholesome pub grub dishes. He was wielding his order pad and asking, 'Did Kit tell you the specials tonight?'

'Not yet, Finan,' Kit replied. 'It's my individual steak and pastry bakes with blue cheese,' they told the group.

'You'll be wanting fish and chips, right, Annie?' Harri said with confidence, adding for Kit's benefit, 'She loved a chippy tea when we lived together in Wales.'

Annie looked straight at Harri with a fixed smile and announced that she had a hankering for Kit's steak bake, actually.

Harri wondered why he felt stung. He fell quiet while Anjali explained she didn't eat meat and asked for the roast Mediterranean veggie pasta. Kit said they'd join her; they weren't all that hungry after cheffing all day. Last of the group, Harri placed his order for his long-awaited cod and chips with tartare sauce, and extra mushy peas, his favourite.

He realised his cheeks hurt a little from trying to smile. Was he being weird? How come Annie managed to be so calm in situations like this? She was already set upon interviewing Kit about the tattoos across the backs of their fingers, which spelled out the letters of their name with tiny blue swallows in flight.

Harri watched as she very nearly touched her fingertips to the inked spots, unaware it was awakening something within him that he wasn't used to dealing with. It would be a good fifteen minutes before he recognised it for what it was: jealousy. And he wasn't proud of it.

Anjali had drunk all her coke. They'd covered where in Wales Harri was from and she'd discovered he made coffee for a living, and he'd learned how she'd lived all her life along the promontory and that her dad was a vet and her mum was a surgeon.

'My mam's a housewife and Dad installs conservatories,' he said, killing the conversation dead.

Across the table Annie was still pumping Kit for information. It was part of her charm offensive. Ask them all about themselves, people love that. It disarms them.

Kit, however, Harri was fascinated to realise, wasn't one to be swept off their feet by an extrovert taking a deep interest in them. In fact, Kit looked overwhelmed.

'When did you know you loved cooking?' Annie was asking, and Kit hurriedly drank from their glass before answering like they were on a quickfire TV quiz show.

'Um, I don't know, when I was at school?'

Harri couldn't help sneaking looks to watch the situation unfold. Kit was pressed into the furthest corner of their chair while Annie was leaning towards them, her chin propped on her hand and her eyes alight. Harri had seen her like this so many times, but usually the subject of her interest was leaning closer and closer to her, flattered and drawn in, desperate to share themselves with a stunning Texan woman with a drawling voice like smoke and bourbon.

'Are you… enjoying your holiday?' Anjali broke through his thoughts. When he met her eyes, she looked a little desperate.

'It's been fabulous, thanks.' He smiled, bobbing his head to make up for his lack of words. It was like he'd forgotten how to talk like a normal person. 'Annie's the bookseller,' Harri added at last, and it cut his friend off mid-interrogation.

'What's that?' Annie asked.

'I was saying how you're the natural when it comes to bookselling. I'm better in the cafe. You're great at knowing what books people want. Always was.'

Kit and Annie only smiled politely, and it dawned on Harri he'd singlehandedly stopped the entire date in its tracks. Now no one had anything to say.

Thankfully Finan was back with their food, and everyone pushed it around their plates; everyone except Annie who hoovered up her steak pie with the blue cheese oozing out from a golden pastry lattice.

'Oh my god!' she said between bites. 'Kit, you're a genius!'

The chef accepted this with a shy grin.

'You know Harri bakes?' Annie said across the table to Anjali, sounding like a proud parent.

'That's… nice,' said the accomplished, professional Anjali, clearly unsure how she was supposed to respond to the information that a grown man possesses a basic life skill.

Why did Annie have to go and say that? Like Minty said at the village meeting, you can't force things, attraction just happens, and it clearly wasn't happening for Anjali.

'So you went to uni together?' Kit asked, trying to rescue things.

'We sure did,' Annie grabbed at the topic. 'No clue how we got as far as graduation; we missed so many classes to fit in work.'

'And gigs, and hangovers,' said Harri, before adding wickedly, 'thanks to Annie. She's a bad influence, this one.' It sounded odd and overly familiar, even for them.

Generously, Annie scoffed at this. 'Hardly!'

'Oh yeah?' Harri brightened. 'Who was it that had to fake your doctor's note that day you sneaked out to see Christine and the Queens when you were supposed to be in our Shakespeare final?'

'Who was it came with me to see them?' she challenged back, eyes shining. 'Was it fake laryngitis?'

'Glandular fever.'

'That's it! And because we missed the exam, we got to spend the summer in Wales having a blast... and doing our re-sits.'

'*Such* a bad influence,' Harri said with a '*tisk tisk*' and a head shake.

'I regret nothing.' Annie laughed, but it faded fast when she realised their dates were sitting courteously by, listening to them showing off.

Harri inhaled through his teeth, shooting his eyebrows up. 'Soooo,' he said pointlessly, unable to come up with another topic.

Nobody talked until Kit threw a lifeline, saying they were thinking of adopting a dog.

'Really?' Anjali's face transformed with happiness, before launching into telling Kit all about the two fosters she had at the surgery at that moment, two elderly greyhounds, ex-racers, both needing a quiet life with beach walks and plenty of naps.

'I had to stop Elliot taking them both,' she said, and Kit laughed and remarked how Elliot and Jude had already rehomed three dogs. 'That's probably enough to be getting on with.'

Annie finished her food and quietly crossed her cutlery on her empty plate.

'More drinks?' Harri said, and Anjali momentarily stopped describing the dogs' various ailments to say she was fine, thanks, and Kit asked for a second cider but kept their attention fixed on Anjali like those old greyhounds were the most fascinating thing in the world.

'I'll help you,' Annie said, springing to her feet.

'So… what do you think?' she asked in a whisper as soon as they slid onto stools at the opposite end of the bar from Bovis (who probably thought he was texting surreptitiously; no doubt updating the gossipmongers of Clove Lore).

'Think of what?' Harri said, taking an exaggerated interest in the different ciders in the pumps.

'Of Kit? They're super cute, right?'

'Sure.'

'What do you think of Anjali? She's gorgeous, right?' she pressed.

Harri screwed his nose. 'Yeah, she's lovely.'

'But?' Annie leaned closer. Her warm almond blossom perfume swelled around them.

'But, things aren't exactly flowing,' he said, amazed she hadn't picked up on that.

They both glanced back at their dates who were leaning elbows on the table now, mirroring each other, exchanging easy conversation. Anjali was more animated than she'd been all evening.

'Besides,' Harri put in, 'I thought we were just here to get off the hook with Mrs C. You're not really into Kit, are you?'

Finan made his way down the bar and took their drinks order, preventing them getting into it further. They kept quiet while he worked the pumps and took their money.

'Would you have been up for a thing with Anjali?' Annie whispered, as soon as Finan left.

Harri shrugged. It might have been nice if she'd liked him a tiny bit. Maybe he would have asked her out for a proper date. 'Would it have mattered?' he said, taking his drink in his hands but not wanting to go back to their table for four.

'What? To me?' Annie seemed confused. 'Why would it matter to me?'

'Because we're on holiday together? Would you have minded if she'd been into me?'

Annie's expression was unreadable, and a little alarm bell sounded in Harri's brain warning him not to pursue this, whatever it was, any further.

'I want what's best for you.' Annie shrugged. 'Do I think a rebound holiday fling would be good for you? Probably not, but I wouldn't stop you.'

Harri took a quick drink from his cider, unaware he was jogging his feet up and down on the footrest.

Annie glanced back at their dates. 'They've forgotten we're here. I guess there's going to be another match made in Clove Lore. Dunno if Mrs C. will be pleased or not?'

Harri sniffed a wry laugh. 'Jowan will be pleased. He did say his money was on us two.'

He wished he hadn't said it. He was being a dick. And yet, inside he was fighting a losing battle with the self-sabotaging part of himself. *Don't say it*, the gentler part was warning. *Don't say it*. But the ill-fated double date and seeing Annie flirting with Kit, and of course, the cider, had loosened up the words, and out they came, all in a rush. 'Annie, when did you have a crush on me?'

Annie's eyes narrowed. 'Huh?'

He pulled his lips together, regretting all his life choices. He knew he was being petty but evidently couldn't stop himself. 'It's just I heard you talking the other night at the Big House, saying you had a crush on me, back in the day.' He forced cheerfulness into his voice, but Annie wasn't easily fooled.

'Oh, that was nothing,' she said, shrugging it off. Annie stood and lifted her drink. Harri followed, only just remembering Kit's pint as well as his own.

'I'd have known,' Harri said briskly, wishing he could shut up.

Annie stopped in her tracks, right in the middle of the bar room, fixing him with a look both pleading and impatient.

'If you liked me. I'd have known,' he said again.

'Well,' she said with a wry smile. 'I guess you don't know everything about me.'

That was a warning shot, he knew. Yet still he wasn't satisfied. 'On what day was it that you liked me?'

'Does it matter?' Annie was on the move again back to the table.

'Seriously, when?' This time it was insistent. He hated himself for it.

Their eyes locked. Annie's were fierce. 'Right before you met Paisley,' she blurted. 'At the beginning of third year, okay? Happy now?'

She left him standing there, absorbing her words. Not just the words. *The tone*. Her voice had cracked. She was upset, and she was cross.

He watched her rejoin the others. She looked so incredibly tired all of a sudden. *Shit!*

He thought of his mum on Friday, still reeling from the news he'd split with Paisley, and telling him not to go upsetting Annie, like she'd instinctively known he somehow would.

Mournfully, he took his seat and listened to Anjali and Kit enthusing about their childhood pets like they were the only two people in the world.

Annie didn't meet his eyes once, not until they had skipped dessert, said their goodbyes to their oblivious, absorbed dates and made their way silently up the blustery slope, discovering the lights in the bookshop still ablaze when they got there and Jowan dozing with Aldous on his lap by the fire, no sign of anyone else.

'You're still here?' Harri asked him when he jumped awake, and Aldous let out a sharp bark of alarm.

Jowan told them in a whisper how they'd waited all evening for officer Zoë to ring them back with an update, now that they knew the man's name. 'But nobody's looking for him.'

'No one?' Annie said, moving closer.

'There's no missing person's report. He hasn't gone AWOL from a care home or ward, nothing. He doesn't seem to be from anywhere. And he's got no ID on him, so,' Jowan shrugged, 'he's being picked up by Social Services in the morning.'

Harri looked around, suddenly suspicious. 'Where's he now?'

Jowan tipped his head towards Harri's bedroom door.

'He's in my bed?'

'Come on, Aldous,' Jowan said, still whispering. 'We'll leave you to it. Mr Sabine's had his dinner and his antibiotics and is fast asleep after a bath. You'll have to listen for him waking…'

Harri didn't know how to baby-sit a grown adult. 'Do I… go in there with him? Watch him?'

'No, no, you two get some sleep, an' keep an ear out for the door in the morning.'

Harri was a few steps ahead. He'd have to sleep out here on the armchair. And after weeks spent sleeping on the couch at Paisley's. He was ashamed to recognise that he felt sorry for himself. This evening was doing nothing for his sense of selflessness.

Jowan, with Aldous at his heels, bobbed out the door and was gone. Harri thought he might have seen a smirk at the corners of his mouth, and couldn't account for it until Annie spoke.

'You're sharing with me, then?'

Harri stared back blankly.

'There's only one bed now,' Annie said, matter of factly. 'You'll freeze to death sleeping in the shop.'

'Uh…' He ran through how awful he'd been this evening, showing off how well he knew his friend, trying to spite Kit, probably making Anjali feel rotten, and then he'd pushed and pushed for the grim details about Annie liking him once upon a time when they were basically kids.

'You comin'?' Annie was at the foot of the stairs.

Harri meekly followed.

Tucked up, two wide-eyed faces peeped over white covers in the dark, and four hands clutched at the edge of the duvet, as they lay ruminating, listening to the creaking in the rafters as the wind buffeted the Borrow-A-Bookshop.

Annie's annoyance had ebbed away ages ago. She wasn't the sort to hold a grudge. Besides hadn't Harri been through a lot recently? She should have known a date was too much for him to handle, should have put her foot down and protected him. He wasn't ready to be out there again.

She thought of Kit and how attractive and friendly they were, and yet, she wasn't all that sure she'd been seriously into them, and why having thoroughly scared Kit off, she'd insisted on flirting so madly. She'd wanted to push Harri, she supposed, after the whole 'Annwyl' revelation.

In the dark, Harri rolled his head to look at her. Annie flicked her eyes shut.

'I'm sorry about tonight. I was being a twat,' he said.

'You were such a twat,' Annie drawled, her eyes still closed, her body still. 'But I forgive you.'

She heard him chuckle, hoping he would drop the touchy subject of how she'd liked him back in third year. She didn't like to remember it, the way the crush had struck her, all of a sudden, back when fancying Harri had been the strangest, simplest thing.

It had come towards the end of the May break, the night before their assessment results were coming out. Harri had been confident he'd be fine; Annie, less so. She'd worked hard enough but had missed a few Classics lectures and had only read the *SparkNotes* on *The Oresteia Trilogy* instead of reading the plays.

Harri had been confident generally that spring term. She'd noticed a change in him. He was smiling more readily, his body seemed relaxed in a way she'd never noticed before, and yes, his shoulders were noticeably broader, and she was sure he'd grown taller. He'd been making more of an effort picking out clothes too.

One day, as his Waterstones shift was ending and hers was beginning, he'd breezed past her in a rush, the neck of his shirt open. She'd never noticed the thickness of his throat or the hard curve of his Adam's apple before. He'd had his hair cut with velvety-looking buzzed sides that seemed to her in that moment very strokable. He'd smelled good too, of something new. 'No time to stop,' he'd said, and he'd kissed her cheek as he ran past, and she'd felt a curious weakness in her knees.

That had been her first inkling of really *noticing* Harri. Then, waiting for their results to come out that night in the flat when everyone else had gone out to the pub, she'd been struck with the period cramps that could ruin whole days at a time, and he'd not even had to think about it, hadn't even asked, he'd just grabbed his wallet and disappeared, coming back half an hour later with a box of Cadbury Creme Eggs (one of her absolute favourite things about living in Wales), salt 'n' vinegar Chipsticks, and, bless him, a big blue packet of Bodyform Night Time towels. For some reason he'd gone for the twenty-four pack, not the eight, and somehow that had made her glow with affection. He'd stood there, not wanting praise or thinking he'd done anything particularly special, and he simply handed them all over and said one word, 'Tea?', and that's when she melted for sure.

It had been, she could admit to herself now, excitingly painful to fancy her friend. She'd talked it over with Cassidy on whispered Skype calls late at night.

'You gotta tell him!' Cassidy had insisted.

'But how do I tell him? He sees me as a friend. He'll think I'm a creeper, crushing on him all this time. I'm like a sister to him!'

'He's a guy; he'll love it.'

'Harri's not like that.'

'Says who?'

'Says twelve yellow roses on Valentine's Day. Says him brushing his teeth and scratching his butt in front of me for two whole years. Says us being work colleagues *and* roommates. If it was going to happen it'd have happened by now.'

Annie conveniently left out how she'd only recently started to like him, and she'd never even considered sweet, funny, friendly Harri as a potential boyfriend until then, and that she'd never given him any indication she liked him whatsoever, so how could it have happened before now?

Besides, this was Harri she was talking about. Lovely, nerdy Harri. Her best friend on this side of the globe. She could flirt with other people around campus, but not Harri. It'd feel artificial somehow and, well, icky.

Annie distinctly remembered Cassidy accepting her list as very good reasons not to tell him, and instead of protesting that if she liked him she should tell him, Cassidy told her it'd be best not to blow the friendship.

Undergraduate Annie, only just embarking on her twenties, had let it go, suffering in exquisite silence for weeks until the reason for Harri's newfound confidence presented herself in the flat one morning.

Annie had heard the giggling and Harri's throaty laughter over the sounds of the shower running. Later, they'd emerged, their hair wrapped up in matching towels. Harri had introduced the woman wearing his Swansea City football top as, 'Paisley, my girlfriend.'

Annie had to throw her hands to her cheeks thinking her reddening face was about to crack from smiling so fixedly. Paisley must have read the situation correctly; she hadn't liked Annie on sight.

So, she'd deliberately shrunk into the background, minimising her feelings, trying to ignore how mortifying it all was, staying late at the library to avoid overhearing Harri and Paisley in the room next to hers. It had been kind of hideous, but come autumn when the new semester began, after a summer of angst and longing, mixed with Harri-avoidance and self-denial, Annie told herself sternly that enough was enough.

Paisley was hanging around every day by that point and Harri was happy, which was all that mattered. Annie congratulated herself on beating her crush, and she didn't dare think of it again. Not until Sunday night at the village meeting when Jude was prying it out of her, and the confession had felt innocent enough. She'd liked him once, but they were better off as friends. She hadn't intended him to overhear. That had been stupid of her. But what she'd said remained true, nonetheless. Friendship was all that mattered.

Tonight had proven that Harri wasn't emotionally equipped for a relationship, even a casual date had been too much for him. The last thing he needed was more complicated feelings on top of his Paisley heartbreak, and god knows, she couldn't bear to lose another friend after the mess with Cassidy.

'We okay?' Harri was asking now, lying by her side in the dark, a large expanse of no-man's-mattress between them.

Annie considered for a millisecond addressing the way he'd let her think 'Annwyl' was just his cute nickname for her when all along it may have signified something more, but she squashed the urge.

'We're good,' she told him, walking her hand along the top of the covers to his. She closed her fingers over his and squeezed them tight, hoping Harri, who had fallen silent now, couldn't feel her body sending out hot crackles of electricity, surprising in their intensity. She released him, just in case.

She glowed wordlessly in the dark until, deep in the night, she finally fell asleep, forgetting all about their guest in the room downstairs, thinking only of the next ten days of bookselling and how she was going to get through them unscathed.

Chapter Twelve

William, Claimed

Harri waved disconsolately at the retreating car ambulance as it carried William Sabine up the slope in the still dark morning. Minty watched it go with her arms folded across her Barbour windcheater.

'This isn't at all what I wanted,' she was saying. 'He came to *us*. He was one of us.'

Mr Sabine had refused Harri's offer of cornflakes and orange juice at seven this morning when he'd heard the old man rattling around downstairs and sprung silently from Annie's bed, leaving her breathing softly in her sleep.

There'd been a minor tussle when he'd offered William his arm at the foot of the spiral staircase to help him up to the bathroom.

'If I can manage an elephant ladder, I can make it up these stairs,' he'd grumped and Harri hadn't pressed him on what exactly an elephant ladder might be and quite how many of them William had climbed in recent days.

Annie slept through the whole thing, which was surprising after she'd passed out pretty much as soon as she lay down in the bed next to him last night. She'd not moved a muscle, lying like a wrapped mummy; she must have had nine hours' sleep, at least. Harri remembered how fitfully she used to sleep back at uni. Maybe she'd changed? Was Annie becoming more restful?

Harri, on the other hand, had finally drifted off at around four, having lain awake burningly aware of Annie next to him, terrified of disturbing her. He was, after all, a bed-crasher and a pretty rubbish friend with a lot of making up to do today. He supposed now that Mr Sabine was being carted off to the hospital, he'd be back in his own room tonight, and of course that was a good thing.

'Got your bags?' the agency social worker had asked William out on the slope. Even Harri thought the guy looked fresh out of college, and Minty had stated the fact out loud. The ambulance driver had stayed in the car, no time to waste.

'He came to us with only the clothes he was wearing,' Minty had said with some force. 'Doesn't it mention that in your notes?'

The young man pulled a clipboard from under his arm, scanned the pages and shook his head. Harri could see the names of umpteen people on his caseload and hoped they weren't all to be visited today. Something in the social worker's harried, efficient demeanour told him they probably were.

'Right you are, Mr Sawyer,' he'd said cheerily, opening the rear door.

'It's Mr *Sabine*,' said William, not at all pleased about any of this but stooping to get in, nevertheless.

The social worker's shoulders had dropped with what must have been relief as he realised this old guy wasn't going to give him any trouble. 'Right you are,' he'd said again in the same tone of voice, like he was talking to a child.

Harri felt a twinge of worry. 'You will let us know how he's getting on?' he'd asked, while William slapped the social worker's hands away from his seat belt.

'Not if you're not family,' the young man had replied.

'How can you be reached, if we uncover any more information?' said Minty.

Closing the car door, he replied, 'There's no direct line. You can ring County, leave a message for the social work team. Someone will ring you back eventually.'

'I want *you* to ring me!' Minty scolded, but the young man ignored this, and climbed into the passenger seat, looking at his notes once again.

Harri had heard him say, 'District Hospital, then?' before pulling his door shut.

The engine started and the car crawled off Up-along, the cobbled path only just wide enough for the slow-moving emergency vehicle. Eyes watched on from behind the blinds and curtains of every cottage on the slope.

Harri waved feebly at the back of William's head, realising that for the first time he found himself in agreement with Minty. William Sabine felt just as much a part of Clove Lore as any of the other misfits and madcaps. With no family or friends claiming him, and no notion of his address, where was he going to end up now?

'We could have helped him, somehow,' Minty said sadly, and after squeezing Harri on the elbow, began her trudge Up-along. 'You did well,' she said as she left.

Harri didn't think he'd done anything at all, and he turned to the bookshop with an unsettled feeling that wouldn't leave him for the rest of the morning.

Chapter Thirteen

Cupid's Arrows

The morning stayed dry and mild that Wednesday; last night's wet weather having blown itself out somewhere over the Atlantic. Annie's fifth day in England was brightened by the arrival of a pale blue sky and white wintry clouds.

She kept the door propped open onto the cool courtyard all morning, not so much out of a need to air the stuffy bookshop, but hoping it would usher in some clarity and calm. The fright of last night had reminded them both of the need to be careful with one another's feelings. Two weeks spent in close proximity and then unexpectedly sharing a bad after their disastrous dates was not an easy feat, and today Annie felt her way around gently and slowly as though the stacks of books concealed coral snakes.

They'd sipped mint teas and nibbled Harri's fresh Welsh cakes (he was branching out from hangover buns). 'A batch of forty should see out the whole day,' he'd told her. They picked a playlist of jazz covers of pop songs for the shop, all the time talking to each other kindly. Customers who happened to overhear them wouldn't for the life of them be able to detect any awkwardness.

She'd taken her time dressing that morning too, going for jeans and a white shirt tucked in with her blanket coat on top, and, for a change, her beat-up white cowboy boots that had been vintage when she'd thrifted them back in Amarillo years ago. She loved how they elevated her, and today she needed the confidence of being a tall girl choosing heels. It helped, unquestionably.

The bestsellers today were the Valentine's cards and love poetry, either in slim volumes or fat anthologies. Harri kept serving the drinks and warming the Welsh cakes. Annie could hear his cafe till ringing at regular intervals until noon.

Together, after the lunch rush, they'd hung the rest of Minty's Valentine's décor around the shop, finally placing the ceramic chubby cherub amongst the display items on the table by the door.

'There,' Annie said with pride. 'Lookin' good.'

The cafe was empty now and a few browsers made their way quietly between the stacks. Annie lifted *The Young Man's Valentine Writer* from its riser and, opening it, discovered an illustrative sketch of another little Cupid.

She showed Harri, who glanced at it while running a duster over the cash desk.

'Says here that the Cupid of classical mythology had two types of love arrow,' she read in a deliberately bad English accent. 'One is barbed and golden and makes the person struck fall instantly in love, and the other is blunt and leaden and causes the victim to lose heart and fall out of love. And here was me thinking Cupid was some cute, helpful little angel!'

'Nope, he's a total pain in the arse,' Harri said blithely.

'Do you think people can simply stop loving someone, just like that?' Annie said, putting the book away, not nearly as amused as she thought she'd be by it.

Harri didn't reply. He'd busied himself right along the cash desk and into the kids' section where he was now wiping up the soot from the hearth.

'Where'd Jowan say the firewood was kept?' he said, without looking around.

'Dunno.' Perhaps it was for the best he hadn't seemed to hear her question.

'I'll go look,' Harri concluded. 'There must be a log store round the back or something.'

He pulled on his coat and was gone so fast Annie didn't have time to say anything else.

—

As soon as he hit the slope Harri forgot all about the firewood. It had been an excuse to get away. His feet were doing all the thinking now, carrying him away from the shop and Down-along. He registered blue sky, huge white clouds way out on the horizon, the white fronts of the cottages and the sound of the waves making their way into his brain. He wanted more of that noise, his feet concluded, carrying him all the way down onto the seawall.

Dogs dashed here and there on the wet sand. Small boats strained at their ropes as they bobbed on the tide. He didn't know if the sea was coming in or retreating. He didn't care.

His walking boots crunched and squelched pleasantly as he marched out along the beach. Hardy holidaymakers in winter woollies laughed and chatted on the Siren's benches at his back. He focused on the sounds of the gulls crying on the wing and the hard shushing of the waves.

He passed the cliff waterfall he'd seen mentioned in Jowan's Borrowers' binder, hearing its music only in so much as its gushing eased his mind. On he went until the Siren's Tail was just a blurry image done in watercolours when he glanced behind him. The insistent feeling that had carried him away from the bookshop began to ebb.

His feet slowed to a stop, and he stood for a long time staring blindly at the wormcasts around his boots. Clean, cold, salty air swirled around him. He could breathe at last.

When he looked around again he realised he was deep in the curve of the Clove Lore bay, and he was all alone.

That was when he became aware of the strange, dull pain that had made him run. Right in the centre of his chest. Unzipping his jacket with a sharp tug, he wrestled it off, letting it fall to the sand, not even slightly aware he must look crazy, shoving his hand under his jumper, rifling under his t-shirt, pressing his palm to the sore spot between his pecs.

Nothing there, and yet… He tried to make sense of it. Annie's words about that troublesome Cupid had sounded exactly like a little bowstring straining, tiny fingers releasing a feathered flight that had crossed the bookshop and struck him hard in the heart. He rubbed again at the spot where he'd felt sure he'd find a leaden, blunted arrow, the kind Cupid fired when he wanted to stop love in its tracks.

What had Annie said? *Do you think people can simply stop loving someone, just like that?*

His hand pushed reflexively into his jeans pocket, pulling out his phone, fingers jabbing at the name stored at the top of his contacts list, his next of kin, his emergency number for the last decade. He only truly awoke from his confusion when the call connected.

'Paisley?' he asked, desperately.

Chapter Fourteen

Austen back in the Bookshop

A young woman bounded into the Borrow-A-Bookshop in a burst of colour, announcing she was here for the children's Poetry Time session. Annie had forgotten all about it until that very second.

'Can you be bothered with another volunteer sticking their beak in?' the woman said in a Manchester accent, holding the door open for yet more people behind her. In followed a little girl of no more than seven or eight, and another woman, also all smiles.

'You're the new Borrower,' the little girl informed Annie. 'I was a Borrower too, years ago, when I was just *a baby*.' She said the word with evident disdain for all babies. 'My name is Radia Pearl Foley.'

'Got it!' Annie said with delight. 'And I am Annie Luna. Who've you brought with you, Radia Pearl?'

'That's Austen,' she replied, pointing to the poetry session woman with the bundles of paper under her arm wearing a berry-pink puffa coat and big plasticky eyeglasses. Radia pointed in the face of the second woman, darker, wilder, and dressed in red dungarees and combat boots. 'That's Auntie Patti. You should just call her Patti, though.'

Through smiles indulgently acknowledging the preco-
ciousness of the little girl, everyone nodded their greetings and Austen went about setting up for the poetry
session that had been her own especial responsibility on
the volunteers' rota for the last eighteen months, except
when she was visiting her parents and leading writing
workshops in her native Manchester.

'So, do I do anything?' Annie asked, remembering that
the little shop she'd come to think of as her own little
sanctuary was still very much a co-op and she was, in fact,
just passing through.

'*You* can make the strawberry squash,' Radia told her.

'All right, bossy boots,' her aunt intervened. 'Why
don't *you* make the squash, Rads?'

Patti parted with a grocery bag of, it turned out, all
kinds of British biscuits, most of which Annie hadn't seen
in nine years. 'But usually someone does put the kiddies'
biscuits on a plate,' she told Annie.

Radia was making a dash for the cafe, so Annie
followed her in search of a plate.

The shop had fallen completely quiet now that it was
almost four. Thankfully, Annie had easily managed both
the cafe and bookselling by herself as Harri still hadn't
returned from his search for firewood.

He'd messaged a while ago to say he felt like some
'alone time'. She'd only really minded his absence when
the cappuccino orders were coming thick and fast around
two and she'd been forced to tell a teensy lie about the
machine being broken and how she could only offer teas
and hot cocoa.

Still, it was getting late now. Where was he hiding
himself? Before sorting the biscuits, she checked her
phone again and found something new there that made

her gasp: a blue 'thumbs up' on the photo she'd sent to Cassidy, the one of her and Harri turning the shop sign on their first morning here.

This, Annie had excitedly concluded, was a break-through. She'd immediately messaged back with a tumble of words.

> Cass!! R u OK? Can you talk? I'm still in England. Msg me any time. I miss you!!

There'd been no reply but her message was marked as 'read'. She'd taken this as encouragement and not a further knockback. Cassidy was out there making contact in her own way. She only worried what it meant for her safety. Was Deadbeat Dave still hanging around watching her every move?

'You're mixing up the chocolate fingers with the Jammie Dodgers!' a small voice shrieked, pulling her focus back to her job.

'Shouldn't I be?' Annie asked the solemn little girl.

She was making a big mess of her own at the sink with a jug of sticky pink syrup, and the cold-water faucet was running way too hard and splashing all over the counter. 'Show me how you do it, then.' Annie turned down the water pressure then let Radia take over biscuit-arranging duties.

When they presented themselves back in the shop with the drinks and plastic beakers on the tray that Radia had known the precise location of, Annie heard Patti excusing herself, saying she had to get to the Big House for the test run of the outdoor cinema projector. Jasper Gold was waiting for her, she said. Patti had kissed Austen on the mouth in such a way that made Annie's heart heavy. Was literally everyone in Clove Lore loved up?

'You guys make me feel more single than ever,' she said, making the women beam.

Patti blew a kiss to Radia and left, telling the little girl that Austen would be taking her home after poetry time.

Austen was saying something about being all set up, just waiting on the kids to turn up, when Radia spoke over her. 'We live in the cottage with the red door, Down-along.'

'All of you?' Annie replied.

'Yeah, with Mum and Monty,' the girl said, taking a couple of Party Ring biscuits, just to test them out. 'And Austen sleeps over when she's not in Manchester.'

'That's nice.' Annie reached for a chocolate finger since they seemed to be fair game. 'I love these. These and Creme Eggs,' she said conspiratorially.

Radia wasn't much interested. 'Mum and Monty are having a baby,' the little girl put in.

Annie had never heard the word 'baby' infused with so much horror. She glanced at Austen who confirmed it was true. 'Yep, and she's not quite adjusted to the idea yet, have you, Rads?' Austen's accent was so different to Harri's, thought Annie. She sounded more like someone from *Coronation Street* (one of her old favourites back in Aber), than anyone she'd ever met. It truly was a marvellous voice.

'Ah!' Annie said, crouching down beside the child. 'I don't have brothers or sisters. I always wanted one. You might find this baby's kinda fun to have around… eventually.'

The look on Radia's face said she'd heard all this before and it was *not* helping.

'Maybe not.' Annie stood again and bit into her biscuit.

'You got the pens and paper ready, Rads?' Austen asked, and this pulled the little girl out of her anti-baby funk, setting her to work.

Austen had finished arranging the chairs and beanbags into a little circle near the stairs and came to stand beside Annie, grabbing a Jammie Dodger as she went. 'Are you staying for the session?'

'I don't know. What do folks usually do?' said Annie.

'Depends. Some Borrowers stay and man the tills in case customers come in; some lock up, take the opportunity to do some sightseeing?'

They both turned to look out at the dark afternoon outdoors.

'Some go to the pub?' Austen added with a light laugh.

Annie weighed up leaving to hunt down Harri in the dark or staying here in case he got back and found her gone leaving a shop full of kids. 'Does anyone stay and take part in the session?' she asked.

'Are you wanting to help?' Radia interrupted from her spot on the green armchair by the fire. 'Because I'm the helper, actually.'

'Oh, no, I uh, I thought I might participate?' Annie hazarded. 'I love poetry, you know?'

Radia seemed to consider this, giving Annie a long look. 'All right then. You can sit…' she looked around, before purposely choosing the beanbag next to her chair, '…down there.'

'Rads!' Austen said in a warning voice just as a family arrived with two hollering kids.

'It's okay,' Annie said. 'I worked… I mean, I work with kids, in a school library, so I get it. Kinda.' She may be comfortable around middle graders, but these little kids were a whole different crowd.

Annie took her place beside Radia who graciously selected a marker pen for her and a sheet of paper, and she watched in wonder as the little girl directed all the new arrivals to their seats, making sure the mother with the baby asleep in a sling sat at the farthest point away from her. 'Babies stay over there,' Radia said with a glower.

Soon there were local kids sprawling across the other beanbag, or perching two-per-chair. Some were sitting cross-legged on the floor, munching biscuits and making crumbs all over the place. Two cups of squash had been upset over the floor by the time Austen announced the session was about to start and Radia had twice, like a little martyr plagued by silly children, tutted all the way to where the mop was kept.

'Who's ready to write some poetry?' Austen asked. 'Today's theme is friendship.'

Annie checked her phone for notifications, and finding none, switched it to airplane mode and, with Radia eyeing her primly because phones were *not allowed*, slipped it into her pocket.

'There's a saying about friends,' Austen said, 'which is going to inspire today's session. It goes, *Friends come into your life for a reason, a season, or a lifetime*. Can anybody help us understand what that means?'

Radia's hand shot straight up.

–

'Harri!'

When had Paisley last said his name with this much affection? Harri could have sworn she really was glad he'd called.

'Hi,' he said, cupping his hands around his phone to protect their conversation from the blustery wind coming in off the water. 'Is… is this a bad time?'

'Of course not. Are you okay?' She sounded girlish, like she had when they first met.

'I don't know,' he said, a strangled laugh working its way out. He didn't know why he laughed. Nothing felt funny. 'It's so nice to hear your voice.'

Paisley laughed too; a bubbling, slightly tearful sound. 'I've missed you.'

'Oh my god, me too! So much.' The words came easily.

'Where are you?' she asked.

He looked up at the dripping fern-covered cliff wall. 'I'm on a beach.' It sounded as odd as if he'd told her he was on the moon. He was so very far away from home and its familiarity and routines. 'What day is it?' he asked.

Paisley didn't seem to think this was a strange question. 'Wednesday,' she said simply.

'Your half day?' he said. 'Are you at home?' *Home*. As though he still lived there too.

'Actually, I'm in Cardiff. I called in sick and I took myself shopping.'

'You did?' Harri had never known Paisley take a sick day in all the time he'd known her.

Her voice shook. 'I earned it, I reckon.' Her accent, so familiar, and so gentle, soothed him. When had they last talked like this? Without the tension and cool civility?

He rubbed at his chest where he'd felt that arrow strike.

'Got my hair done,' she said. 'And I went to Wagamama's.'

'On your own?'

There was silence on the line. The waves broke on the shore and retreated all the way out again, dragging a hundred thousand tumbling pebbles, dragging the breath from Harri's lungs. He shouldn't have asked that.

'Was there something you needed?' she said.

Harri didn't know why he'd called.

'Are you all right, Harri? Is Annie there?'

Now she sounded like the Paisley of recent months. It woke him fully. 'She's at the bookshop. Listen, Paisley, can I ask you something?'

'All right.' There was caution in her voice.

'Did we just… fall out of love?'

This brought a small gasp, and silence again.

He wasn't going to chicken out now. 'It's just, I don't really know what happened, and now I'm wondering if…' He had no idea what the right words were.

'If we got to the end of us?' Paisley said.

'Right. Did we?' His throat thickened with the need to sob.

He let her think, listened to her breathing. Eventually she said, 'I think so.' She sounded so sad.

'Do you think we could have stopped it? Could *I* have stopped it?' he asked, fearing the answer.

'Maybe,' she said. 'Actually… no. Probably not.' He hadn't expected her to laugh at this, but she did, and it sounded good and wry, like they were moving past something.

'I wasn't the best…' Harri began, but she cut him off.

'We both did our best. We were kids.'

'Nearly thirty-year-old kids?'

'Naw, we were doing our best with what we had.' There was no mistaking she was crying now and trying to keep it out of her voice.

'Paisley,' he began, wondering where his tongue was taking him. 'I don't think I'll be coming home, to Port Talbot, I mean.'

'You took most of your stuff,' she said. 'I didn't think you were coming back.'

He let silence fall between them. The sky seemed bluer over his head. The air sharper. He pressed the phone closer to his ear. She was listening too, no need for words. It felt absolutely natural to be quiet together for a while. Harri realised his face was wet from tears. They stayed like that for a long time.

Eventually, Paisley asked if he'd let her hear the beach sounds, so he held out his phone to the shore.

After a while they said a few words about the weather. Her mum and dad were doing fine, thanks. She'd had her hair bobbed that day and he told her he was sure it suited her. She guessed he'd already had fish and chips and extra mushy peas, and he'd swallowed the lump in his throat.

'Paise, did I waste your twenties?' he said suddenly.

'Not unless you think I wasted yours.' She was so assured when she said this, it took away a little more of the dull arrow's ache.

'I need you to know, I was all in.'

There was silence on the line. A dart of panic went through him.

'I know that,' she said eventually, and it was emphatic. She must have understood he needed to hear it in her voice.

It wouldn't hurt like this if he hadn't been in love with her, if he hadn't been all in. She wasn't a distraction either, never second place to a dream of having Annie.

'I was your number one person,' she said, and he wanted to crouch down to the sand and cover his face in his hands.

'Will you be okay?' he asked her instead, knowing they couldn't stay like this much longer.

It was starting to hurt in a new way now, the way it feels when love really is irrecoverably gone and you have to walk away for the very last time.

He knew she was nodding down the line. 'Yep,' she said at last. 'I'm going to find out who I am on my own.'

'Me too,' Harri said.

'I think you already know,' she said with a new kind of arrow-like precision.

'We'll talk again, won't we?' he said.

Neither of them really believed it, but both let the lie settle between them for the sake of the last ten years and all they'd shared.

They both cried when Paisley at last hung up. Harri let the phone drop to his side and he scuffed his boots and skimmed stones on the beach for a long time as the dark afternoon drew in around him, thinking the whole time that he could only be true to himself, and fair to Paisley, if he resolved to be content to be alone. No more dates, no more sleeplessness, no more clinging to a humiliating hope that a teen crush would miraculously become an adult commitment. He willed the tiny part of himself he'd held in reserve for Annie Luna to dissolve. He wouldn't hold on to guilt about failing Paisley any longer, but he also couldn't carry on walking around with this tiny barb in his chest for Annie either.

His unburdened heart beat anew.

–

'Jonas is my best, *best* friend,' one of the children, Barney Burntisland, declared, only to be cut down by Radia telling him imaginary friends don't count.

'Who's your best friend forever, then?' Barney shot back, making Radia even crosser.

'I'm friends with everybody in my class.' It didn't sound convincing to Annie's expert ears, putting her in mind of some of her middle schoolers who couldn't quite negotiate close friendships yet. They were the kids who drifted between groups, never quite bedding in. Radia, she suspected, was destined to spend a fair few lunch breaks and recesses hiding out in the school library. She knew the type. She'd been one herself, still was, even if everyone mistook her for an extrovert. She'd spent so long as a kid cultivating her convincing happy-go-lucky demeanour, most days even she believed it.

'Let's focus on the words, shall we?' Austen said over the chatter.

Radia did a good show of modelling attentiveness for the other children, sitting bolt upright, eyes fixed on Austen, her felt pen poised. The others, all eight of them, ranging in ages from five to nine, and all pupils at the nearby primary school, fell in line.

'Can anyone tell me what it means to have a very best friend?'

One of the blond Crocombe boys, brought today by their mother, the school's headteacher, raised a tentative finger.

'Yes, Charlie?' asked Austen.

'Somebody to play football with,' he said.

'And trade Pokémon cards?' his older brother put in.

'Nice! So someone you can play with, and someone you can share things with? Let's write that down,' Austen said, marking the words 'share' and 'play' on the flip pad she held facing the group.

'Anyone else? What is a friend?'

The room was quiet until another child said, 'A friend plays with you.'

'We've already had that!' complained Radia.

'Any of the biggies know?' Austen encouraged, lifting her eyes to the adults watching on.

The younger Mrs Crocombe and Monica Burntisland, one of her school's teaching assistants, who'd been catching up with whispered conversation standing at the back, didn't even notice her asking, so it fell to Annie to help out.

'Um, how about... friends forgive each other?' said Annie.

'Ooh, good one!' Austen enthused, writing the word 'forgiveness' on her pad.

This opened up a heated debate, ignited by Radia, on how you shouldn't forgive anyone who picked on you or pushed you over, and the whole thing descended into a lot of noise and disagreement, until Laura Crocombe was forced to break off from talking with her friend and intervene.

The children, chastened by the shame of their headteacher telling them off outside of school – and when she was wearing her out-of-school clothes like she was a real person – brought a new type of focus, and they sat with fingers on their lips for as long as they remembered to and everyone was suggesting 'good friendship vocabulary' at Austen's urging.

'Caring?' the oldest of the bunch said.

'Telling jokes,' said the eldest Crocombe boy.

'Invites to birthday parties,' another suggested, and so on, until Austen's paper was covered in ink.

'Let's use some of these good friendship words to craft our own poems, okay?'

'Like, how?' said the littlest Burntisland.

'Well, like this one.' Austen pulled a notebook from her pocket. 'This is one of my own poems and it's going to be printed in a magazine next month!'

This prompted a lot of impressed oohing and a smattering of applause from the kids and Radia loudly announcing, 'She wrote it for *my* Auntie Patti, you know?'

'Okay, thank you, Rads. Anyway, it goes like this.' Austen cleared her throat and leaned closer to her attentive audience.

'Before you, I didn't know the sky was blue.
Before me, you told me, you'd been lonely.
Before us, there was a long waiting.
Now there is summer in winter and only the briefest, passing,
scudding clouds.
Lonely no longer.
Forever after, us
Beneath a blue sky.'

Austen closed the book with a smile and looked around the group. Annie clapped, but the children didn't move.

'Scudding?' asked the smallest Crocombe.

'Here we go,' said Radia, doing a dramatic eye roll. 'You've set him off again.'

'Scud, scud, scudding,' the boy went.

'Very good, Charlie, well done! Take that energy and write your very own poem. You've got five minutes, starting...' Austen looked at her bare wrist. 'Now!'

The swiffing sounds of felt pens moving over paper overtook everything. All their little heads were bent over, tongues jutting from the corners of mouths in concentration.

'You too, Ms Luna,' said Austen.

'Oh! Right, of course.' Annie, who'd been enjoying the sweet ease of the afternoon and the familiar feeling of being surrounded by young people again, jolted her eyes to her blank pad. 'Write something about friendship, yeah? Sure, okay.'

Radia shushed her.

There was only one thing Annie could think of writing. It welled up in her and before she'd even got the first line down her eyes were wet with tears and she'd forgotten where she was entirely.

> *Cassidy, I miss you.*
>
> *Why aren't we talking?*
>
> *I know I was rough on you, telling you how I felt about Dave, and when you'd just broken up and all, but I never imagined you'd be getting back with him. But we don't have to talk about Dave because no matter what, I'll always like you and approve of you.*
>
> *Being in England makes me realise how far apart we are and the missing you is only getting worse now I'm here.*
>
> *So, here's my promise to you. Even if you can't forgive me, even if you're with Dave for life, I will still be your friend, even if you can't reach out to me. If you're ever ready to talk, I'll be waiting because we're best, best friends forever.*
>
> *Please hold on to the part of yourself that loved me because I can't bear to lose you.*

Now I've got to find a way to mail this to you.
I hope you can find a way to reply. X

When Annie lifted her head, tears were tracking down her cheeks and she had to wipe them hastily away with her sleeves.

The kids had already finished their poems and were sharing them. It took her a long while to zone in on them again and when she did she realised she felt lighter, somehow, and she had a new tiny flame of hope inside her.

'Friends scudding stones on the scudding shore,' Charlie was reciting, much to the delight of Austen.

His poem went on for some time, but Austen never lost her genuine smile, and she led the group in applause when he sat down with a proud, gappy grin.

'Nice one, Charlie! And you've added a new word to your vocabulary! Who's next?'

Radia had waited impatiently to read hers to the group and she stood to do it.

'A little girl went around the world and now she goes to school,' it began, but at that moment, Annie's attention was pulled to the opening door and Harri stepping inside, his hood up, bringing the cold of the dark afternoon inside with him.

Annie was on her feet to meet him. 'Excuse us,' she told the group and walked with him into the empty cafe.

'What happened to you?' she said, still holding on to her letter.

'Sorry about that. I was on the beach.'

'O–kay?' she said, dragging out the word. There was more to it than that. He seemed wired and tired, like he'd been awake for days.

'And I spoke to Paisley.' He stood like he was fixed to the stone floor.

'And?'

'And it was good,' he said. 'And a bit sad, but mostly good.'

Annie nodded, not sure what he was telling her. 'You guys are… friends again?'

'I think so, maybe. Something like that.'

There was something different about him. Before he'd been strung out; now he was worn out.

'Oh, Harri, come here.' Her heart swelled for him and she pulled him into a hug. 'Well done for speaking with her. That can't have been easy.' He gripped the backs of her arms as she held him, his head resting heavily on her shoulder like he'd had too much to drink. He hadn't, she was certain. Harri was just weary.

'You need some cherishing,' she told him.

In the next room, the kids were noisily getting into their coats, chairs were being scraped across the floor, mothers were issuing instructions, and someone else had knocked over another cup of squash. Harri didn't seem to register any of it.

'Cherishing?' he said, drawing back to look at her.

'Yep, come on. We'll get these guys out, lock the doors, and order takeout. There's a TV in my room, let's see what the reception's like. Reckon we'll pick up the BBC out here? Maybe *Happy Valley* is streaming on demand?'

'Should be,' Harri said, thawing.

'The *Great British Bake Off*, after? Then *Homes Under the Hammer*?'

He smiled at this, remembering their favourite shows from a decade ago. 'Oh, I stopped at the shops,' he said, remembering himself. 'Got us these,' and from his coat pocket he produced the box.

Annie's heart lifted at the sight of the Cadbury Creme Eggs.

'Five pack, since it's been a tough day,' he said.

She hugged him again.

'Did you happen to pass a post office in Clove Lore?' she said when he drew back to look at the paper crumpled between them.

'You've got something to post?' said Austen at the cafe door. 'I can take it, if you like? Sorry, didn't mean to interrupt.'

Why did everyone in Clove Lore always think they were interrupting something between them?

There followed a lot of activity. Annie left Harri in the cafe with instructions to call the Siren's Tail and order the scampi and chips with extra mushy peas for her, and she made her way with Austen into the shop, now almost emptied of families.

She took a Valentine's card from the display and folded her letter inside, inscribing the card with Cassidy's name and the words, 'I'm here.' She wrote the familiar Amarillo address on the envelope and handed it to Austen, who insisted she didn't want any money for postage, it was her pleasure, and off she went with Radia buttoned up in her winter coat.

'See you next week, same time!' Austen said cheerily as she and the yawning Radia left.

Annie bolted the shop door behind them, deciding to leave the tidying up for tomorrow. She had a friend to comfort right this second and a cosy evening ahead.

'Pop the kettle on, luvvie,' she called to Harri in her worst Welsh accent, and he laughed hard and shook his head, hanging up after his call to the pub.

'Dinner's on its way,' he said. 'Time for PJs and a brew?'

'Definitely!'

With that, the two friends settled back into their easy old patterns learned years ago.

–

Annie didn't know the time when she woke, but the building was still shrouded in winter darkness and all was quiet, except for Harri's steps on the stairs. He must have woken her coming out of the bathroom.

She listened to his feet padding down the spiral stairs as slowly as he could. He was trying not to disturb her.

It had been a perfect evening of good food and easy conversation during the ad breaks, propped up on pillows on Annie's bed.

At eleven they'd been hardly able to stay awake and she was vaguely aware of the yawning Harri turning off the TV and tucking the duvet over her before making his way to his own room. Blissful, full-bellied sleep had settled over her, but now she couldn't help pushing the covers back.

Harri hadn't talked much more about his disappearance, other than saying he and Paisley had, 'sorted some stuff out'. She'd been happy to see him looking relieved, somehow freed up and more relaxed than he'd been since their arrival in Clove Lore, but she couldn't help the twinge of regret either.

Was he getting back with Paisley? Just like Cassidy had reunited with Deadbeat Dave? She couldn't pry and she couldn't make her true feelings felt. She'd learned that the hard way with Cassidy. In her letter she'd said nothing of her feelings about Dave, about how she feared he was controlling her, making her think things not in her nature, turning her against the people who loved her best. If she was going to reconnect with her friend, she wouldn't achieve it by badmouthing the man who was still under her skin. So, she'd chosen to write about the preciousness of their friendship instead. She hoped it would work.

She was learning to hold back. This was progress. If she could speak her mind to Harri she'd tell him to take his time, to enjoy being single for a while, that loneliness was only natural after so long in a relationship, but if he just let things settle, he'd be happier. Rushing back to Paisley would be a mistake.

She couldn't say any of it. But she could at least check in on her friend now. Why was he up in the middle of the night? She tiptoed to the top of the stairs.

Harri wasn't going back into his room. He was making his way across the shop floor barefoot in the dark.

Annie didn't understand why she did it, but she impulsively crouched unseen at the top of the stairs, spying on him through the bars.

He switched one lamp on beside the display table. What was he doing?

She shifted for a better view then wished she hadn't seen him flicking through the Valentine's cards. He pulled one out, turning it in his hands for a long moment. She saw him make to put it back, hesitate, then change his mind.

Then he was opening it, writing something inside, enclosing it in its envelope, running his tongue over the glue. Suddenly, as if wary of her presence, his eyes darted to the stairs and she drew herself back into the shadows, holding her breath.

What on earth was she doing, acting crazy? But she couldn't help looking once more as Harri, satisfied he really was alone, flicked out the light and carried his Valentine's card off to his bedroom.

She sat, clasping her knees to her chest at the top of the stairs for a long time.

He'd been writing to Paisley. After their talk today, he'd been lured back in. He loved her, after all. *Of course* they were reuniting. Wasn't Harri just the sort who couldn't miss Valentine's Day? Would this be his and Paisley's tenth?

There was always the possibility, a hopeful part of her brain suggested, that he'd simply been feeling sentimental, and he was sending Paisley a friendly token of his affection, for old time's sake.

Whatever was going on in his heart, Annie was astounded to realise how much she hoped that, come Valentine's morning, Harri would be giving that card not to Paisley, but to her.

The realisation was enough to send her straight back to bed in contrition where she scolded herself for a long time.

It was Clove Lore that was responsible, and this book-shop. Being in England in the slowest days of winter, being by the rugged coast, and around Valentine's Day too. None of it was helping. Throw in her tendency towards Anglophile romanticism and she was *way* too susceptible to silly daydreams.

She had to fight back. Get a grip again.

She could get through it, she reasoned as she lay in bed.

There were only nine full days of their holiday left and, so long as they avoided romantic moments, beautiful places, alcohol, and anything remotely cosy, she'd get through it, safe and sound.

Eventually she slept, finally back in control of her over-active imagination and believing herself immune once more to those stupid, inconvenient things she'd briefly felt for Harri long ago.

Chapter Fifteen

Castle Lore

Sale of Contents
Viewings: Saturday 8am–1pm
Public bidding on selected lots: 1pm–9pm
Pre-arranged guests only

'We're definitely late,' said Annie, reading the sign at the entrance.

'Check your bag, Miss.'

'You have security at auctions?' she said, stopping under an archway where a burly man in black blocked their way.

The man didn't reply, only casting a detection wand over Annie's shoulder bag and then down her body.

'They do when it's a place like this, I guess,' said Harri, taking in the gatehouse with its portcullis drawn up over their heads. 'Can't have just any scruffy so-and-so walking in.'

'How come we're here then?'

Harri presented the man with their passes; the ones Jowan had given him when he picked them up in Minty's Land Rover for the short journey down B roads and along the back fields, heading inland.

Harri had insisted they'd get a cab back down to the village after the auction ended tonight; it seemed unnecessary, making Jowan leave home on a dark winter's night when there were perfectly good taxi apps.

'And you've got the credit card?' Annie asked, while the man made Harri turn, patting down his pockets.

'Woah! Easy there!' He would have glared at him if he wasn't so massive. Instead Harri indignantly tugged at his coat to straighten it out and led Annie away as soon as the man was satisfied he wasn't a threat to Devonshire's security. 'And we can spend up to two grand on book stock, right?' he said.

'Particularly books relating to Devon.' Annie knew their mission too. Jowan had been very clear.

'Yep,' Harri confirmed. 'History books, maps, local legends, that sort of thing, and absolutely anything that references Clove Lore and literally any fiction. The more antiquarian the better. And no old dictionaries, bibles or encyclopaedias, because they don't sell.'

The security guard grunted in their wake, and they followed the signs through the gatehouse and across a small bailey courtyard of bare dirt. This was no stately home with modern adaptations in the living quarters, manicured lawns and a gravel driveway for a Bentley; Castle Lore was a grey stone Jenga tower reaching into the even greyer afternoon sky with crumbling arrow slits, gargoyles worn away to faceless, obscene stumps, and rooks' nests and weed clumps peppering the masonry where the mortar holding it all together should be. One whole side of the old heap was propped up with wooden scaffolding that looked like it had been there for decades.

Even in the wintry daylight, the lamps glowed orange and inviting through the castle's few glazed, narrow windows, and there was a loud hubbub of voices coming from inside.

'Sounds like a party,' said Annie as they climbed the worn steps and through the arched open doors.

'Ah, good! You're our last arrivals,' said a woman tapping on a tablet behind a table positioned between two suits of armour, their helmets lolling forward like soldiers propped up while dozing. Her ID said she was Katie Barnes of Blazey, Barnes and Blazey, Business Liquidators and Private Auctioneers, Totnes.

'Has the bidding begun?' Annie asked.

'Not yet,' Katie replied cheerily. 'These are your complimentary drink tickets. One each. And you'll be at table eighteen. You are blue guests.'

'Okay.' Harri looked at the seating plan on its stand. Table eighteen was at the back of the room, furthest from the auction block, and it was coloured in blue like their drink ticket. The tables closest to the front were yellow. Harri guessed they were for the big buyers.

'It's too exciting!' Annie didn't seem to mind that they were very much the bottom of the bidding power pile. Katie handed Annie a card with a large number printed on both sides.

'What's this?'

'That's your registration card,' said Katie.

'Nope, still no clue.' Annie flashed her white teeth.

'You hold it up when you want to bid.'

'Right, of course, sorry.'

'Shall we?' said Harri, crooking his arm. Annie accepted it with a gracious nod and they walked past the foot of a carved wooden staircase towards what a sign told them was the grand reception room, and where all the noise was coming from.

He'd resolved to try to match Annie's energy the last couple of days when they'd been busy and peaceful in the bookshop and the volunteers had thankfully left them alone.

They had been re-treading the easy, well-worn grooves of their bookselling days in Aber. Thursday and Friday had been counted in cups of experimental latte recipes and iced hangover buns, modest daily totals (who knew the ninety quid takings of day one would be a record for their holiday?), and a continuous round of tidying and reshelving, shopping for cafe ingredients and cooking dinners eaten together. Harri had read in the evenings alone in his bed while Annie had held her book closed on her lap and watched the flames in the shop fireplace until she gave up kidding herself she wanted to read and took herself to bed to watch British soaps and quiz shows until she fell asleep.

Things had been easy once again, and today was set to be even easier. It's not every day you get free rein to rummage through the contents of an ancient country pile.

'Top three books about creepy-ass castles?' Annie joked as they turned into the reception room, all dark wood panelling, ceilings as high as the room was wide, with antler chandeliers hanging above them.

'Easy peasy,' he began. Harri reeled off his favourites. *Dracula*, obviously. *The Castle of Otranto* would come a close second place, and he couldn't not have *Howl's Moving Castle* in there. He'd read that in high school, and it had stayed with him ever since.

Annie had been about to add her own favourites when a voice called out to them over the hubbub.

'It's the young'uns!'

The animated face of the elder Mrs Crocombe with her headscarf knotted under her chin loomed out of the crowd and following behind came Mr Bovis dressed as though for a day's gamekeeping in tweed knickerbockers and long woollen socks. His Harris coat carried the smell of mothballs with it.

'So, my dinner date didn't go quite as planned?' said Mrs Crocombe, blocking their entry further into the room.

You mean *our* dinner date, Harri wanted to say, but he only pulled his lips into a straight smile.

'Turned out all right in the end, though, didn't it?' Bovis put in. 'We saw young Kit and Anjali in here earlier. They were leaving when we arrived, looking every bit like love's young dream.'

Mrs Crocombe was smiling thinly. 'Not one of us had money on the pair of 'em, but we shan't hold it against them. Love's a funny thing, does what it wants.'

Annie wasn't smiling quite so delightedly as Harri would have expected and she'd dropped Harri's arm upon sight of the troublemakers. Maybe the novelty of the Clove Lore busybodies was wearing thin, or worse, maybe she still remembered the hurt he'd caused the night of their date with his jealous behaviour? He'd noticed Annie had been prone to quiet moments these last few days and he'd accounted for it by guessing she was still hurting for Cassidy, though he harboured a sneaking feeling there was still something he was doing wrong that was making Annie occasionally quiet and sad, even if she'd tried to hide it.

He watched her now.

'Aren't you going to stay for the bidding?' Annie was asking.

'Oh no, we're only here for a nosy,' said Mrs Crocombe.

'Can't be spending money willy-nilly,' Bovis threw in, rocking on his feet. 'Not when we've been saving up…'

Mrs Crocombe shot him a glare that was hard to miss.

'Oh! Uh…' Bovis collected himself. 'Not when my old Land Rover's needin' new…' he hesitated, '…brakes?'

'Ah!' Harri made the sort of interested sound he thought was expected of him, but really his attention was drawn to the extraordinary sights around the room.

A suddenly very flustered Mrs Crocombe was hastening Bovis away saying, 'You young'uns be sure to enjoy yourselves.'

If he'd been paying attention, Harri would have heard the chastened Bovis receiving a ticking off as she bustled him away. Annie turned her head to watch them go, bemused, but Harri had already forgotten about them.

'Woah!' he said under his breath as the room revealed itself to them fully. 'What do we do now?'

'Treasure hunting?' Annie hazarded.

What followed that afternoon was an astonishing insight into what happens when a very lonely old man, the last of his line, dies all by himself leaving a crumbling castle full of treasures to be sold off in recovery of his ancestors' ancient debts.

Everything he once owned was catalogued and laid out for the world to pore over. Harri and Annie shuffled around the numbered items, reading aloud their descriptions in the catalogue.

There were fat West Country salmon mounted on plaques with the dates from a century ago when they were yanked out of something called The Bridge Pool, Bideford. These leaned up against grimy family portraits of stern men and feeble, sallow women all bearing the once-impressive name of Courtenay. There were unwound clocks with stilled hands, chairs too weak with age to sit on, silver dinner canteens tarnished black, delicate Chinese tea sets so transparent they might disintegrate upon use, bright oriental rugs that looked like they'd spent their lives rolled up and never been walked on, fine smoking jackets, parliamentary robes, ribbons and medals, hunting pinks and riding crops from the turn of the last century, unsmoked Cuban cigars in exotic boxes, crates of stoppered cognac, lots and lots of antiquated guns and swords, and then boxes and boxes of foxed letters and estate records shoved in a corner beside a pile of neatly folded flannel bed sheets.

Finally, awfully, amongst all this musty old stuff, stood the curiously out of place field hospital bed, a small television, and a rickety wheelchair with a silk smoking jacket folded over its backrest as though its owner was coming back for it at any moment.

'I don't know if I like this,' Harri whispered, seeing these last possessions of the hermit Courtenay.

'Yikes!' Annie exclaimed, her face in the catalogue. 'They want twelve hundred sterling for those awful taxidermy foxes over there. Why are they all snarling like that?'

'You can put in a bid, if you like? Take one home?' Harri teased, wishing he could enjoy the novelty of it all as much as Annie.

'Christmas gifts? Dad would *love* that.'

'Do you think he was unhappy?'

'Who? Dad? Most definitely, if his voting record's anything to go by.'

'No, this Courtenay guy. Isn't it a sad way to live and die? All alone?'

Annie considered this, letting her eyes dance up to a brass coronet candelabra and the dusty stucco plaster between the vaulted beams. 'I dunno. He was a recluse for a reason, right? If he needed people, he'd have looked for people.'

Harri wasn't so sure. 'Would you be happy rattling around a draughty, creepy castle by yourself all day?'

'Do I have Uber Eats?'

'*The library is open for viewing!*' came the voice of auction assistant Katie over the heads of the milling people, marking up their catalogues, some making phone calls, probably to their private buyers overseas.

'*Ooh!* That's us. Go, go, go.' Annie took Harri's hand, pulling him ahead of the slow-moving crowd. 'Is the library upstairs?' she asked the auctioneer.

'This way, please,' said Katie, turning on her heels and guiding them up the wooden staircase with its boxy turns and bowed, flaking plaster. The wool carpet, once red, was worn beneath the banisters on both sides, but Harri could make out the repeated pattern of a coat of arms depicting an open book and two heraldic hearts pierced through with swords beneath the letters 'C. L.'.

'Clove Lore?' Harri said to Annie.

Overhearing him, Katie answered. 'Courtenay-Lore. The family have lived on this site since it was first built in the late-fourteen hundreds.'

'Jeez!' Annie sucked air through her teeth. 'How is the place still standing?'

It was growing colder as they climbed. Harri became aware of footsteps behind them, hurried ones. Glancing back, he saw two men, one owlish in round glasses and tweeds, the other eagle-like in a dark suit and stiff collar.

'Mind you don't trip, please,' instructed Katie.

Cables ran up the stairs, taped down here and there. They brought illumination to harsh spot lamps clamped to the spindles.

'The library and upper bed chambers have always been lit by candlelight,' said Katie. 'Anyone buying the tower will need to do a full electrical installation.'

'They'll need to knock it all down and start again,' quipped the Owl behind them.

'Are you book buyers too?' Harri asked the men, but neither obliged him with an answer, the Eagle overtaking them on the stairs, determined to get the first look at the library. The Owl awkwardly cut in around them as they reached the upper landing with a, 'Sorry, chaps.' At least he was apologetic about shoving in.

'They're not here to make friends,' Annie whispered for Harri's ears only, and he smirked back.

'They want to beat us to the Penguin classics and Lady-bird books, I bet,' Harri joked, just as Katie was turning her key and pushing apart double doors to reveal a sight Harri would never forget for as long as he had breath inside him.

—

'Oh. My. Lord!' gasped Annie, frozen on the threshold of the candlelit library.

The Eagle and the Owl were already pulling on white conservators' gloves and dispersing into the stacks, immediately setting to work.

Annie had no such prey instincts. All she could do was gape and stare around, stuffing her hands into the gloves

Katie was insisting upon, taking in the dark wood library shelving that lined the walls, all packed with orderly old tomes in leather bindings. Wax tapers glowed in candelabras and sconces all around the time-capsule room and, as Annie's eyes adjusted, even more detail came into focus; tapestries and heavy furniture, rugs and long red drapes, each one with a numbered auction ticket attached.

She wasn't aware of Harri's eyes fixed upon her, alive with something soft and admiring. In fact, he had barely registered the room, preferring instead to study the look of wonder on Annie's face. It was this he could not draw his eyes from.

Unaware, Annie stepped further into the room. She had seen 'old' back in Aberystwyth where she'd walked amongst historical architecture daily. She'd had access to wonderful antique shops any time she wanted, but this place? This was time travel. This was stepping into someone else's life entirely, a place utterly untouched by modernity. This was immersion in a forgotten way of life.

'Now *this* is a library,' she whispered to Harri, now standing by her shoulder.

'This is like *church*,' he said. He was still gazing at her, but she had no idea.

She thought, however, that she knew exactly what he meant. They'd always shared an awed reverence for bookish spaces and this had to be the best place they'd ever stood together.

Annie noted the misty winter's twilight and deep navy blue sky through a window of leaded diamond panes that rose from the oak floorboards to where the ceiling beams disappeared into cobwebbed darkness. At the centre of the window was the same crest she'd seen woven into the carpet; two hearts of glass pierced through with swords over an open book, its pages curved like a moustache.

A low fire crackled invitingly under a marble mantle and next to it stood a heavy, highly polished desk with a book propped open with weighted beads on a library cushion next to a pair of half-moon spectacles, as though their owner had only just left off reading.

She approached the book, poring over its words and recognised the text in an instant. It was Oscar Wilde's *The Picture of Dorian Gray*, a favourite of hers since she first discovered him as a teenager hungry for Victorian decadence. She read under her breath a passage that shone out from the page, drawing her eye like a beacon.

'As for being poisoned by a book, there is no such thing as that.' She allowed her fingertips to lightly graze the black type. 'The books that the world calls immoral are books that show the world its own shame. That is all.'

Annie drew out her phone to take a shot of the page, but was halted by Katie clearing her throat. When she glanced around, the auctioneer wordlessly held up her catalogue to show the 'no photographs' sign on its back.

'Got it,' she mouthed, slipping her phone into the pocket of her blanket coat and stepping deeper into the inner sanctum.

A new kind of silence descended as the book-lined walls dampened the gliding footsteps of the Owl and the Eagle. Annie forgot everything as she approached a great antique globe suspended on a brass stand. There was no sign telling her not to touch so she risked turning it, slowly letting Europe rotate away, her gloved fingertips tracing the wide Atlantic all the way to the Americas and past them once more.

'Got the whole world at your fingertips?' came Harri's voice.

'*What's the starting bid on the globe?*' The Eagle bellowed, as though this place wasn't some wonder of a lost world magically preserved against the odds, but carrion to scavenge.

She couldn't help glaring at the man, fighting the urge to 'shush' him. Not something she'd ever do in her own noisy, bright, lively library back home.

Katie was talking to the Eagle now, turning pages in her catalogue. She was telling him that the cabinet under the globe couldn't be unlocked, there seemed to be no key, and that was detrimental to its sale value, but Annie's mind was drifting further away as Harri stood by her side and together they wordlessly turned the world on its axis.

Annie loved the hubbub of her school library. Anyone could talk there. Heck, they could vocalise and stim and sing as much as they wanted. It had been just as much of a sanctuary as this old place, more so, as far as Annie was concerned, since it served the needs of so many young people. Far better than this damp treasure trove shored up to please only one rich old man.

The contrast hit her now. Even in this antiquated dream library with its elegant ladders on tracks that ran along the tallest stacks, she longed for her lanyard and plastic keycard, her pencil behind her ear, the tapping of keyboards as the kids worked on assignments, and all the questions and chatter of school life, and especially she missed the library lurkers. Those were the kids who'd skip lunch to slouch in the stacks, huddled over a book, trying to raise their grades or avoid the bullies, escaping into their imaginations. They were the ones forever asking her to order in the latest titles, making balancing the meagre budget hard, but she'd done her best to meet their needs.

Annie knew all the things a library could be for kids who didn't feel at home in school (and plenty of them didn't even feel at home in their own homes). She could tell you every one of those kids' favourite series and when the next instalments were due for release.

She'd known some of their problems too; she'd been just as much a safe space as her library was for them.

'*Overstepping,*' the complaint had said. '*Undue influence over young minds.*'

Her heart plummeted like a broken elevator to think of it now, just as it had done that day she and the rest of her colleagues had been handed the letters on the library steps and Sally the school administrator had taken possession of their keycards until 'the necessary inquiries are concluded'.

She hadn't replayed that moment until now, having blocked it out in her rage. It had been too painful to think of what she had lost, of what those kids had lost, when the complaint came in and her senior colleagues had dug in their heels and refused to concede to an external audit of their library purchases over the last few years. They were going to do it anyway, of course, armed with their new lists of banned books currently circulating amongst concerned parent groups online and getting longer by the day.

'Annie?' Harri was watching her, his eyes soft with concern.

She blinked at him through welling tears, coming back to herself.

'Are you okay?'

'Harri,' she began. 'There's some stuff I didn't tell you.'

Chapter Sixteen

A Lot More Than They Bid For

They'd been summoned to the bidding by the sound of a gong before she could say anything more, and Harri had taken her arm and walked her down the creaky stairs.

He'd been concerned, of course, but she couldn't have known where his mind had gone when she told him she had secrets to share. The little key in his heart had turned and sprung the lock, letting out a rush of hope despite all the promises he'd made himself at the beach after talking with Paisley.

There'd been no time for talking, however, as they were ushered to their table of bidders. The blue seats.

Katie closed the doors upon the room once everyone was inside. Her colleague took his place at the rostrum, introducing himself as 'Colin Blazey of Blazey, Barnes and Blazey', and proceeding to talk for a very long time about the ancestry of the Courtenay family, which could be traced back to Agincourt, and then there was a lot of talk about provenance and estate inventories and the declining fortunes of the little known Lord Courtenay who'd passed away five months before, leaving no will, no heirs, and no money.

Castle Lore, the Borrowers learned, was as yet unsold, but listening to the whispers of the antique dealers at the table around him, Harri gleaned there'd been some interest in the land from developers keen to have the site for rental chalets and caravans, letting the castle moulder on, uninhabited, as a picturesque ruin at the centre of their holiday park.

Annie didn't seem to be listening much to any of it, sitting now with her head lowered and her hands in her lap.

Even when the auction began she was subdued, though Harri was fascinated by the auction-goers in the yellow seats hastily claiming lot after lot. The cold businesslike way it was all conducted astonished him.

The furniture went first, then the weaponry and armour. By the time they got to the contents of the library, Harri's thighs were numb and Annie was slumped in her seat, her coat wrapped tightly around her. Harri had considered offering her a spot in the nook under his arm, but something stopped him, even though they'd done just that the other night, snuggled up together like the oldest, most innocent friends as they watched TV on Annie's bed.

'Lot sixty-six, first editions of the Marquis de Sade in their original French.'

This made him sit up.

'Shall we start at eighteen hundred?'

'Oh!' Harri's shoulders dropped and he watched as the Eagle and Owl fought it out until the Owl was beaten and the Eagle had promised twelve grand for the titles.

'Don't think that's the kind of thing Jowan was after anyways,' Annie whispered, amused, as though they could have afforded it if it was.

The auctioneer worked his way through the library contents. Bound manuscripts, illuminated scrolls, titles in Latin and Greek selling for prices that had Harri plumping his bottom lip in incomprehension. A huge old bible with the family's coat of arms embossed into leather went for only a couple of hundred quid, which he couldn't believe, and as soon as volume one of something called *The Yellow Book* and a water-damaged, incomplete Shakespeare's *Folio* sold for eye-watering amounts, to the Owl, as it happens, both of the bookish birds of prey got up and left the room, their business concluded.

'Maybe now we'll stand a chance?' Harri whispered to Annie.

The lots got smaller and induced fewer gasps from the crowd, until finally there were books the Borrowers could afford. With Annie's encouragement, Harri claimed two lots of assorted three-volume melodramas and Mudie's Circulating Library editions of forgotten novels once popular in the nineteenth century. Annie did the maths in her head while Harri raised the card to claim collections of obscure European poetry, histories of the British Isles, naturalists' yearbooks, almanacs and what the auctioneer called 'railway novels' in gaudy jackets. Finally, they snagged some Devonshire history books that nobody else bid on.

'We've only a few pounds left,' Annie warned him, just as the auctioneer presented a cardboard box, soft and bulging with damp.

'Assorted library papers, uncatalogued, largely foxed, dating from this century. Do I hear twenty-five pounds?'

Harri glanced at Annie. She shook her head.

'Ten?' the auctioneer tolled. 'Do I hear five, then?'

'Five!' said Harri, his card lifted.

'Sold.'

As the hammer fell, the Borrowers rose to settle the bookshop's debt at Katie's station by the doors.

Harri claimed their free drinks and the pair took their seats again for what the catalogue described as 'the prestige' lots of the day. There were mayoral chains of office and a rope of Jacobean freshwater pearls allegedly seized after Bannockburn; six fine portraits in miniature of eighteenth-century Courtenay women in feathered hats, and an impressive oil-painting of a pointy-bearded Royalist Courtenay in a high lacy collar. This bidding had been accompanied by bursts of applause and a lot of boozy hilarity from the yellow tables.

Annie and Harri watched on, spent out and sleepy. Their table had emptied ages ago. The auctioneers were preparing to open the bidding on the contents of the stable block, which included an engineless, tyreless Rolls-Royce.

'I'm surprised Minty didn't want to come to the auction,' Annie said to Harri, dabbing at her mouth with her cocktail napkin because that's what they did in period dramas and it seemed like the proper thing to do now. 'I guess they wanted us to enjoy the experience. It's certainly been eye-opening. Kinda sad, though.'

'I know what you mean,' said Harri, though he wasn't sure if she was referring to the sorry state of the Courtenay estate or to the other, secret thing she'd wanted to tell him.

Annie looked across the room and, spotting the waitress clearing glasses onto a bar trolley, an idea seemed to strike her.

'Excuse me,' she was whispering to the woman, before Harri could work out what she was up to. Annie rummaged in her bag as the waitress pulled her trolley closer. 'We used up our complimentary drinks passes. We're lowly *blue* guests, but...'

The bored girl had let Annie have the bottle of wine in exchange for a tenner, which went straight into her apron pocket with a surreptitious glance around, and Annie turned around triumphant and grinning, holding her prize.

'What's happening?' Harri said, eyes narrowed and suspicious, but definitely up for a bit of scheming.

'You want to go look at that library again?' she said, suddenly driven by a new impulse, not her old mischief, rather something reckless within her; her old carefree self fighting to get out, perhaps?

Harri thought about it for precisely one second. Standing and taking Annie's bag, putting it over his shoulder, he said, 'What about the security guard?'

'Just walk like you own the place,' instructed Annie.

As they left the room Katie was busy taking auction payments and stifling her yawns. Everyone else was engaged in draining their bottles and preparing for the very last round of bidding.

Annie led him to the foyer at the foot of the stairs and peered up into the dark space above them.

'No one around,' she hissed, reaching for Harri's hand.

He held on as she led the way, tiptoeing as fast as they could up the stairs. The rigged-up spotlights had been switched off and Harri lit their way with his phone. They laughed and shushed one another all the way up to the library doors.

The key was still in the lock and Harri turned it, again letting Annie peek in first.

'Coast's clear,' she said, and as he followed her, he made sure to lock them inside the silence of the library. The mechanism clunked into place and he knew for sure nobody could disturb Annie's impromptu escapade.

Doubtless, they'd only stay twenty minutes, long enough to take the photos Annie hadn't been allowed to earlier, and to have a proper snoop around.

Pocketing the key, he followed Annie towards the fire-place where the last embers glowed amongst the cooling ashes. All the candles had been extinguished, no doubt by the efficient Katie, and the room was lit only by the stark wintry moonlight through the window.

Annie lifted some kindling from the basket by the fire, since there were no logs, and stuck them into the grate. The flames slowly sparked back into life and Harri crouched by her side to watch them as Annie piled on more of the soft wood. Then she lit a candelabra of three slender white tapers using the fire, wax dripping onto the stone hearth. Harri didn't suppose it mattered.

'They're going to strip this library apart in the morning. We might be the very last people ever to see it like this,' he said.

This stopped Annie in her tracks.

She was beautiful in the glow from the fire and candle-light. He determined not to mention that fact as he sat himself down on the fireside rug and cracked the screw top on the wine bottle, handing it to her.

'Here's to poor old Sir Courtenay and his library,' he said.

Annie sat by him on the hearth rug and, setting the candlestick down, took a swig before handing it back. 'Here's to him.'

When he'd taken a drink, he watched Annie arrange her long coat and skirts. She hugged her arms around her legs where her long leather boots laced up her calves.

'So do you want to tell me now?' he said.

Annie seemed to take a second to work out what he was asking. She lunged for the bottle and drank with a grimace.

'Cheap Shiraz,' she said. 'Dad would not approve.'

Harri laughed and reached for another drink, this time glugging it with deliberate relish to spite judgy, cold Mr Luna.

Annie's laugh told him his joke had landed.

'Go on then,' Harri prompted. 'I'm listening.'

His friend exhaled hard. Whatever she had to say, it wasn't easy for her. Harri didn't try to rush her, tipping his head and waiting for her to find the words, trying to stop his heart jumping to conclusions and hoping for too much.

'I'm not on vacation leave,' she began. 'I was… we were all suspended from the library service.'

'What! How come?'

In a shaky voice, she told him the whole sorry story of how her colleagues had been sent home from their jobs, and most likely wouldn't return, having been found to have stocked numerous books that went against parental tastes, and when they all flatly refused to participate in submitting the library's future acquisitions for the approval of a hastily thrown-together committee of concerned parents, 'things had got real crazy, real quick.'

'But you love that job,' Harri said.

'I know. We were family. But what do you do when the community turns against you, and suddenly you're not the cornerstone of your school anymore? You're just a dangerous snowflake pushing your own agenda?'

'Jeez! What exactly did you do?'

'Nothing!'

'I mean what books were you giving these kids?'

'I dunno, most of the ones they objected to were written by or are about LGBTQIA plus folks or by Black and Indigenous people and people of colour. They're well-written books with some great representation, as far as we were concerned.'

Harri nodded along. 'I've seen this on the telly. Parents trying to ban books in schools.'

'Yep, happening more and more. In some places they have the law on their side, and they can whip up pretty nasty campaigns about a person.'

Harri shifted closer. 'Is that what they did to you?'

Annie nodded. 'To us, all the staff. It was constant. There were emails, letters sent to school... one mom even came to our houses with a petition she'd made. They were saying awful things about us. Obviously, none of them were true. We were just curating a library of books relevant for our kids.'

'So, what are you going to do?'

'Do?' She shrugged. 'I could appeal. Argue that I was wrongfully suspended. Argue that even if you don't want to read a book it doesn't mean you have the right to stop other folks reading it. I could take it to the Library Association... but...' Annie's shoulders slumped and her words turned into a hard sigh.

'But?' Harri coaxed.

'But without Mom and Dad supporting me, and without Cassidy, it didn't seem possible somehow. And I was tired and scared. And I've seen what happens to some of the librarians who fight back. They get crushed. Their faces all over the news. I guess it's hard for you to get it, when it's not really happening in the UK. Not yet anyways.'

Harri's heart cracked. 'What about your colleagues in the library?'

'I haven't heard from them. We were told to go home and not to try organising anything.'

'So who's running the library?'

Annie raised an eyebrow.

'Ah! Right. Some parents? But they're not trained librarians. What do they know?'

'They know plenty, apparently.'

Harri watched her drinking from the bottle, weighing up if he could ask what was on his mind. He risked it. 'Why didn't you say anything when it was all kicking off? I could have helped?'

'Could you?'

'I mean, not with the school and the parents, but I could have helped you, I could have carried a bit of this worry for you.'

Annie didn't say anything at first, only taking another drink. Distantly, out on the roadside, Harri registered car doors shutting sharply.

'I didn't want to admit I was losing,' Annie went on. 'I'm supposed to be Annie Luna, the gutsy one. I'm supposed to be brilliant. And I was scared, and I was embarrassed, actually. Yeah, embarrassed, and I was ashamed. It felt like my own community thought I was some creep, pushing inappropriate books at kids, but they were just books, *kids'* books!' Tears rushed out as fast as her words.

'Oh my god.' Harri shifted to her side and threw his arms around her.

'You *are* the gutsy one!' Harri said, his head against hers. 'You're Annie Luna! School Librarian extraordinaire! I've always been so proud to know you.'

This made her sniff back her tears and she managed a little laugh followed by a sorry groan. 'I really miss the kids,' she said, her eyes sadder than Harri had ever seen them.

He pulled her closer. 'What did they say about all this?'

'The kids? Some of them sent me messages, saying they felt bad it was happening. Most didn't say anything. How could they? They're just kids. Some of them were shouting at the school gate with their pissed parents and their placards. The school authorities said they were worried for our safety and the safety of the school, so they sent us all home until it blew over. They called it a suspension to keep the parents happy, but they're removing books at the parents' requests anyway. I don't know if I have a job to go back to, and I don't know if I wanna go back.'

'You should have told me.'

'You had your own stuff going on.'

'Oh.' Harri drew his neck back. 'With Paisley, you mean? But I didn't tell you things were rocky with Paisley.'

'A girl knows.'

'Right.' Harri let this sink in. Everybody had known he and Paisley were doomed, long before he'd been able to admit it to himself. A flash of headlights passed over the library wall, followed by another, but neither registered it now. 'I could still have helped.'

Annie made a cynical snort and reached for the bottle. 'There's nothing anybody could do.'

'And your parents didn't stick up for you?'

Annie's eyes fell. 'Nope. They were embarrassed, I reckon. They don't see things the way I do. They don't think it's important that kids see themselves and their lives reflected in books. Most of all, they'd prefer I didn't bring a big, public fight to their door.'

'You deserve better than that.' He tamped down the livid feelings. How could anyone treat Annie like that?

They passed the bottle between them, and Harri loosened his hold on Annie. The auction sounds and the distant milling of people had faded, but Harri only vaguely registered this fact. He didn't care if they were the last to leave. He'd call a taxi soon enough. For now, he had to comfort Annie.

'Tell you what, though, if you *do* go back to face them, now that I know, you have me on your side, all right? You're not on your own.'

Annie nodded, fixing her eyes on the fire.

For a long moment no one said anything and Harri moved to throw some more kindling on to the flames. 'We'll be out of sticks in ten minutes at this rate,' he said, coming right back to her side where he'd been a moment before. It suddenly felt very, very close, now that Annie's confession and crying fit had passed.

He wriggled an inch or two away from her side and she definitely noticed. A line appeared between her brows. Harri had to look away. He'd gone and made things awkward again, so he shifted his body back, right into the nook by Annie's side, and her warmth reached his limbs where they almost touched.

'Did you, um, hear from Cassidy at all?' he tried, hoping the moment would pass and be forgotten.

'Oh, yeah, I did actually.'

'No way! What did she say?'

'It was just a thumbs up emoji, but that's still progress.'

'Did she know all this stuff was happening to you?'

Annie sighed again. 'Pretty hard not to know. It was in the Amarillo papers and there wasn't a person who wasn't talking about it.'

Harri was overtaken by a feeling of injustice. 'I don't like that,' he said, and his jaw set like a clamp as he shook his head.

'It's okay. Deadbeat Dave might have stopped her reaching out. Or maybe she thought it was my fault, bringing it on myself? No, actually, no. There's no way she'd think that, even if that would suit Dave perfectly. She knows me, and I know her. She'd be mad too.'

'*Are* you mad?' Harri said.

'Of course I am!'

Harri looked at her for a long time, his eyes searching her face for the spark. Where had her fight gone? Had it really been that bad? That she'd lost it completely?

'I'm just taking some time,' she said defensively. 'To regroup. Like you are.'

'The Annie Luna I know fights for what she wants.'

'Does she? Or does she wait around, for years and years in some cases, waiting and hoping that she'll get what she wants?'

'Huh?'

'Nothing, forget it.' Annie moved to stand up.

'No wait, what are you saying?'

'I...' She looked desperate, like a trapped animal. 'I...' Her whisky-coloured eyes turned dark as her gaze flicked to his mouth. It took a fraction of a second to register the change but it was enough to set off a hard primal fire in Harri's gut. He was already lifted onto his knees and drawing Annie to him with his hands spreading over the small of her back.

She breathed hard, inches from his face, both frozen, all thoughts suspended, only their nerves and instincts speaking. Her eyes lifted from his lips, which had fallen open with the force of his breath.

He was waiting for any signal from her when two came at once. Her pupils shrank to a pin sharp intensity that shot straight down his spinal column landing heavy and low where he hardened, and she gave the clearest nod of permission before their lips met in a sudden crash with the force of a decade's waiting behind them. He couldn't help the moan that came from deep within him as they kissed and Annie answered it with her own.

No words, no thoughts, nothing held them back as they kissed harder, and their hands roved. He pulled her against where he was aching for her and the burst of heat coming off her filled him even fuller with wanting. She rocked her head back when he put his mouth to her throat. He was reading her, responding to what she needed.

How they were lying down, he didn't know, but he was on top of her. She tugged his shirt loose and yanked at his belt, stopping only to run her hands over him, driving him close to blacking out. He'd pulled up her skirts with her nodding the whole time, kissing him between her gasped, 'yes,' and suddenly there was nothing between them at all. She was reaching for her bag, rummaging inside, all sorts of crap spilling out of it.

'Dang it, where are they?' she said, laughing, but Harri wanted her to feel how much he wanted her, so instead of helping, he took her arms in his hands, feeling his way to her wrists, bringing them over his head, pressing her fingers to the nape of his neck until she understood and held him there. He kissed his way right down her body from her neck to her navel, through her clothes and over her bunched skirts until his mouth was exactly where he wanted to be and he ran his tongue in relentless sweeps letting her, his Annwyl, know how much he'd wanted her all this time, making her trust his touch, making her gasp for it, promising her he could do this to her whenever she wanted.

Just as she was drawing her thighs closer, almost losing it completely, there came the unmistakable sound of a key turning in the library door, and the echo of the mechanism unlocking, reverberating through the library.

The pair jumped apart.

'Oh my god! Someone's coming in,' cried Annie, hauling herself back into the shadows to fix her clothes.

'Shit! Shit! shit!' hissed Harri, scrabbling to button and zip himself back together, straightening his glasses, wiping at his face. It had to be Katie doing a last check. The auction must be long since over.

The door was creaking open, the glow of a torch lifting the gloom. If he wasn't so alarmed Harri would have laughed at the sight of Annie emerging from the shadows, a picture of hastily poised serenity, pretending to inspect the big globe in the middle of the room.

'Who's there?' came a crotchety voice. Definitely not Katie.

A figure presented itself now; hunched, shambling, all in black.

'Mr Sabine?' cried Harri and Annie at once.

Chapter Seventeen

A Library Sleepover

William Sabine set down his torch and moved slowly around the room, lighting the candles from a pocket matchbox.

'What are you doing here? I thought you were in hospital?' said Annie, following him.

'What are *you* doing here, Annwyl, *hmm*? In my library?'

'Your library?' repeated Harri, trying hard to recover his composure. He could still hear his own pulse hammering in his ears.

Mr Sabine shuffled towards the desk. A stricken expression passing over his face as he surveyed the open book and the spectacles arranged on the display cushion. He closed *The Picture of Dorian Gray* and held it in his hands, his eyes settling on the spectacles.

'Nicholas's library,' he said, sadly.

Harri flicked his eyes to Annie. Her cheeks were flushed pink but there were no other outward signs of what they'd just been doing. A shudder of wanting shocked down his spine. He tried to hide it.

'Sir Nicholas Courtenay? You knew him?' Annie's brain was evidently working far better than Harri's;

amazing considering how close she'd just been to coming apart completely against his lips.

Harri tried to concentrate. 'How did you get here, Mr Sabine?'

'I walked, mostly,' he said, like it was the most obvious thing in the world.

'But that must have taken all day!' Harri was already reaching for his phone. 'Mr Sabine… do you live *here*?'

The man nodded.

'I'll find Katie,' said Annie, jolting into action. 'She's the auctioneer, Mr Sabine, she'll need to know we're here…'

'Save yourself the trouble,' said William, softly, staying her with a lift of his hand where he held a big key, very much like the one Harri had put in his pocket. 'They've all gone. I let myself in.'

'I don't understand,' said Harri. 'You live here? But they're selling the place, aren't they? Are you a Courtenay too?'

The old man chuckled at this. The chuckle turned into a cough and he reached for a box of freshly dispensed pills, still with their white sticker over the seal.

'Get me two of these please? And there's a Marsala in the cabinet.' Harri took the packet from him and William produced a smaller key, giving it to Annie. 'Over there, beneath the globe.'

Annie took the key, her face all curiosity and concern, but she still did as she was instructed. The hatch beneath the globe sprung open and, sure enough, there was a decanter and goblets inside.

'Should you have alcohol?' Annie asked.

Mr Sabine only raised a wild eyebrow and Annie gave in, pouring him a little of the tawny wine.

'Mr Sabine,' said Harri after a glance at his phone screen. 'It's gone nine o'clock. We need to decide what we're doing tonight. Where are you staying? Can't we take you back to the hospital? Or at least, to the bookshop?' Where was Minty when you needed a responsible adult to delegate? Harri didn't have a clue what to do.

'*Tsh!*' tutted Mr Sabine, before washing down in one gulp the pills Harri had popped for him.

'I'm not the only one enjoying a nightcap, I see?' William said mischievously, nodding to the open bottle of red wine by the hearth next to Annie's bag, its contents spilled everywhere. Seeing their blushes, he let out a laugh. 'I may be old and unnecessary, but I know a hawk from a handsaw.' He dropped himself into the fireside armchair with the sigh of a man arriving home after a long time away.

Harri smiled at this. He was quoting *Hamlet*. He couldn't be so ill and confused if he was able to do that.

'You seem better,' said Harri.

'I'll never be better.' He held out his empty glass for Annie to refill. 'But yes, they helped me with my prescriptions and the doctors reached their diagnosis. A water infection,' he said in a low voice, not for Annie's hearing, 'and a lack of sodium, apparently.' He chuckled and scratched his bare head. 'The marvellous complexity of the human body, and it can be poleaxed for the lack of a few grains of salt.'

When Annie came back her demeanour had shifted. She stood by Harri's side and handed over William's glass, filled halfway this time. 'We would have been locked overnight in the castle if you hadn't shown up.'

Harri felt a sudden flush of warmth emanate from her. She had to be thinking of what would have happened if they hadn't been interrupted. Her arms were by her sides now and his whole soul wanted to reach for her hand, to let her know it wasn't over. They had left everything To Be Continued, only she took a quick step away, leaving a cold space between them.

He didn't know what would happen if they didn't get the chance to talk it all over, and the sooner the better, but a feeling of unease was making its way inside him now.

Annie couldn't look at him even though he was blatantly looking right at her. Was she embarrassed? Regretful? He needed to know.

'I watched from the gatehouse until the last car was gone and I let myself in,' William explained. 'It's my right, after all. I've lived here these last fifty years.'

Annie crouched by his side.

Harri felt like he was watching from behind glass. He had to talk with her. But how, when they had poor Mr Sabine to sort out?

'Nicholas and I were companions,' the man was telling Annie fondly.

'You were…' Annie began, before stopping herself.

'We were the closest of friends, which is better than whatever is running through your head, young Annwyl.' He smiled sadly and his whole face transformed into a picture of softness. 'You young people might want to imagine us being more, but friendship was all we ever needed.'

Harri wished he wouldn't call her Annwyl, even though it was only the old man's way of teasing him. It made him feel even more ridiculous than he already did.

Annie was smiling back at William. 'You didn't seem to know any of this when you appeared at the bookshop.'

Mr Sabine huffed out a breath and shook his head. 'I remember the day they took Nicholas away. I'd been looking after him here. He hated hospitals, begged me not to let them take him. He wanted to die at home, with me.' Tears filled his eyes, and he pulled a handkerchief from his pocket.

'You looked after him?' Annie was saying.

'We looked after each other. And when the ambulance men took him out of here, he was already unconscious. I knew he wasn't returning. And after that, I... let myself slip.' He wiped at his eyes. 'I didn't see the point in keeping up with my pills. Nicholas always saw to that sort of thing. He saw to everything. This last year or two... we had both let things slip.'

'Oh, William.' Annie reached for his hand, holding it fearlessly.

Harri still couldn't quite function, an awful desperation was setting in, and guilt too. His main concern should be William, like it was for Annie. She seemed to have forgotten everything that had happened.

William talked softly on. 'I did my best by him. He was agoraphobic, you see? Always was. Even in seventy-six when I responded to his advertisement for an antiquarian and steward. The outside world drove the fear of the devil into him, so we kept our own company here.'

'Minty said he was a recluse, a hermit?' said Annie.

William laughed sadly. 'He can't be blamed for that. Have you seen the world? Oh, we had doctors stop by, over the years, and they questioned and prodded, psychoanalysed and so on, but the truth of the matter was, Nicholas didn't need the whole world; he only needed his own little kingdom.'

'And you were part of it,' said Annie.

'I was half of it,' he corrected, sorrow splitting his face as his eyes filled. 'Oh dear, oh dear, what would Nicholas say if he could see me now?'

Annie looked to Harri and the pain in her eyes startled him into action. Harri came to crouch by the man's side too.

'He'd say how glad he was to see his old friend still here, I imagine,' said Harri.

'But they're selling it all out from underneath me, aren't they?' said William, with the look of a child.

'They auctioned off the house contents today,' Harri said, and a fresh wave of remorse came as he remembered the bidding and how easily he'd helped break apart the estate with the wave of a card. 'To recover some… debts.'

'But they can't sell the castle,' Annie put in. 'Not yet. There's some legal stuff stopping it. I don't really understand.'

'Because Nicholas died intestate,' Harri put in. 'No will.'

William kept his eyes on the handkerchief in his hand. 'The castle will be sold by the Crown. It *is* beyond repair. Perhaps it is for the best.'

'But where will you live?' said Annie, her voice swelling with emotion. 'Have you no family?'

William shook his head and looked around his library like he was watching ghostly scenes playing out everywhere. The place was haunted with his memories. He smiled at them as they danced across his vision. He and Nicholas by the globe, lost in conversation; his friend pacing with his hands behind his back, William smoking by the fire, debating some idea from a dusty old tome open upon the desk; the pair of them pinpointing a spot on a map and sharing their knowledge of the place, all gleaned from books, never from travel or experience. Their experiences were those recounted by authors and adventurers told in manuscript and print. They were collectors, connoisseurs, bookish companions. They had everything they needed right here in Castle Lore.

William would receive from Nicholas a list of treasures to hunt down on the first Monday of every month and he'd add them to his friend's other requests, writing off letters to collectors and repositories across the world looking for them.

Nicholas would have the sole pleasure of unpacking them when they arrived, and so the men would have new material to read, new matters to discuss, and life went on, full of interest and intellectual endeavour. Their friendship had been their lives' work, the rarest treasure they had.

'I'll stay another night,' said William. 'To say goodbye.'

'We'll stay with you, then,' Annie replied, without asking what Harri thought.

'And then tomorrow, we'll all go back to Clove Lore and decide what's to be done,' Harri put in softly. '*You'll* decide. If you don't want to go back to the hospital or wherever Social Services put you, I don't see how they can make you. And you don't *seem* ill.'

'I'm not,' he snapped. 'I'm old and alone, that's all.'

'You're not alone,' Annie insisted, still holding his hand. 'You have new friends now.'

The three of them prepared for a night at Castle Lore, William showing them where the woodstore was and how to toast bread on the library fire. There was loose tea in a silver caddy and, Nicholas's favourite, the last of the Marc de Champagne truffles they'd have sent over from France, and as everyone busied themselves with settling down to sleep – William insisted on sleeping by the library fire, so

Annie and Harri took the other armchairs — Harri felt his opportunity slipping away to talk about where he and Annie stood now that they had absolutely overstepped the boundaries of the friend zone (and Annie looked nothing but relieved not to have to talk about it).

They all slept, Annie and William more soundly than Harri, until the winter morning came. Clove Lore Castle had housed its last ever overnight guests.

When day came, it was no longer a home, but a relic out of time, its library collection hours away from being packed up and scattered across the four corners of the earth, a testament to the friendship of two men who found a whole world in each other and which had been adventure enough for both of them.

Chapter Eighteen

Reaching Out

Everyone was soon alerted to William's reappearance at the Borrow-A-Bookshop. The village's (self-appointed) authorities in these matters had concluded that a few days' rest by the sea would do him good. A room was reserved for him at the Siren, what with it being their quiet time of year, though Finan the landlord pointed out his pub was booked out for the upcoming Valentine's weekend so he couldn't stay indefinitely.

William had said he might like to spend some of his daytimes at the bookshop amongst the stock. Perhaps he could make himself useful, he'd said.

His presence had been enough to bring nosy locals descending upon the bookshop to learn more about him, while Harri and Annie tried their hardest to keep the place running as normal.

Without the need to discuss it, William had remained tight-lipped about Harri and Annie being discovered in a compromising predicament in the library of Castle Lore long after the auction ended. Annie had taken his placid smile, aimed at her across the bookshop hubbub, as confirmation that their secret was safe with him.

After that she'd kept out of everyone's way. There was the silent book club coming up that evening and a lot to prepare, or at least she made it look that way, fussing in the kitchen, rustling up her mother's recipe for devilled eggs and cleaning the already very clean glasses, and she'd insisted on the shop opening as usual, even when there was a crowd of nosy parkers surrounding William in his armchair by the fire, no one more incredulous than Minty that he could have been living in their midst these fifty years and no one had laid eyes on him. William didn't mind the news circulating about his former residence; as far as he was concerned it had never been a secret.

There'd been a few comments noting Mrs Crocombe's absence. Why wasn't she here to interrogate poor Mr Sabine when that sort of thing was right up her street?

'She's got the Ice Cream Cottage to run, and her Valentine's flavours to perfect,' Jowan concluded. 'Never missed a day's trading these thirty years,' he added.

It was left to Izaak and Leonid to unravel the mysteries of the life of Mr William Sabine. They winkled it out of him that he was a French national and that he'd arrived with no passport and no papers with the rest of the back-packers and youth hostellers of the Seventies.

He'd received no formal education after the age of sixteen but was considered something of a genius by his teachers, though a worry to his mother, displaying an aptitude for ancient languages that really warranted a university career and could easily get him into the Sorbonne, but he'd struggled with the demands of directed study and preferred to suit himself.

Whilst visiting the libraries of the British Isles, he'd come across Courtenay's appeal for a companion in private intellectual pursuits and with that he'd sunk into the pleasant daily rituals that kept him holed up at the castle, living in ease and contentment.

Jude Crawley, for she was here too, had wondered aloud about how they could have afforded to live, and William hadn't liked the intrusion, pointing out that Nicholas Courtenay was a gentleman of some small means and although he had never paid William for his services, he'd taken care of all his worldly needs.

Elliot, Jude's husband, had stopped the clamour of questions this provoked by pointing out that it was 'no one's business but William's' and they'd all pretended to be chastened until he left for work at the veterinary clinic, and they'd started up again.

Meanwhile, Harri was distracted.

'Are we going to talk about it?' he tried, catching Annie as she flitted between customers and her event preparations.

'Can you make a batch of cookies?' Annie replied, feeling the heat along her hairline, even in the February chill. 'I know we told everyone to bring potluck baking, but it's better to have too much than not enough.'

'Annie…'

He'd tried to detain her but every fibre in her being was telling her to shut it down.

'I don't think we need to go over it,' she hissed, checking for prying eyes and ears. 'There was wine and firelight and a crazy Gothic library like a movie set, and we got carried away.'

'Right, but if we hadn't been interrupted…' Harri had his hand clamped to the back of his neck and the tips of his ears were pink again. Only, he looked exasperated rather than embarrassed.

'Thank god we were stopped!' Annie cut him off. 'We could have really done something stupid and spoiled things for good.'

This seemed to draw Harri up. She felt his eyes on her as she scurried away, folding paper napkins and piling them pointlessly on a tray. Annie wasn't sticking around to dig deeper into her mortification.

As she bustled around, her phone rang in her pocket. Drawing it out, she saw the words that made her momentarily forget everything: *Cassidy calling.*

'Cass? Are you okay?' She'd grabbed her coat and headed right out the shop door into the noon drizzle.

'I'm good, I'm good. You?' Her friend's voice vibrated with emotion like she'd been crying.

'What time is it in Amarillo?' Annie held her phone from her face to check. 'Seven? You're up early.'

'I got your Galentine's letter.'

'You did?' Austen must have mailed it expedited. These locals really took their roles as Borrower Support Team very seriously.

'Remember last Galentine's?' Cassidy said, sniffing through tears.

Annie didn't miss a beat. 'Those watermelon cocktails? I could take a couple of those now.'

'Right?'

Annie listened to the fresh silence down the line, not wanting to spook her friend when she was reaching out.

'I kicked him out,' Cassidy blurted.

'Okay?' Annie knew to be cautious. There'd be no premature celebrations this time. No commiserations either.

'He's gone for good this time, Annie. I promise.'

'What happened?' she tried, keeping her voice neutral.

'Remember Becky from the juice place?'

'The blonde one?'

'No, the other one. *She* happened.'

'Ah! When did you find out?'

'A week ago. Kinda hard not to find out when he was sneaking her out the back door when I came home from work.'

'Shit!'

'Yup! Shit.'

'Are you okay?' Annie was still cautious.

'Yeah, I'm…' Cassidy was trying to sound blasé, but she was breaking. 'I'm so sorry…'

'Hey, shush now, it's fine.'

'It's not. I wasn't there when you needed me.'

'It's all good, honestly.'

Cassidy's guilt wouldn't be easily placated. 'Dave was tough to live with, you know? It was difficult to get away and see you…'

'I know. It's okay. I meant what I said in my letter. I'm here for you anytime.'

'I'm not taking him back. Dad helped me change the locks. He's gone for good. Becky can have him.'

'He should come with a warning,' hazarded Annie.

'Like a pet passport from the pound. This dog has fleas.'

'And needs a muzzle.' It was happening again. She was being drawn in to the break-up revenge trash-talking. It had felt so good before, but Annie couldn't shake the fear he'd be back and she'd be the one locked out again.

'Cass, you know I don't want to interfere but please, please don't even see him. If he comes back with his sad eyes wanting to explain. Don't hear him out. Please.'

'I won't. Your letter was like a light coming on, reminding me how much I let him change me, how much I lost myself. I'm never going back to him. Besides, Kenny's moved in for a few days, so there's someone else here.' Kenny was Cassidy's skinny brother. He'd be no match for Dave in a fight, but at least Cassidy wasn't alone. 'Annie?' Cassidy's voice faltered. 'I'm sorry I wasn't around to help with everything at school. I should have been.'

'Oh, that? It's okay. I'm just taking some time out. Why? What did you hear?'

'That you and the senior library staff were suspended. That there was some kind of investigation going on. I should have called. Dave convinced me not to. He had this way of making me forget myself and the things I need. He knew exactly how to control me.'

'I know.'

Annie wandered down the passageway that led to the breezy slope. The cobbles shone with slippery wetness under her feet. It didn't stop her turning Down-along to face the harbour.

Being suspended from the job she loved had hurt all the more because Cassidy hadn't reached out to check on her, and yet she'd already forgiven her. That's what friends do.

She couldn't help following her runaway thoughts. If Annie could brush Cassidy's great big neglectful betrayal under the rug, Harri could surely forget their teeny tiny misdemeanour last night, for the sake of their friendship?

Annie tried to stick to the matter at hand. 'It's not your fault. Dave was a… lapse in judgement! And heck yes, he *was* controlling, and hot in a hottest-deadbeat-you-ever-saw kind of way. That's a deadly combo.'

Cassidy laughed, thank goodness.

As Annie passed the wide window of the Ice Cream Cottage, she was too absorbed to notice Mrs Crocombe and Mr Bovis behind the colourful display of ices in the refrigerated cabinet like a kid's paint palette of pastel colours, suddenly spotting Annie and in a panic Mrs C. whipping something small held between them out of sight behind her back. Neither did she see the look of relief on Mrs Crocombe's face as she glanced at Bovis.

Annie passed on down the slope entirely unaware of whatever it was those two old buffers were intent on concealing.

'Are you coming back to school?' Cassidy was asking her.

'I… I truly don't know. Do I even want to work in an environment like that? With a handful of parents running the halls?'

'Both Kimmy and Linda were reinstated. Did you hear?'

'No! When?'

'Yesterday. They're holding community meetings next week to talk it all out. The Library Association reps will be there too.'

'They will?'

'Yeah, and you saw the kids' protest, right?'

'The what?'

Annie's phone buzzed as Cassidy sent her the images. Her little band of library lurkers, holding banners, standing with their families around the school gates. There were so many of them.

Now it was Annie's turn to cry.

'It's not as bad as you fear,' Cassidy was saying. 'If you come back, you'll see. There's more support than you think. And I'll be there this time, whatever happens.'

Annie huffed a breath and looked down to the wide horizon over the Siren's roof. A blue-grey line cut between the green sea and the clouds heavy with yet more

February drizzle. It looked like it was setting in for the whole day.

'I don't know if I have the strength to take on all those other folks, Cass. And Mom and Dad, they've not exactly been supportive.'

'But your mom is, secretly, right?'

'*Hmm*.' Annie thought of her mother always telling her not to rock the boat, especially at home with her father. 'She's with me in private, but Dad was furious, couldn't understand why I'd bring the fight to his door. *It's only a few books*, he said. *Stock them, don't stock them, what's the big deal?* He doesn't get it.'

'Come back,' Cassidy pleaded. 'See how things are. You're more ready for this than you know.'

'That's what Harri said too,' said Annie, wryly. What did he know about how brave she was? She was a coward. He should have figured that by now.

'Oh yeah? How are things with him?'

'He's kind of beat up. He's on a break with Paisley.'

'No way! Because of the bookselling vacation thing?'

'I had nothing to do with it,' said Annie, a little too primly.

'That's not what I said, but... was it?'

Annie groaned. 'Maybe. They split at Christmas, but he's been living in their flat share ever since.'

'And they're definitely taking a break? Are they talking?'

'They've talked since I got here.'

'But he's with you right now, not Paisley, right? If he wanted to be with her, wouldn't he be?'

'We're having some friend time. It's been good for us.'

'*And?*'

Annie knew that tone. It meant trouble. She could imagine Cassidy's dark brow arching in suspicion.

'And…' Annie faltered.

'Oh my god! There *is* an and!'

'We might have… had a moment last night.'

There came a squeal of excitement down the line. Annie would have stopped her friend's speculating dead if it weren't for how good it felt to be confiding in each other again. It was like old times. Like there was no distance between them at all.

'Was it a *good* moment?' Cassidy pried.

Annie kept moving down the slope. She wanted to be out of the hearing of everyone in England if she was going to admit this.

'It was… *so* good! We kind of got locked in an old library together at night…'

Another squeal.

'It's a *long* story. Anyway, we were drinking wine and one thing very quickly led to another, and he was kissing me, and then he was, you know, moving his mouth lower and…'

'Oh my gawd! Go Harri!'

'Quite,' Annie said in a prudish way, even though she was smiling and enjoying this. She wasn't on her own with it anymore. She had her other best friend in all the world back. 'He was…' Annie glanced around the harbour wall, covering where her mouth touched the phone with her hands. There were families nearby on the sand and kids in waterproofs barefoot in the rockpools. '…seriously good, and things were about to get crazy serious, like I was in my bag looking for birth control and then… we stopped.'

'Why?'

'I didn't want to stop, believe me, but it's for the best we did. It was a good reminder about how important he is to me as a friend. Actually, this whole trip's been one big reminder after another that I need my friends around me.'

Silence down the line told her this had landed with Cassidy how she'd needed it to. It wasn't a barbed criticism; it was the truth. She needed friends more than she needed excitement or adventure or unbelievably hot and intuitively good head from Harri, even if she'd never wanted someone so much in her entire life than she'd wanted Harri last night when he'd made her forget where she was. Heck she'd forgotten her own name!

'Annie?' Cassidy's voice broke through.

'I'm still here.' Annie shook away the memories, standing at the edge of the shore. 'Listen, do you need me to come home early? I can change my flights.'

'No way! Don't run from this.'

'I'm good at running. When are people going to realise this? I'm not as brave as you think I am.'

'If Harri really is your best friend, don't you owe it to him to stay and prove it?'

This silenced Annie.

'And if there's actually something more, and things between you are as good as I suspect they must be, well… don't you think it's worth the risk to find out?'

'I don't want to lose him.' That was the bottom line. Annie feared his loss more than she dared risk exploring the growing attraction.

'If your friendship is so important and so strong the thought of losing him makes you this afraid, how could telling him you like him possibly spoil things? Look at us, we're friends, right, no matter what?'

'Right.' Annie wanted to protest that Harri was a different matter entirely, but she didn't. She only watched the gulls in the sky, her shoulders dropping. She suddenly felt very small and very stupid indeed.

Cassidy wasn't done yet. 'If he's love-of-your-life material, you don't want to pass up the opportunity to find out for sure.'

'I'm flying home Saturday. What can possibly happen before then?'

'It sounds like plenty's already happened.'

Annie wanted to dream and confide and giggle like a kid with her old pal, but she forced herself to face facts. 'I saw him pick out a Valentine card for Paisley.'

'Was that before the library thing?'

'Yeah,' Annie said grudgingly.

'Well then. Things can change.'

Annie took a deep breath of salty sea air and released it in a sigh. 'I hear you.'

'I don't know much, but I know you and Harri, and I've never heard you in a fix like this over a guy. He's got under your skin.'

Annie huffed sadly. Cassidy knew her better than she knew herself. 'I've missed you,' she told her friend.

'Me too. So much. Thank you for forgiving me.'

'Nothing to forgive.'

They talked more about the shop and the English seaside, and Annie told her all about William, the silent book club tonight, and the Valentine's movie night on Friday, and Cassidy tried hard not to get carried away and say how it all sounded like the most romantic thing she'd ever heard of, but Annie could tell that's exactly what she meant every time she remarked it sounded 'so cute' and Annie 'deserved every second of it'.

When they hung up, Annie found herself staring into a rock pool, catching her reflection in the ripples with the grey sky above her. The Cassidy-shaped hole in her heart was filled up again, and now there was something new troubling her; the battle between her fears and the great big aching wanting she had for a sweet, nerdy Welshman who, after last night, she couldn't help but appreciate in a whole new light.

She lingered on the sand for a long time trying not to feel anything at all. For a supposedly simple bookselling vacation with an old friend, she'd seriously got more than she'd signed up for. It was a lot to take on board.

Added to that, the situation back home had clearly moved on. Was her community really coming out in support of the library? The kids had made their voices heard. Her colleagues were taking the high ground and inviting discussion and understanding. Was there a place for her amongst it all? Would her father be ready to get on board now? Could she face it all now that she knew Cassidy was waiting for her and Dave was out the picture?

It would still be so hard. Why on earth did everyone think she was so brave? She was afraid, and she was tired and, above all, confused about literally everything.

Chapter Nineteen

Sunday's Silent Reading Club

Something strange was happening to Harri.

Here he was with an evening of cosy company and quiet reading stretching out ahead of him and he couldn't get past the same paragraph his eyes had skimmed at least twenty times. Nothing was going in, and it had everything to do with Annie Luna who, right this second, was curled up on one of the beanbags by the fire, her nose buried deeply in a bonkbuster novel from the Eighties, and she really *was* reading. He could tell. She was devouring that thing.

He didn't know whether to be glad Annie finally seemed to have her bookworm mojo back or whether he was offended that she wasn't lost in the same struggle between brain, book and the blazing fire inside his body, ignited last night in the Castle Lore library and still burning out of control now.

Had anyone else noticed? They must be able to see he was consumed with it? But the other Clove Lore residents were deep in their books too.

The lights were up in the shop and the pink and red love hearts strung around the shelves and hanging in the windows created a bright, festive feeling. Everyone had arrived an hour ago, bringing their baking and snacks, blankets and cushions, determined to throw themselves into the spirit of Annie's vision.

She'd been busy like a bee, of course. Too busy to talk with Harri beyond the details of where the chairs ought to be set out and delegating the hot chocolate duties to him.

There'd been William to see to as well. He was currently in the green leather armchair, a blanket over his knees, looking very much at home with his tiny gold specs on his nose, reading some dense old volume of Roman plays in the original Latin and chuckling every now and again like he was listening to a comedy podcast.

There'd been a buzz of interest, led by Minty, about where on earth Mrs Crocombe had got to, and nobody had seen Mr Bovis either. They'd never normally miss a community event like this.

After some initial speculation, Minty had settled down to read. She'd brought the latest copy of *The Lady* and was tucking into a bag of pink bonbons with surprising relish. She looked as contented as can be with Jowan by her side with his works of John Donne, which he'd picked from the top of the bookshop's poetry shelves remarking out loud to the volume, 'Still here, my old friend.'

Aldous was at their feet with a rather revolting butcher's bone keeping him occupied, not an easy thing to crunch, having no teeth to speak of.

Annie had been delighted to welcome Kit and Anjali when they arrived on what was clearly another date. They were currently cloistered in the furthest corner of the cafe and whispering together, their books unopened.

Austen and Patti were arranged on the stairs, limbs everywhere, both stuck into beach reads and looking just as happy as they always did.

A pregnant woman who Patti had introduced as her sister, Joy, had followed them inside with a wavy-haired man in a fisherman's jumper. His name was Monty, and while Joy read something very intently on her Kindle, he made it his sole responsibility to top up her hot chocolate, prop her feet across his lap, and make sure that little Radia had everything she needed as well.

Radia had brought her entire *Isadora Moon* collection from home and was making a show of speed-reading her way through them under a blanket tent she'd constructed between two chair backs. There's nothing like reading in public to bring out the performance in precocious types.

Harri couldn't help sneaking peeks at the little family, so self-contained and protected as though they had a bubble of love around them. It was so unlike his own experiences growing up with his dad always occupied elsewhere with the conservatory business and always inclined to pick faults in him.

Jude Crawley was here too, having brought homemade iced gingerbread biscuits in the shape of open books. She was languidly turning the pages of a dog-eared copy of *Persuasion* with a look on her face that suggested this wasn't her first time reading it; she wasn't gripped so much as she was comforted and happy. Elliot, her long-haired, outrageously handsome and muscly husband, had his arm around the back of her chair, his EarPods in, reading an audiobook. Every now and then he'd absently stroke his hand down her hair and she'd squeeze his thick thigh. Such a power couple. This evening wasn't doing anything for Harri's nagging feeling of seriously missing out on life and love.

Closest to the door, Izaak and Leonid were lost in their books too. Izaak was nearing the end of a paperback titled

Swimming in the Dark with a serious expression, and his husband was taking notes on his phone as he read an illustrated guide to rhododendron growing. They'd brought a huge poppyseed loaf cake sent from Izaak's mother in Poland. Harri still had some of the seeds stuck in his teeth from the first slice and was considering a second, it was so delicious.

So what if he was trying to eat his feelings, as his mum would say? Anything felt better than being cheerfully, wilfully ignored by Annie and being forced to sit here in public feeling utterly skinless in complete silence.

Why wouldn't she talk with him this morning? Ten minutes and they could have cleared the air, surely? Though, when he tried to rehearse what he wanted to say, he couldn't quite find the words.

He tried to picture himself telling her how he'd not wanted to stop last night. He'd loved it, and he thought she'd been loving it too – if the way she'd scraped her nails through the short hair at the nape of his neck was a good indication of enjoyment. She'd whispered his name too, many times. He could hear it now, *dammit!*, breathy and frantic. His whole body answered the memory.

He fixed his eyes on the same paragraph. His face burned hot. Somebody was going to notice. That's when Annie, stopping at a chapter's end, turned her page and lifted her eyes to survey the room.

She'd seemed so proud of what she'd achieved tonight. She'd certainly motivated the whole community to turn out. Harri hadn't met half the locals occupying every corner of the bookshop and there were a couple of holidaymakers in from the Siren too.

Harri could feel her eyes land upon him, but he couldn't look back. He scratched his chin in a pretence of reading something fascinating. He narrowed his eyes and nodded as if to show his thoughts. *Hmm, interesting*, he tried to convey. He was overdoing it for sure.

That's when Annie's laugh burst into the silence. Harri couldn't resist looking up. She'd thrown her hand to her lips.

'Sorry,' she whispered.

She didn't drag her eyes away, but kept them fixed on Harri. She'd laughed at him and his ridiculous behaviour, and now Harri was grinning too.

The pair of them stayed like that, fixed on each other across the bowed heads in the bookshop, and sure some of the nosier locals were smirking in a knowing way at one another, but Harri didn't care. He was telling Annie with his eyes that he liked her, and she was exploring his face in her familiar, frank way.

Waves of affection passed between them, and then the other feelings kicked in. He saw it in her lips parting. She was glazing over. She was remembering him touching her. And she still wasn't looking away.

The bookshop disappeared around them and Harri knew she was thinking the same thing. Tonight, when everyone had left and William was safely conveyed back to his room at the Siren, upstairs in Annie's big white bed they'd pick up where they left off and this time there'd be no stopping them.

Were her cheeks pinking up? Were her pupils dilating to pinpricks? His own had to be. The way she was staring and smiling told him so.

His heart was thumping, turning over hard and rhythmic like an engine. He was going to mouth the word at her. Tonight. He knew it would land how he wanted it to.

He hadn't imagined any of it. They'd been incredible together. But as he wet his lips to silently convey the word, glancing surreptitiously round the room to be sure everyone else was reading, the phone in his pocket rang.

All eyes flew to him. Annie laughed again. She was enjoying his discomfort, no, she was sharing it, and it was kind of funny.

'Oops, sorry you guys,' he said, smiling goofily until he saw the name on the screen. Paisley.

He hadn't meant to, but the look he threw Annie communicated everything. Her face fell as he pulled the phone to his ear.

'Just a sec,' he whispered down the line, and as quick as he could, he carried his conversation out into the dark courtyard leaving Annie watching him, crestfallen in her spot under the stairs, her eyes slowly dropping, falling back to her book, looking very much like a woman who knew she'd almost made a second huge mistake.

Chapter Twenty

Things Back Home

The struggle was easy enough to ignore. She'd settled it while the rest of Clove Lore slept.

Last night, at the silent book club, she'd let the serotonin take over, watching Harri when he was pretending to have forgotten all about the thing in the library.

The call from Paisley was the reminder she'd needed to listen to her amygdala. That was the part of her brain that knew best. It carried the memories of all the times she'd been hurt, burned, scared and scarred. It was the part that learned from mistakes, that created inhibitions. It was the part that was going to stop her destroying her friendship with Harri. It was currently telling her to stop being horny and start being hardworking.

She'd not hung around at the end of her event, disappearing upstairs and into bed behind her bolted door before the last of them had left. She'd witnessed Harri sloping back inside the bookshop after what had felt like ages pacing in the courtyard, his phone clamped to his ear.

He'd returned looking ashen and guilt wracked. She knew him well enough to read his expressions. He'd tried to catch her eye but she avoided him.

Had he confessed everything to Paisley, about their library madness? Had she scolded him? Threatened that this really was the last straw? Whatever they'd said to one another, Harri's guilty look was enough to confirm things were far from over back home.

This morning she'd excused herself from the bookshop and Harri, who had dark circles under his eyes like he had barely slept, had watched her, more than a little bewildered, as she poured the breakfast coffee he'd made her into a takeaway cup, piled on warm layers, and looked out the door into the Monday morning winter glare.

'You coming back any time soon?' Harri asked, dispirited. Annie had no idea of the pains he'd taken to craft the perfect Hawaiian espresso – made with eye-wateringly rare and expensive Mount Loa beans, topped with the lightest slow-whipped, Korean-inspired dalgona creme. She couldn't know how his heart dropped at the sound of it being sloshed into a cardboard carry cup.

'I have some stuff to do,' she said. 'Can you hold the fort by yourself?'

'Course.' He'd shrugged like it was nothing. 'We should talk, though, about last night… and the night before that, and…'

'Can't stop,' she'd said, breezing out the door.

Out on the slope, however, with her bag over her shoulder, she realised she didn't quite know where she was going and for a moment it didn't matter so much because the white cloud cover was broken through here and there, revealing glimpses of watery blue sky and a hazy sun.

In the little front gardens that lined the slope, bare branches covered in spring buds dripped with morning dew and Annie spotted her first daffodils of the year, tiny yellow trumpeters heralding the coming spring.

She didn't have time to stop and stare however, as a bright blur of pink and red was coming down the slope towards her. All smiles and chatter, Austen and Patti seemed to carry springtime with them just as much as the early garden blooms.

'Hey!' Annie called, and they waved back.

'Going sightseeing today?' asked Patti when they drew nearer.

'Actually, I have some work stuff to do. But I can't concentrate in the bookshop.'

She ignored the brief amused glance that passed between the two women. A glance that said they suspected why she couldn't concentrate. Was the whole village whispering about her and Harri? They'd read it so wrong if they were.

'Is there a library round here?' asked Annie, trying to maintain her poise.

'Nope,' said Austen. 'The council closed the library out on the main road years ago.'

'Aww, no!' Annie recoiled. Another one bites the dust.

'Yep,' added Patti sagely. 'It's a Starbucks now.'

'So what does a person do for wi-fi and when they need a place to work? That isn't an expensive coffee shop, I mean?'

With a glance of communication, Austen and Patti reached a wordless agreement.

'Come to ours?' they said at the same time.

–

Meanwhile, at the bookshop, Harri was settling William in for the day. Or rather he was watching on as William made himself at home re-ordering the 'Languages' shelf.

'The *Varronianus* ought to be here with the *Etyma Latina*, keeping David Crystal on English here, next to

Chomsky on language acquisition. You see? It's simple Dewey Decimal four hundred, you know? And what is *this* doing here?' He pulled a Wilfred Thesiger from the shelf. 'Photography section, surely? And this *Galloping Gourmet* cookbook is clearly lost.'

'Ah! We've an expert in our midst, Harri,' quipped Jowan, taking the offending titles to the correct shelves. 'I always arranged things loosely by theme and some cursory alphabetising, but Borrowers over the years have imposed their own order on parts of the shop. One time, a young lass arranged the general fiction by spine colour.'

William shuddered noticeably.

'I know, 'twas a dark day for Clove Lore,' added Jowan with a smile. 'There's bound to be a fair amount of cross-pollination on these shelves,' he went on. 'Being a living, breathing bookshop, our own little garden of books, and not a neat and tidy library.'

Nevertheless, he took instructions from William for as long as it took the older man to find a book that caught his interest, carry it to the armchair and bury his nose in it.

Harri liked Jowan very much, now that all the match-making and betting-book stuff seemed to be forgotten about. He'd made both men espresso con panna at ten, fixing himself one too, even though he had no enthusiasm for it. Even though he really needed the caffeine.

It had been hard to sleep after Paisley's call. She'd been to Neath to drop in a bag of his books along with some clothes she'd found at the bottom of the laundry basket and washed for him, which was really nice of her. Her visit had clearly got Harri's dad worked up. She'd said he'd 'not been best pleased' when she mentioned his son wasn't planning on coming back to their flat in Port Talbot, but more than likely moving back to the family home.

'Just a heads up,' she'd said, and Harri had sighed and thanked her.

It was a timely reminder that the first week of his holiday had flown by and in five more days he'd be standing at the station deciding what to do next. By then, Annie would be on her flight home.

It had been a jolt, but one he needed. This escape was only a passing dream. Reality was just there, waiting.

His mum mustn't have broken it to his dad about the break-up. Paisley had ambushed him with it. He'd have been hopping mad, Harri knew. Mad enough for Paisley to call and warn him.

He'd hoped he might receive at least a neutral welcome home from his dad, knowing it wouldn't be a warm one; but it sounded like he wasn't going to be welcome at all. The call had been enough to send him shrinking into himself, and when he'd returned to the silent reading group and found Annie hunched over, absorbed in her book, having totally forgotten about him, he'd shrunk further still. She'd disappeared to bed with her book leaving Harri to lock up, giving him time alone to lecture himself on how he'd so easily abandoned his promise to let Annie enjoy her holiday untroubled and in peace. *Typical Harri, always letting everyone down*, he'd told himself, picturing how his parents must be at home at that very moment arguing about what to do with their disappointing son when he showed up with all his stuff in a few days' time. He could hear his mum attempting to plead for him, saying how he was just out of a relationship and had nowhere else to go. Harri had fallen asleep at dawn picturing his dad with that firm-set mouth and folded arms calling him 'hopeless' and 'far too old to be so far behind'.

This morning, seeing Annie uncomfortable and desperate to get away from him, he'd vowed to concentrate on the bookselling side of things and less on being a slave to his needy, guilty feelings.

He'd been glad when Jowan arrived bringing William and the boxes they'd won at the auction. Jowan had dragged the boxes right to the door on a little sled like a grizzled Santa Claus delivering Christmas gifts. Aldous had hitched a ride on the sled too and now he was fast asleep by the shop fire.

Jowan hadn't said anything in advance about planning on helping out today but evidently that's what was happening. Harri assumed, since William had no place to be, and he was most likely a bit lonely, he'd be sticking around all day as well. The village elders were clearly claiming him for themselves and Harri couldn't think of a better community to undertake the task.

'Any news on the sale of the castle?' Harri asked in a low voice while the antiquarian read peacefully by the fire.

'There's a public consultation planned for tomorrow,' answered Jowan. 'The Happy Holiday Park seems keen to acquire the land from the Crown. Word coming out of the council offices is that the company has already drawn up plans to develop the site. Eighty-eight static caravans and cabins around a camp hub with indoor heated pool,' confirmed Jowan gravely. 'But you didn't hear that from me, and certainly not from my Mint,' he added, very much like a man whose wife *definitely* knew someone on the council and had wheedled the news from them.

'Sounds quite nice,' said Harri, thinking how it was exactly the kind of place his parents would have taken him on holiday when he was little, when he'd been the apple of his dad's eye, his mini me, before he'd become a worry.

Jowan didn't seem convinced.

'Was there really nothing left for William?' asked Harri in a whisper. 'It's rotten he's lost his best friend and his home all in one go. Isn't he entitled to something?'

'Well…' began Jowan, scratching his chin. 'Mint might have made some enquiries amongst her lawyer pals – and she knows a thing or two about the law herself, having inherited a great big house and a great big debt from her old man. Unfortunately, she's certain there's nothing can be done. Them having lived together, them being friends, him being his *carer* even, doesn't mean he's entitled to a cut of anything. Even if he has just lost his home. The whole estate belonged to the Courtenay family, and now they're gone.'

'What'll happen to William?' whispered Harri.

Jowan inhaled through his teeth like the news wasn't good. 'There's the problem of him being of no fixed abode. He's technically homeless. We can shelter him as much as we likes, but Social Services are still involved. They'll find him somewhere permanent to stay.'

'In Clove Lore?' Harri asked. That didn't sound so bad.

Jowan shook his head and leaned closer. 'You didn't hear this from me, but rumour has it they're looking at sheltered accommodation as far afield as Taunton.'

They both looked at William, absorbed in his book.

'Looks like he's in his element here,' said Harri. 'A bookshop's the next best thing to his big old library. Can't he stay here?'

Jowan raised a sandy brow. 'If this was a novel, probably. But, this is real life an' that man needs looking after. You saw what happened when he stopped taking his medication and wasn't feeding himself proper.'

It was all very well for Harri to wish for more for William, but he was leaving in a few days and was hardly in a position to know what was right for him, or to volunteer the village's permanent residents into roles as his new carers, no matter how well suited they might be for it.

'It just seems a shame,' said Harri. 'How he can't make his own decisions.'

With a hand on his shoulder to show he agreed, Jowan gave him a conciliatory pat.

'Come on, let's unpack those boxes of books you bought for us. I'm sure William can tell us all about them.'

–

Annie pinched at her screwed eyelids and the screen glared blue. Her morning's work had at least been worth the eye strain and the anxiety of opening her inbox.

First of all, she'd logged into her emails to find messages from her senior library colleagues. Cassidy had been right. Their plans to get the community on their side were well underway. A meeting had been called at the school for parents, students and the relevant library associations to attend and share their concerns. The school library had been temporarily closed. None of the volunteer parents were authorised to work the systems and the whole thing had ground to a halt so they'd reluctantly reinstated Linda and Kimmy, just as Cassidy had said.

She'd fired off replies straight away, pledging her support, saying sorry for being so quiet. She'd been frightened. The intimidation was real.

If anyone was going to understand, it was her colleagues. Harri had been outraged on her behalf but he couldn't ever know what it was like to be a woman facing down public humiliation and frightening accusations in a time and place where, all around her, women's rights were being stripped back by cold, careless conservatives, as though decades of fighting for basic freedoms had meant nothing at all, even when Annie knew that as a white, cis woman with a place to live and a university degree she didn't suffer the half of it.

Satisfied that her colleagues couldn't doubt her support, she'd checked the latest news reports about libraries in similar positions to her own, only deeper into the fight. Her heart dropped reading about the librarians whose careers had been curtailed by wildly dangerous allegations. One image accompanying a news story showed a mother on a school yard, their mouth set in a stern line. Their homemade banner shouted *librarians, keep your mitts off our kids.* Seeing it had made her queasy with indignation and dread.

There were stories of support too. Of librarians who'd taken on the book bans and won, but it had come at a cost to everyone involved, and most especially to the kids at the centre of all this. Kids who, Annie knew, deserved books they could read for free, housed in a safe, well-resourced library that belonged to them, and with a book collection as diverse, wonderful, entertaining and unique as them.

Annie's jaw was clenched hard when Austen brought her a sandwich and tea at twelve. 'Snack for the workers,' she said in her *Coronation Street* twang, plonking herself on a stool next to Annie at the kitchen bar.

Being a Monday, Radia was at school and her mother, Joy, was working at her little tech-support station in the bedroom she shared with Monty. Patti had gone up to the Big House a while ago to show a prospective bride and groom around the wedding facilities. This had been exactly the headspace Annie needed.

'Thanks for this,' said Annie.

'Ach, it's just a crisp and cheddar butty an' a brew,' Austen replied, squashing her crisps between thick, white, buttered bread slices with a satisfying crunch before taking a big bite.

'No, I mean this,' said Annie. 'Letting me hide out here… Hold on! Crisps and cheese? That's genius.'

'I know.' Austen took a big bite. 'Has to be salt and vinegar, mind.' She let Annie enjoy her first taste. 'Good, right?'

It really was good. Annie hadn't had time for breakfast in her hurry to get away from the shop this morning and her stomach had been growling as she worked. Harri's consolation prize coffee had turned cold in the paper cup.

One of Annie's favourite things about Austen, aside from her generosity and her taste in snacks, was that she didn't ask prying questions. Anyone else in Clove Lore would want to know why she was hiding out from Harri. Having been a Borrower herself, maybe Austen could appreciate how stressful it was when the whole village tried to insert themselves into the lives of their vacationers.

'You looked busy,' Annie said between bites.

All morning Austen had been curled up on the sofa at Annie's back, with headphones jammed over her ears, taking handwritten notes from a textbook.

'I've got an assessment coming up. Bibliotherapy.' She took a slurp of tea and caught Annie's questioning eyes. 'What's bibliotherapy, right?'

'Yeah. Sorry. Haven't heard of it. It sounds like something I should know about.'

'You'd love it. I'm doing an online course just to learn the basics, now that I'm running loads of creative writing workshops and things.'

'You were so good with the kids the other day,' Annie cut in.

'Thanks. They're easier to handle than an adults' creative writing circle, that's for sure.' Austen's laugh was bright and easy. 'But your silent reading night was actually more like bibliotherapy than my kids' poetry session was.'

'It was?'

'Yep, reading for wellbeing,' Austen said.

Annie remembered how much she'd enjoyed sitting by the fire, lost in her novel, surrounded by people who no longer felt like strangers. It had been the first time in months she could read at all, let alone *enjoy* reading. The blockage, whether it had been to do with Cassidy or the school, had shifted that night and she'd simply enjoyed the feeling of her eyes moving across the lines, absorbing the racy, lavish storytelling. 'I think I know what you're saying,' Annie told her.

'It's all about matching the right book to the right person at the right time. It can be therapeutic and healing; transformative even.'

'In that case, I know *exactly* what you mean. I used to be...' Annie stopped herself. 'I *am* an assistant librarian in a school. I've seen kids who hated reading find their way to exactly the right story for them and, *bam*! It's love!' She could picture those kids' faces. She knew that look in their eye when the magic was happening. 'The right book can be a huge comfort.'

'Exactly!' agreed Austen. 'Books tell you you're not alone. That's what this essay assignment's about; mental health and the solace of reading. Reading, letting our imaginations run wild, rehearsing difficult feelings or working through tough situations from a safe distance, all that stuff happens when we're reading, and those processes help us turn pain and trauma into creativity and healing. Happiness too. I can't imagine living without reading. It's like breathing to me.'

'Can I read it when you're done?' The words had blurted out. Annie forgot she was supposed to be reserved around these folks, but Austen seemed delighted.

'I would love that! And any feedback you've got?'

'You want to know what I think of it? Really?'

Austen mugged amazement. 'You're an actual librarian, aren't you? Of course I do!'

The tiny ember of determination that her morning's work had ignited within her burst into a flame now. 'You're right,' said Annie, resolutely. 'I am an actual librarian.'

She opened her emails again and started to compose a message.

Dear Principal Johnson, it began.

Chapter Twenty-One

Unpacking

'Book stewardship, you see,' William was explaining, having at last put his book down and settled to a little work, hunched over one of the open boxes from Castle Lore, '...is both a vocation and a calling.'

Jowan made a gruff sound to show his agreement while William pulled out paperback after paperback looking at them like they were old friends.

'You chose well, young Harri.'

'I didn't do much.' It was awkward riffling through the titles that, until last week, had been in William's care. Harri wanted to do nothing but apologise and offer them all to William to keep, but the antiquarian had a different take on things.

He saw the bookshop's purchases as a rescue of sorts. 'They'll do well here on your shelves. One day just the right person will come for each one and Nicholas's books will gradually become dispersed into libraries everywhere. That's no bad thing.' But it didn't stop him looking fondly at the book in his hand. 'General Fiction, H,' he said, passing Harri a Radclyffe Hall to shelve.

'Ah, *The Well of Loneliness*,' said Harri. 'We studied this at uni.'

'It was banned, you know?' said Jowan.

'Obscene Publications Act, eighteen fifty-seven,' said William in an offhand way. He really was a walking encyclopedia. 'Ah, I'm glad you saved these!' William pulled out Harper Lee and two Iris Murdochs. 'Oh, and here's a Huxley. A particular favourite of Nicholas's. *That man could see the future*, Nicholas used to say.'

It was small, but Jowan spotted it, the pinch of stress and sadness between William's brows.

'You are welcome to keep any of these books, you know?' said Jowan. 'T'would be our pleasure to return them to their owner.'

'No, no,' said William, swiftly wiping his eyes with his handkerchief. 'Let us carry on.'

He had a tireless energy for unpacking and correctly cataloguing the works on the shop's stock system, telling Harri their publication dates and rough value without having to consult any databases or compare prices across book merchants.

William lifted the very last title from the second to last box. 'John Donne. A favourite of yours, I believe?' he addressed Jowan. He remembered him reading a collected works at the silent reading night.

' 'Twas the favourite of my Isolde,' said Jowan. 'My late wife. My late *first* wife,' he clarified like a man not quite used to saying the words yet. 'We set up the bookshop at her insistence. Oh, she was some woman! A poetry lover.'

'I was never one for Metaphysicals,' said William, unromantically, but handing the Donne to Jowan nonetheless. 'Perhaps you should keep this one?'

'Thank you, but I only care for the collected edition, up there on the top shelf. It's overpriced so no one buys it, but I like to keep it in the poetry section so anyone that needs it can find it.'

William nodded his understanding and Jowan flicked through the book. He thought hard for a little while before passing the book to Harri.

'Poetry shelves, please.'

Harri entered the book's details into the shop laptop.

'You know,' said Jowan in a pointed way. 'My Isolde and my Minty were great friends.'

This stopped Harri on his way across the shopfloor with the book. 'They were?'

'Aye, and for a long, long time after Isolde's passing, I found I couldn't even entertain the notion of my liking Minty.'

William motioned for Jowan to cut the tapes on the last box, marked 'miscellaneous'. Romantic stories evidently weren't for him. Jowan worked the scissors as he talked.

'Mint and I were great friends for a long time. She helped me so much with my grief, maybe because she shared it? After losing Isolde, I couldn't bear the thought of losing Minty, my friend and my comfort, as well. But my avoiding loving Minty almost broke us apart anyway.'

'It did?' Harri couldn't help asking.

Deep laughter lines radiated out from Jowan's eyes like sunrays as he gave a throaty chuckle. 'Got to the point where I'd gone way past liking Mint as a friend, and we were both dancin' around each other, trying to avoid our feelings. I loved her, deep down, and I knew if I couldn't have her, my wanting her would break us anyway. So, I chose to tell her. It was a risk, of course, but I was going to lose her completely, the way things were heading.'

Harri's shoulders dropped. He knew exactly what Jowan was up to. He shelved the book without another word.

Jowan wasn't done yet. 'Came a point where I had to ask myself what would happen if she met someone else and I missed my only chance,' he said.

William looked up from the box as though wondering why they were still on this topic when there were deeply fascinating library papers to sort.

'Luckily for me,' Jowan continued, 'she was of the same mind, and we married soon after I confessed my heart.'

'*Pfft!*' William evidently didn't agree with this strategy.

Harri was grateful for William's curmudgeonly insistence on starting the unpacking of the last box right away. It would at least prevent Jowan talking about friends becoming lovers as if it were an easy thing to navigate, as though it weren't in fact near impossible.

Harri plunged his hands inside the last box, his fingers falling upon a yellowing packet. He handed it to William right away.

'Ah!' William's voice shook as he pulled a photograph from the envelope.

Harri caught sight of the image, faded with age, as William examined it closely. Two men, both in rolled white shirt sleeves, open collars and shabby trousers. One, unmistakably a young shaggy-haired Sabine, stood with his arms folded and legs apart like a school sports team photo, and seated nearby, on what Harri recognised as the steps of Clove Lore Castle on a summer's day, was a thin, pale fellow in a Panama hat, a pipe in his mouth, slouched, a book open across his lap. Around him on the steps were piled numerous books, most of them open as though the men were reading all of them at once.

The mood in the Borrow-A-Bookshop fell as dark as the wintry afternoon outside now that the sun was setting.

With some difficulty, William rose to stand, the photograph still in his hand. 'I'll retire to the Siren now, if you don't mind. It's been a long day after all.'

Jowan signalled for Harri to find the man's coat and the new woolly hat, scarf and gloves that one of the villagers, Caroline Capstan, the launderess, had knitted for him.

'Come along, Aldous,' called Jowan. 'We'll walk Mr Sabine down the slope.'

William didn't thank him. He'd turned distant and sorrowful again, like he had been on the day he first arrived, only now that the medication was keeping his mind sharp, the pain was written on his face.

When Jowan held the door open for him, with Aldous zipped up inside his jacket for warmth, William asked that Harri leave the rest of the box for unpacking another day.

'Mr Sabine?' Harri said, before he was gone. 'I'm not sure if anyone's actually said it to you yet, but we're all very sorry for your loss.'

William's chest heaved but he was determined to maintain his dignity. 'Thank you. It isn't so sad. We had each other for a very long time. How many people can say that? Friendship is the most important of all relations.'

He passed down the shop steps and into the darkness, Jowan nodding a farewell, before closing the door, leaving Harri in the empty shop.

When he propped himself up behind the till and opened his book he found once more that he couldn't get far in his reading as the older men's advice – he'd been smart enough to figure their storytelling was giving advice about him and Annie – circulated in his brain.

Tell her before the wanting breaks your friendship apart. What if she meets *the one* while I'm debating what to do?

Don't risk spoiling things. *Friendship is the most important thing.*

He pictured himself as an old man like William. He didn't know where he'd end up at his age, the future was a blank for him, but he knew he too would live a life measured in books and coffee cups.

Imagine, he told himself now, how incredible things could be if he cherished Annie's friendship, cherished *her*, for all his life. Imagine if he worked hard on staying in touch. He could be her greatest supporter, and she for him. It could be wonderful. Wouldn't that be just as special, and safer, than risking it all on a love affair that might burn itself out, especially with an ocean between them?

He didn't absorb one word of his book or taste a note of his coffee that afternoon as these thoughts turned in his mind.

–

When Annie returned from her day at Austen's, he had dinner ready for both of them. As they ate, she told him all about the email she'd sent the principal, letting him know for sure she was coming home to the school library after her leave of absence.

She'd let her boss know she was committed fully to participating in the community meetings to find a solution to their problems, and she'd made sure he understood she had no intention of shying away from a fight if the book banning was to escalate.

She was ravenously hungry and dreadfully tired. He'd listened to her, all fire and enthusiasm even though she was yawning her head off, and he topped up her tea and made sure she knew he'd be there supporting her through it all.

They'd read by the fireside after dinner until Annie was nodding off. She'd started on a new novel – an English translation of a story set in a dreamy Korean bookshop – devouring it as hungrily as she'd eaten her food. He'd noticed her yawning as she closed its covers with a satisfied smile and told her to head up to bed.

'I'm gonna save the last chapters for tomorrow. Don't want it to end too soon,' she drawled, her eyes heavy-lidded, her head propped in her hand.

William and Nicholas would be so proud of them, he felt sure of it. Jowan and Minty, on the other hand, might have other opinions, but for tonight at least, it was very easy to ignore them.

Erring on the side of caution and friendship felt like the steady, comforting, kind thing to do for both of them.

That night he went to bed with something in his heart that felt close enough to contentment to allow him to sleep in peace.

Chapter Twenty-Two

Homesickness

The first flush of daffodils was spreading Down-along, lighting up the little gardens that lined the sloping path with a buttery yellow, made brighter still against the slender stems of white snowdrops. The village ravens, crows and rooks were busy repairing their nests and hungrily hunting for food all along the slope.

In the front garden of the Clove Lore Ice Cream Cottage, just a little way downhill from the turning into the Borrow-A-Bookshop, a single flame-red tulip streaked with vivid orange was opening its petals for the first time in the mild morning air.

It was a beautiful, bright, late-winter morning, but Mrs Crocombe wasn't there to witness it. In fact, no one had laid eyes on the old matchmaker. The ice cream parlour was locked up, its shutters drawn, and the building as quiet as the grave.

Her absence was all anyone could talk about, excepting William Sabine who wasn't remotely interested, up at the Big House ballroom where the developers were holding their first public consultation on their proposed plans for Clove Lore Castle.

'Mr Bovis not here, neither?' said Caroline Capstan, Samantha's mum, and owner of the Clove Lore Laundry

Company, leaning back in her seat to address the gossips in the row behind.

'Strange,' replied the village postie.

'Nobody knows where she is,' joined Minty, slipping into the row behind, making no pretence about her eavesdropping. 'Her own daughter, Laura, the headteacher, hasn't heard from her, can you believe? Doesn't know where her own mother might be.'

'An' she made no mention of taking an 'oliday,' threw in Jowan, settling beside his wife, Aldous trotting to a stop unhappily between the chair legs, wondering why his morning walk had been curtailed with a boring delay in his own ballroom.

'Mrs Crocombe's Ice Cream Cottage has been open every day for decades. That woman doesn't know the meaning of a day off, let alone a holiday,' added Mrs Capstan.

'What are we talking about?' said Estée Gold, getting in on the gossip in a magnificent white kimono with bright red flowers in her hair.

Minty gave her friend an appraising, surprised look but kept any comments to herself, instead letting her know that she was worried about Mrs Crocombe and Bovis. Missing a meeting on the fate of a local landmark wasn't like them at all.

'Ran off together, have they?' Estée said salaciously, only to be tutted at by the lady of the manor. 'What? It's more than possible they've taken themselves away for a dirty… I mean a *romantic* break.'

'If that's all it is, why the secrecy?' said Jowan. 'There's not one of us doesn't know those two are paired up like doves in that shop. No, I reckon there's more to it than that.'

'Harri mentioned something about Bovis saying the brakes on his Land Rover were on the wonk,' put in Samantha, artlessly, as she shuffled down the row, coming to join her mother. Jasper Gold, Sam's boyfriend, wasn't much interested in the planning meeting and had stayed away to prepare for his Valentine's movie night, only three days away. He was outside on the lawns now, setting up his projectionist's booth.

'I hates to say it,' began Jowan in a knowing tone, 'but she has been prone to rash decisions in the recent past.'

Minty tutted. 'The fling with the sea captain?'

Estée sat up all the straighter at this. 'An affair?'

'He was an old fraudster, turns out,' Jowan added, stroking at Aldous's beige head by his knee. 'But he's long gone, back to sea, and our Bovis has been a steady companion to her ever since. I'd say they are good influences on one another.'

'I'd say they are as thick as thieves,' Minty put in.

'An accident, then?' Estée began, spreading her hands before her, painting the scene. 'It's easy enough to picture. Night-time, a country lane. A rickety old Land Rover trundles through the sleet and snow.'

'Hasn't snowed in Clove Lore these fourteen months, Estée,' attempted Jowan, only to be cut off.

Estée was still caught up in the drama in her imagination. 'An owl hoots, the driver, an elderly, red-faced and very silly man, is momentarily distracted. A tyre hits a patch of ice, they skid, he brakes, the brakes fail, his passenger screams, they hit a wall, stones and metal crunch horribly, a whimper...'

'Thank you, Estée! That's very... vivid,' put in Minty, a hand to her temple as if to soothe a headache. 'I'm sure we'd have heard about any accidents in these parts.'

'That is, if they haven't skidded into a flooded quarry, or a reservoir?' Estée enthused. 'My character in *Destiny's Peak* lost her second husband in just such an accident when his Porsche went to the bottom of Lake Tahoe with him trapped inside… or so we thought!'

'Ooh, are we talking about *Destiny's Peak*?' said Izaak enthusiastically, as he took one of the last available seats, right next to Estée. He had remained her biggest fan, next to his husband Leonid, even while becoming one of her only friends, now that she was a skint ex-celebrity long since abandoned by her A-list mates. 'How did the scriptwriters get him out of that one in time for season five?'

'Amnesia, of course,' said Estée very seriously.

Pained, Minty shook her head.

The developers were taking the stage. Three white men, all in dark suits, were tapping lapel mics and fiddling with a laptop and projector before spreading into a line before the assembly.

'Picture this,' said one, the mic boom in the speakers drawing the room's attention.

'Castle Lore like you've never seen it before,' said another.

'None of uz have seen it,' shouted one of the old timers from the front row.

William Sabine, seated next to him, didn't respond to any of this, only clasping his hands on his lap and listening.

Undeterred, the third man took over. 'Picture our castle ruin, a magnificent historical backdrop to a modern, fully accessible holiday resort, open year-round, bringing visitors to Clove Lore and employing people from across the region.'

The first speaker took over again as the Happy Holiday Park logo onscreen behind him melted into an artist's vision for the resort. 'Complete with step-free splash park and pool, snack bar, restaurant, tennis courts…'

On they went, painting a picture of a holiday heaven on earth. William sat still and unreadable. At the end, when some of the villagers were longingly eyeing the complimentary pastries and biscuits on the table by the fireplace and others were completing their handwritten notes like there was going to be a test, the presentation leader brought his hands together in a satisfied clasp.

'If we're successful in our acquisition, that is what you can expect from Devon's next big family holiday destination. Now, I think we have time for a few questions. Anyone?'

He only staggered a little when nearly every hand in the place shot up.

–

Knowing the whole village would be up at the Big House, Harri and Annie had taken the consultation as an opportunity to sleep in late and they'd emerged from their separate rooms all the brighter for it. While Annie showered, Harri worked on a new coffee.

'Ta-dah!' He proudly presented his creation as Annie appeared downstairs at ten. 'This is my all-new smooth peanut butter and Kenyan espresso mix with almond milk over ice, topped with a whipped Devonshire double cream swirl with a dusting of cinnamon. Go on, try it.'

He didn't look away as she drank.

'I'd pay seven bucks for this, easy,' she said.

Satisfied, Harri tried his drink. 'I came up with the idea overnight.'

'You dreamt about making coffee?'

Not quite. He'd dreamt about making coffee *for Annie*. He knew that would sound weird if he told her, so he gave a laugh instead and rummaged for his tasting notes app, typing some words. 'If the Port Talbot coffee shop wasn't a chain with a set menu, I'd suggest this to my manager.'

'This,' Annie took another sip, 'with an almond croissant would be…' She made a chef's kiss with her fingertips.

'I was thinking a crumbed almond shortbread finger,' said Harri.

Annie observed him as she drank, before saying, 'You got a whole dream coffee shop going on in your head.'

Harri pulled a contemplative face. 'Maybe I do.'

His manager had told him loads of times he should apply for his own franchise, run his own branch. He'd won all those barista competitions, hadn't he? He showed up day after day for work and the novelty of improving his skills still hadn't worn off. He hadn't applied for so much as one other job since his Master's graduation. He'd put it down to laziness. Or at least, that's what his dad put it down to. Paisley hadn't understood it at all.

'Maybe I just like making coffees?' he said, as though to himself.

He'd never considered his manager's suggestion seriously, but the last few days had shown him he could make a go of it, in theory.

'I've enjoyed running my own little bookshop cafe,' he said, louder now, making Annie smile. He didn't add that he'd loved it precisely because Annie was right next door behind the till, and he'd been driven to experimenting with his drinks menu so he could offer Annie something new to make her happy. Plus, he'd liked the freedom to serve whatever he wanted. The cafe had kept its own

243

hours, nothing about it was dictated from a faceless team from head office like his role at the chain coffee shop. If he wanted to experiment here, he could. If he wanted to rustle up a quick batch of Welsh cakes, he'd done it. They went especially well with the single cream caffè breve he'd been convincing customers to try instead of their habitual latte. It had all felt like one long, fun game of playing shop.

'I guess it's easy when you don't have to worry about overheads,' he admitted.

All the money going through the till went straight into the Borrow-A-Bookshop Charity Trust, and his baking ingredients were subsidised by petty cash (and the occasional donated cake, like the one Jude Crawley had brought). It would be a different matter altogether if the shop's livelihood was reliant on sales, and his salary was earned cup by cup.

Over the last few years, he'd grown used to his wages depositing in his bank account, the same amount every week. He'd chat with the customers, knew his regulars' orders by heart, petted their dogs, learned all about their jobs and their kids. It was a nicely contained way of remaining sociable and connected, all while making money. He even liked going on the training days, up at the corporate HQ training kitchen. It was his job to learn and then demonstrate the new menus for the other staff back in branch. He looked forward to those days, now he came to think about it.

His manager, on the other hand, didn't have nearly so much fun. He was forever grumbling about sales targets and losses and visits from Regional checking up on him. None of that appealed, but that, he figured, was the reality of running a business. Here he was only playing, risk free.

His heart fell a little now that the thought of returning to work in a few days had lodged itself in his brain, though that had just as much to do with Annie going home too.

Annie didn't seem to be thinking about home, right this second. She had her eyes closed dreamily and was taking another approving sip, slow and smiling. An intrusive thought said he wished he could watch her like that all day.

That's when the locked door rattled.

Jowan was behind the glass, holding up Aldous so he could look inside. William lurked behind them.

'The workers have arrived,' said Harri, snapping out of his caffeine dreams and letting them inside.

-

The day stayed dry and bright. The good weather brought the day-trippers out, so the shop was busy all morning.

William was more animated than the Borrowers had seen him yet. Right this second, he had his nose buried in the Chaucer from the display table.

'Has anyone partaken of this little wonder?' he asked the room. The tourists browsing the shelves ignored him, not knowing what to think.

Annie was closest and peered at the cover. '*Parliament of Fowles?* Nope. I did wonder what it has to do with Valentine's Day.'

William very kindly suppressed the little impulse within him to call them all philistines. 'This, in my opinion, is Chaucer's finest work. A poem celebrating the time of year when birds typically choose their mate.'

'Valentine's Day?' asked Harri from the cafe door where he was drying off washed baking rings. That morning he'd attempted a coffee cake frosted with butter-cream, with moderate success.

'Chaucer exercises some poetic licence, but yes, the feast of Saint Valentine was typically associated in the fourteenth century with the beginning of avian life cycles. Chaucer perhaps popularised the notion.'

'Doesn't sound *super* romantic,' observed Annie.

'If you don't read it, you'll never find out.' William tapped the book to the side of his nose and put it back on its riser. 'Valentine's traditions are rather curious,' he went on. 'Especially in this region.'

'Devonshire?' Jowan asked from the middle of the floor where he was sweeping up sandy footprints with a long brush.

'Hmm,' the antiquarian agreed. 'Valentine's Day is deeply rooted here, more than many other places. Nicholas and I made the ritual our especial study for a period in the early nineteen-nineties.'

Annie and Harri exchanged a smiling glance. The more they learned about those two curious old book-worms, the more they loved them.

'Did you know the Valentine's greeting has its roots here in South Devon? In the nineteenth century, letters containing a love device of some kind or another were sent in vast numbers in this region, paving the way for these...' he touched his fingertips to the Valentine's cards in the rack, '...commercial Valentine's.' He evidently did not understand the need for them at all.

'I've long said we are a more romantic sort round these parts than those 'uns up country,' joined Jowan, resting on his brush.

'It may well be attributable to the longer, lighter days in the South West,' explained William dryly. 'Spring arrives earlier here than other places. It is lusher and wetter, brighter, more clement. Thrushes, finches and wood-peckers were all conspicuous in their mating at this time of year, back when our bird populations were healthy. As a consequence, nests were feathered earlier, chicks hatched sooner; the first bees were flying by February some years.'

'The lovers out-of-doors all the earlier, meeting in hedgerow trysts?' Jowan said, throwing an irreverent wink to Harri who rolled his eyes.

Annie's laughter fluttered through the shop.

'It is true, we can only attribute the survival of Valentine's rituals to certain… impulses of nature awakened by the springtime abundance,' William said primly. 'Especially given the attempts to ban the feast of St Valentine altogether.'

'What?' This caught Annie's interest.

'Edward and Elizabeth both abolished the holy day,' tolled William, steepling his fingers in front of his tummy like a minister ending the sermon. 'But it seems,' he cleared his throat, '…amorousness continues regardless.'

'Lovers will find one another.' Jowan clicked his lips and rushed his sweepings right out into the courtyard. They promptly blew back inside again before he had a chance to swing the door shut.

Annie remained fixed on William's words. 'Seems to me there's always someone set on banning all the good stuff just 'cus they don't like it for themselves?'

William inhaled as though ready to begin a lecture on the topic, but Jowan made the very good point that not one of them had had a cuppa this past hour, and Harri took his cue and refilled the kettle, but Annie stayed silent for a long while, thinking hard, interrupted only by a customer wanting to pay for a 1977 *Blue Peter* annual and a book about collecting Tonka vehicles. The woman explained in a shifty whisper they were a birthday present for her husband, and asked Annie to wrap them quickly before he emerged from the stacks and saw what she was up to.

When the couple left, the shop fell quiet and a warm three o'clock stillness set in. In contrast to the bright, blue-sky morning, the afternoon felt deeply dark. Venus was already shining brightly overhead by the time Harri emerged with the teas. Annie switched on the lamps one by one around the shop and now the Borrow-A-Bookshop basked in a honeyed glow. Harri had also baked millionaire's shortbread before the lunchtime rush and the sweet vanilla caramel aroma hung in the air.

When William spotted the glossy chocolatey triangles on the tray in Harri's hands, he confessed to feeling a little peckish and rushed to his armchair by the fire. Annie put another log on the fire to keep the flames roaring, and all four drew closer to the heat, lifting their steaming mugs appreciatively.

Aldous paid particularly close attention to William, who always dropped crumbs down his front. It was a waiting game, but he'd be snuffling those up as soon as the old man nodded off. Then the pair would have a glorious afternoon nap in peace, so long as no kiddies came in to disturb them. Aldous was not alone in observing that this newest villager had very much become a fixture of the place.

'How was the consultation?' asked Harri, leaning on the side of the shop counter nearest the fireplace. Annie slumped in a beanbag, a big bite of chocolate caramel shortbread already in her mouth.

William gave a dismissive grunt, so Jowan had to answer.

'Seems they've a strong vision for Castle Lore as a sort of…' he glanced at William from his spot by the fireplace, '…a sort of picturesque centrepiece for their holiday park.' He took a long drink while everyone panicked about what to say next.

'It is my home no longer,' William said, with no particular intonation in his voice.

Annie and Harri exchanged glances in the silence that fell. Annie knew he must miss the only home he'd known for decades. She knew he must miss his friend even more. Rather desperately she said, 'We're lucky to have you here, William. Our very own antiquarian expert.'

Now Harri and Jowan looked at one another. Harri seemed to be trying to communicate something, but Annie didn't know what.

'Uh,' Harri managed, 'home is wherever we happen to be.'

'*Pft!*' objected William before drinking his tea.

Annie watched as Harri's shoulders slumped. 'Okay, I don't really think that. I have the worst case of *hiraeth* whenever I'm away from Wales.'

This made Annie lift her eyes from her cup. The Welsh word had been a familiar one back in Aber. She hadn't heard it in years. 'Homesickness?'

Harri nodded. 'Only, I haven't felt it quite so much since I came here.'

'That's the Clove Lore magic,' said Jowan, dunking his shortbread before taking a sopping, melty bite. '*Mmm,*' he chewed. 'Though I've never left home *to* feel homesick, but I did feel something very much like it, I reckon, for my Isolde. Still do, and yet here I am, at home.' He looked around his bookshop. 'An' I wouldn't be nowhere else on this great globe.'

To Annie's surprise the usually reticent William nodded at this, as though homesickness for Nicholas and not the old castle explained precisely how he felt.

This set Annie thinking. There was a strong tug within her to get back home, but it wasn't driven by the wish to see her family as such, but to get to work. It had been building ever since Cassidy told her about the changes at the library and the growing resistance to the book bans.

She realised Harri was watching her now, something questing in his eyes. 'First thing I'm gonna do is hit *Buc-ee's* for a brisket sandwich and their glazed pecans,' she blurted, knowing he was expecting something on the topic of her impending homeward journey. 'With Cassidy, of course,' she added.

Harri smiled thinly, and she thought, a little sadly. She wished she hadn't spoken so glibly. Leaving here, leaving Harri was going to be far tougher than the first time she left him, back at uni. She let her eyes drop to the mug in her hands. 'I wish I could stay here *and* go home,' she said, before realising that was stupid and she laughed at herself.

'I hear you,' Harri said quickly.

After that there didn't seem to be anything pressing to say or do, and everyone fell to watching the fire and letting the warmth and sweetness of a dark afternoon in their bookshop seep inside of them. Annie closed her eyes, trying to absorb it, willing the comfort of being here with Harri and her new friends and all these wonderful books to stay locked within her. She'd need the strength of it when she was alone again, jetting across the Atlantic, steeling herself to face her community – and her adversaries.

Chapter Twenty-Three

Counting Down

Austen Archer beamed through the glass door of the bookshop the next morning. When Annie let her in, she brought with her the force of a whirlwind, she was so enthusiastic in her mission.

'Right, you two!' she said, as Harri emerged from his room pulling on a brown cardi over a t-shirt. 'I've been sent to give you this.'

Austen forced a basket into Annie's hand. 'I'm on the rota for today. You're going out. See some sights. It's a bookselling *holiday*, remember?'

'I've still not seen this volunteer rota everyone keeps going on about,' Harri replied, 'but I don't mind the idea of a day out of the shop, if you don't?'

Annie was already reaching for her slouchy bag, making sure she had her book and phone. 'I'm in,' she said.

As much as she adored working in the shop, the thought of leaving on Saturday had brought a sense of urgency. She hadn't seen much of Clove Lore and she'd arrived under a cloud worrying about Cassidy. Now that was resolved, she wished she'd enjoyed herself more. Who knew when she'd next be taking a vacation? Money could well be scarce when she got back to Texas, if she couldn't keep her position at the school library. If things got worse, not better.

'Bella's walking William up from the Siren in a bit, so I'll have him helping, and I'm doing the poetry session at four, so there's no need to hurry back. Oh, but if you bump into Mrs Crocombe or Bovis on your travels, can you ring the shop and I'll let everyone know?'

'They're still not around?' said Harri.

'No sign of them. Even I'm getting worried,' Austen replied, seemingly surprised at herself. 'Anyway, off you go. The Clove Lore estate gardens are always open. The big glasshouses are pretty at this time of year. And they're heated.'

This was all the prompting Annie needed to carry her out of the shop, up the slope and to the ticket kiosk at the entrance gate to the Big House estate where Izaak waved her and Harri through without asking for any money. He also asked if they happened to have seen Mrs Crocombe on their way here. It seemed everyone was on the lookout for the old matchmaker.

'She can't have gone *missing* missing, can she?' Annie asked Harri as they made their way across the dewy, misty lawns of the Big House.

Harri didn't seem too worried. 'I think folks in Clove Lore can't stand it when they don't know everyone's business twenty-four-seven. If one of your neighbours back home wasn't spotted for a day or two, would you even notice?'

Annie's neighbours' houses were a hundred yards from her parents' place in both directions down an unwalkable road. She'd have no clue where her neighbours were at; couldn't recall the last time she'd even seen them.

'Exactly,' said Harri, noting her silence. 'So,' he cast off the subject, 'what's the basket in aid of?'

'Oh, yeah.' Annie lifted the bright yellow wicker basket so she could prise open the cloth-wrapped bundle inside, revealing heart-shaped cookies, wrapped sandwiches – also cut in the shape of love hearts – and two bottles of chilled peach tea. 'A picnic,' Annie confirmed. 'A *Valentine's* picnic.'

If Harri thought it was yet more meddling, he didn't show it. 'Austen made it?'

'No idea.' It didn't matter either. Even if this was yet another attempt at matchmaking, Annie was just glad of a day out of the shop and some time alone with Harri.

The day was cool and cloudless, the sky a shocking blue. Up here on the springy, damp lawns of the Big House they could see much of the promontory and the tops of the cottages winding down to the harbourside. The tiled roof of the Siren was just visible from here. Way out on the winter horizon, container ships passed one another, only tiny black dashes from this distance.

Annie breathed in the chilly air. It smelled of the estate's woodland, budding rhododendron and heritage pines. Birds sang all around them as they came to a gravelled path that led around the side of the grand house, though Annie couldn't spot any of them.

'William's birds,' she said, listening.

Harri smiled his agreement and reached to take the basket from her. 'I'll carry it for a bit.'

She let him take it, fixing the straps of her bag over her shoulder.

'I saw you bringing a book,' Harri said, gesturing to the bag. 'Thinking I was going to bore you?'

Annie gave a laugh. 'No.' She bumped his arm with hers. 'It's just now I've got my reading powers back, I don't want to be too far from a good book. You get it?'

Harri nodded again. Of course he did. He'd never lost his love of reading in all the time she'd known him.

'I uh…' he began, as they crossed a gravelled knot garden with low parterre hedges forming diamonds with sweet white narcissi boxed inside them. 'The other night, at the silent reading thing?'

Annie's feet stumbled on nothing and she reached for Harri's arm to steady herself, before whipping her hand away again, shoving it in the pocket of her long coat.

'When Paisley rang?' Harri pressed on. 'She was letting me know she'd dropped off the last of my books and clothes at Mam and Dad's.'

'Oh.' Annie hadn't expected this. 'That's it?'

'What do you mean?' Harri stopped briefly at the foot of the stone steps that led to yet more spongy, mossy lawn.

'She didn't want…' Annie felt herself shrinking, '…anything else?'

Embarrassingly for Annie, Harri seemed to catch her meaning. He sniffed a little laugh. 'She just wanted to let me know.'

Annie's chest heaved like she was going to sob. She forced herself to smile placidly. 'I'm sorry about that,' she said.

'Don't be.'

Annie wanted to scrutinise his face but dared not turn her head to look at him. She climbed the steps up onto the higher lawn. The apex of tall glasshouses came into view behind what looked like the remains of ruined stone walls, a damaged building, where two figures sat on one of many wooden pews open to the air, looking out over the estate to sea.

'Is that… Jowan?' Harri was saying.

'And Minty,' Annie added.

They made their way towards them, but as she stepped in silence, Annie ran the math in her head. Her cab was booked for nine on Saturday morning. That left them sixty… eight precious hours of vacation, and here was Harri, finally turning a corner with Paisley. He'd arrived crushed and sombre, guilt-ridden even, but now he was lighter. She sneaked a look at him, the basket in his hand, his other hand shoved casually in his coat pocket, his scarf thrown round his neck, his specs glinting in the glare of winter sun. He was actually smiling at the prospect of bumping into these villagers. He'd definitely changed. He was happy. With the end of their holiday in sight and only sixty-eight hours left to them, he was happy. A strange pang bloomed in her chest. She forced it away as Minty heard their approach and turned to welcome them.

'Our picnickers are here,' she said, and Jowan turned too. Aldous was dozing inside his owner's coat, only the fuzzy beige dome between his ears poking out of Jowan's open collar.

Harri was looking around them at the tiled floor, the broken columns, the altar stone. 'Is this a church?'

'This,' Minty began proudly, 'was Grandmama's chapel. It was destroyed in the Christmas Eve flood, and now it is our open-air wedding venue. Couples come from all over to say their vows here, even without a roof!'

'An' it's the place we wed,' Jowan put in, prompting a smile from Minty. Annie registered how much she looked like a girl in that moment.

'It's beautiful,' said Annie, and she meant it. Even in the cold weather, this was a beautiful spot.

'You're here to sow love apples?' Minty said, utterly throwing both Annie and Harri.

'Sow what?' Harri said, amusement in his voice.

Jowan explained. 'Valentine's is the traditional time for sowing tomato seeds, or love apples as they used to be known. Leonid's set up a potting area in the temperate house so visitors might take home their own little seedling. A souvenir of Valentine's week in Clove Lore.'

'Be sure you take yours, Harri,' Minty added.

It took Annie a second to grasp what Minty was getting at. She circled a finger as she thought it out. 'Ah, US border control?'

Harri clicked too. 'Good point. Doubt you can fly with compost and seeds in your hand luggage.'

Everyone was smiling, but Annie's heart pumped harder at the thought of being processed at the airport. *Sixty-eight hours*, her brain repeated.

Minty hurried them away, telling them to enjoy their picnic, saying it would be warm in the cactus house.

They left the couple enjoying the view from their pew and made their way to the door of the first glasshouse.

Chapter Twenty-Four

Glass Houses

'Okay, top three favourite glass books?' said Harri.

They had closed the doors behind them and were crunching slowly across dry white stones, taking in the long, red-brick raised beds topped with soil from which twisted the gnarled limbs of grape vines bursting with tight purple buds that spread out across the wall and up into the glazed roof.

'Glass books?' Annie repeated.

'That's what I said.'

'Gee, okay. Let me think for a minute.' Annie made her way along the path between the planted beds. Melons and gourds had been trained to clamber up wire supports suspended from the glasshouse's ceiling. They were still small but had the look of vigorous seedlings bursting with strength for their long sprint to the ceiling.

'There's uh…' She swam a hand in the air, thinking. 'The Brontës' *Glass Town*, of course.'

'Ooh, nice one!'

'And the *Charlie and the Chocolate Factory* sequel?'

'*The Great Glass Elevator?*' Harri tried.

'I never read it though.'

'Then it doesn't count,' smirked Harri.

'I read *The Glass Blowers* by Daphne du Maurier last summer. That definitely counts!'

'Yep.'

'And…'

Harri folded his arms in triumph, lifting his chin.

'*Cinderella*,' she said, defeating him.

'I'll allow it.'

More easy smiles, boots softly scuffing stones, amid the rich green new-life smell that only happens in temperate greenhouses this time of year.

'This must be what Minty was on about,' Harri said, stopping in the middle of the greenhouse, where, on a plastic potting tray with raised sides, lay stacked coir pots next to a mound of fresh black compost, two trowels and unopened tomato seed packets.

'Gardener's Delight,' read Annie, lifting one of the packets as she came close to Harri's side. 'Go ahead,' she urged him. 'Get sowing.'

'You can do one for my Mam, if you want?' said Harri, laying down the picnic basket. 'I'll take it home to her for you.'

Someone, Harri assumed it was Leonid, Izaak's gardener husband, had left a notice with neatly written instructions which they followed now, working together to fill two pots, pressing two tiny tomato pips into the soft compost before covering it and adding a fine sprinkling of water from a little plastic can. Harri read aloud the rest of Leonid's sign.

'Shortly after their introduction to Europe, tomatoes were given the name love apples due to their aphrodisiacal properties. Did you know that?'

'Can't say I did,' Annie replied. 'But we should totally bring back the name love apples. Much cuter than tomatoes.'

'There we are. Something to remember our trip by,' said Harri, tamping the compost down like it was coffee grounds. 'I'll send you pictures when they've grown, our little babies.'

Annie, he noticed, wasn't saying anything now, and she'd withdrawn a little.

He wiped the soil from his hands. 'Did you know,' he began, 'I wasn't assigned to our flatshare at Aber? Not at first.'

This made her swing her head to look at him.

'It's true. I was meant to be sharing a private flat with three rugby lads in the town.'

'No way?'

'But Dad thought I'd end up boozing away my degree if I stayed with them.'

'He was probably right.'

Harri played offended, hand clutched to his chest, to make her laugh.

'So I asked to be transferred to campus and...' Harri shrugged at the serendipity of it all.

'And there I was,' said Annie.

'And there you were.'

'So we might never have met if it wasn't for your dad's total lack of faith in you.' She quirked a brow.

'Only you could get away with saying that.'

She laughed again, pushing away from the potting bench and opening the basket at Harri's feet, drawing out a bottle of peach tea that she shook before opening.

'You're lucky I like you,' Harri said. She took a drink then handed him the bottle.

How he wished she was easier to read. Less closed off, always trying to be a one-woman island taking on the world alone. Now she was rummaging in the basket, taking out the sandwiches.

'What are they?' Harri asked.

Annie inspected the package, taking off the wrapping, quickly whipping her eyes to his when she realised. 'PB and J!'

'Your national dish,' he joked.

Annie showed him the heart-shaped white bread sandwiches, nice and big, made from two fat slices. She tore the heart in two and handed him half, smiling wickedly the whole time, doing it to annoy him.

He looked at his torn half. 'Thanks a lot.' He still took a hearty bite and for a while all they did was perch on the low brick walls of the raised beds, chewing slowly, enjoying the feeling of being insulated from the winter chill beyond the thin glass.

'It's not easy having a daddy who's tough on you,' Annie said eventually, not quite out of nowhere. She'd obviously been considering something as she ate.

'You don't need to tell *me* that,' Harri said with a wry smile. 'But you can talk about it any time.'

Annie brushed crumbs from her lap. 'It kind of closes a person off, you know? When there's someone in your life who's supposed to be on your team but all they seem to care about is how others see them.'

Harri nodded slowly, listening, not wanting to spook her when she was sharing her feelings. They'd never really talked like this before, not before they made this trip to Devon.

'And Mom,' she went on. 'She's great and everything but…'

Harri already knew what she was going to say. He knew because his mum was the same. 'But she defers to him?' said Harri.

'Yes! All the damn time. You know the best conversations I ever had with Mom were whispered ones behind my bedroom door?'

'I loved Saturdays at home with Mam,' Harri put in. 'She'd be funny and not loud as such, but louder, and we'd watch cartoons and play games. I remember those times being really relaxed, even when I was tiny. Then at night, Dad would be back, grumping around the house, and we'd both button ourselves up again.'

Annie grabbed hold of the idea. 'And some of us have stayed buttoned up all our lives.'

Harri thought of Jowan calling her a firecracker, but delicate underneath it all. That man noticed everything.

'And yet you're the most outgoing person I ever met,' he said.

'Only when I'm away from home. When I'm not being scrutinised, embarrassing him. Anyways,' she sighed, 'it's hard to rely on anybody when you can't trust the one person you should be able to run to when you need them. When you can't trust them to react the way you need them to, you know?'

Harri heaved a heavy breath and screwed the lid onto the empty bottle. 'I do know.'

'Daddies are supposed to adore their little girls,' Annie added.

'I'm sure he does. How could he not? He just never figured out a way to show it.'

'Sure. I think that's true, but he's had almost thirty years to figure out *some* way. Well, twenty-five. He kinda liked me up until I got my own opinions.'

'He likes you now. He *loves* you,' Harri reassured her. 'He hates me!' Glad she laughed, he carried on. 'Dads are funny things. I always hoped one day mine would be proud of me, or even… vaguely approving. I kind of like being a barista. I'm good at it, and I don't have any other big plans or ambitions. I don't want to sell conservatories or anything really. To be honest,' he thought he could risk saying it, 'the happiest I've ever been is making coffees here while you're selling books right next door.'

'Hmm.' She was nodding now. She seemed to be about to agree, but when she spoke she said instead, 'What kind of people do you think we'd be if we were the apples of our daddies' eyes?'

'I think we'd be pretty much who we are now, don't you?' Harri replied.

Annie thought about it, looking away. 'I know I'd be happier. More daring, maybe?'

Seeing her getting lost in her thoughts again he moved closer, offering her his arm around her shoulder, waiting for her nod before making contact, pulling her into a sideways hug.

'I cannot imagine what an even more daring Annie Luna would be like! In jail most likely?'

'See! Daddy's right to be worried!' She conceded a smile, and Harri pulled her gently with his arm, rocking them both.

A moment of silence passed between them for the relationships that caused pain even while they loved their fathers.

It felt okay, having talked about it, thought Harri. He rarely told anyone things like that.

Annie was still a little slumped and her body wasn't glowing the way it could. He withdrew his arm and reached for the basket, tidying the empty wrappers away.

'I'm glad you ended up in our flat,' said Annie looking dead at him.

He smiled. 'Me too.'

Harri didn't know if it was unconscious or not, but Annie drew her bottom lip between her teeth the tiniest amount, wetting the soft pink there. To stop himself staring he stood.

'Shall we go see these cacti Minty was on about?'

–

Stepping into the blast of warm air in the second tall glasshouse, next to the first, felt like walking across the hazy summer airport tarmac in Texas.

'*This* is what I've needed,' Annie rejoiced, her head back, slipping her coat from her shoulders and down her arms.

'And we've got the place to ourselves too,' said Harri, taking off his steamed-up glasses and closing the door behind him. 'Perks of off-season travel.'

This place was more like a garden than a greenhouse. The entire floor was planted out and covered over with grit. Stepping stones guided visitors around the plants in meandering waves. The silvery trunk of a plant labelled 'bougainvillea' grew immediately by the doors and its long branches were already in shocking bloom with bright pink papery flowers. This, contrasted with the blue sky beyond the glass, gave Annie the feeling of being transported straight into summer. Even the shaggy geraniums that had sheltered here all winter were a picture of lush summer health with their red, pink and white flower heads lifting up over their strongly scented, cloud-shaped leaves.

Annie fingered the budded branches of a lemon tree in a huge terracotta urn. She couldn't help thinking of her parents' garden back home. Heat, red earth, cacti as big as barrels, the occasional glimpse of the shimmying tails of Great Plains skink disappearing into clumps of high grass with dry, rattling seedheads, the aerial orchids hanging down over her mother's shady swing seat and everything scented with blousy red tea roses, a curious mix of the prairies and old England.

Nothing could erase the way she loved Amarillo, no amount of work disputes and family feuding. Not Dead-beat Dave or any number of awful senators and state officials, or those few book-banning parents. It won't be so bad going home, she told herself, taking a deep breath of the fragrant air. Then she caught sight of something even more deeply familiar and her heart jumped. 'Look!' she called Harri closer. 'Do you know what this is?'

Together they approached the great cactus standing with its arms raised, reaching up to the glass roof.

'It looks like a kid's drawing of a cactus,' said Harri, putting his glasses on now the hot fog on the lenses had cleared. 'It's the most cactus-y cactus around.'

'It's a prickly pear,' she told him. 'They're everywhere back home. You can eat every part of it.'

'Not sure I'd want to,' he said inspecting its spikes.

'Ah,' Annie sighed happily, turning on the spot. 'I love it in here.'

'Oh, look out,' said Harri, removing his coat. 'It's happening. Might even have to unbutton my cardigan in a minute.'

Annie gasped in mock amazement.

Laughing, they made their way to the bench right at the centre of the glasshouse, beneath the spreading leaves of date palms.

'What else is in there?' Annie asked, nudging Harri's knee with her own, indicating the basket by his feet.

He brought out the cookies; pink iced love hearts. Annie rolled her eyes but took one all the same. 'If I didn't know better, I'd say Izaak was up at the ticket kiosk telling folks the glasshouses are off limits to visitors today.'

Harri bit his cookie, peering between the leaves to glimpse outside. 'You make a good point. It's oddly quiet.'

'I don't mind,' Annie said, taking another bite.

A low buzzing sound filled the air and a fan, mounted in the glass high above, turned, distributing warm air. Birds sang loudly from the trees at the far edges of the lawns.

'I've had a really great trip,' Annie said.

'It's not over yet,' Harri quickly replied. 'We've got ages left.'

Sixty-seven hours. Annie didn't have to say it. She felt the change in the air between them. Harri held his cookie mid-way to his mouth, thinking.

'We did a lot of cool stuff,' he said.

'We sure did.' Annie thought of only one thing they'd done, late at night at Castle Lore. The prickles on her skin made her certain Harri had thought of exactly the same thing at the same moment. The memory crackled between their bodies.

She glanced aside to check. Yep, he was turning the tiniest bit pink.

'We never did talk about it,' Harri said suddenly.

Annie didn't even try to play innocent. 'I know. But, what good would it do?'

Harri lifted his shoulders, then dropped them. 'Don't know. Just feels like something we should… address.'

Annie took the last bite of her cookie, caution sneaking in again.

'Because it meant something,' Harri went on. 'And because it definitely crossed a line.'

This would be excruciating, Annie thought, if it wasn't Harri. If it wasn't so intriguing a thing to think about, to unpick and inspect. What would have happened that night if they hadn't been interrupted by William's arrival? Annie knew exactly what. She felt her face flush hot.

'Warm in here,' she said, stupidly.

Harri laughed a little, but he had a serious, searching look in his eyes now. He turned his body a little towards her on the bench and *dammit* if her own body didn't automatically do the same thing without her instructing it to. She looked him over.

'Harri,' she began, not quite sure where she was going with this, she only knew that she couldn't have what she wanted. 'I'm going home on Saturday, and I have a bunch of stuff to do when I get there.'

'You could come back, come see me in Wales? Or I could meet you somewhere in the spring? Where's halfway between Wales and Texas? The Malvinas?' He was lost in thought, and looking a little desperate, throwing out potential destinations. 'Newfoundland? Canada? I have no clue!' He was getting agitated, his eyes wild.

'Harri? Harri!' she stopped him. 'I don't even know where I'll be, come springtime.'

Harri drew himself to a pause, thinking, before exhaling hard, his posture crumpling. 'Me neither,' he admitted. Annie couldn't know it, but Harri thought of his cases back at the shop, containing almost everything he owned. He could go on anywhere from this little spot by the sea, it occurred to him, if only there was somewhere waiting for him where he was welcome, where he might thrive rather than just survive, like he'd been doing for years now.

For a moment, a troubling little pathway in Annie's brain was telling her that Harri might end up back in the flat with Paisley but she didn't want to say it out loud. She'd returned the last of his stuff to his parents' place, hadn't she? That must represent real 'getting closure' stuff for Paisley, mustn't it?

'That night at the castle… It's not as though we're like…' she stumbled over the words, '…boyfriend and girlfriend, or anything.' She tried to force laughter into it but it came out sounding glib and weak.

Harri mirrored her. '*Pfft!* It's not like we're walking down the aisle or anything.'

Annie tried to be vehement in her agreement. 'It was just… chemicals firing in our brains, what with the… novelty of it all,' she said.

'And loneliness,' Harri added. 'Plus, there was a fair amount of booze involved.'

'Exactly!' Annie pounced on this. 'And those are a dangerous mix. They can make a person crazy.'

Harri seemed to be running with it too. 'Right. Right,' he was nodding. 'It's not very respectful is it?'

'What? Getting hot for each other just because we're in a strange place?'

'Yeah, just because we're thrown together like this,' he said.

Annie drew her head back, a little humbled. 'Oh! Like I could be anybody and you'd feel the same?'

'Would I?'

'Yes! Definitely,' she said with a conviction she didn't feel. 'Probably. It's lazy, and not respectful, and it's... predictable! A man and a woman, best friends, they take a vacation...'

'In, basically, book heaven,' Harri added.

'Right, and it's so beautiful here and it's winter and it's cosy.'

'We're bound to get stupid ideas?' he said, very much like it was a question.

'My point exactly. I'm glad we stopped when we did, before it got... silly.'

'And now we should stop thinking about each other in that way?' Harri said blankly.

Annie felt an uncomfortable nudge at her heart. She didn't know how she'd stop thinking about Harri. At night, alone in her room, he was all she could think about. 'Right,' she said.

This brought silence, followed by yet more silence. Annie noticed she was wringing her hands and shoved them down by her thighs in tight fists to stop herself.

'Or...' Harri said.

'Yes?' She practically jumped at this. 'I'm so glad there's an or.'

'Or maybe...' Harri was flushing pink now, the spots below his eyes were positively red. 'Maybe the problem *isn't* that we should stop thinking about each other... in that way. Maybe the problem is we should really, *really* think about each other like that.'

'Huh?' Annie felt herself untethering, at risk of letting go the last vestiges of common sense she'd been clinging to.

'Maybe,' Harri went on, 'we need to get any... residual attraction out of our systems?'

Annie blinked abruptly. 'When you say *residual attraction* like that, it kind of makes me want to throw up.' She registered the tiniest flash of disappointment in Harri's eyes. 'Hold up. When you say *get it out of our systems*, you mean...?'

Harri didn't say a word, only looking back at her frankly, making a 'why not' kind of gesture.

'Is that what you want?' she asked, her pulse quickening.

'Is it what *you* want?'

'What if it ruined literally everything?' she said, her voice little more than a gasp.

'Well, we kind of almost... you know, at the castle library the other night and it didn't ruin *everything*. We're still best buds, you just said so yourself. So...' He shrugged, somewhat casually, but she could see through his calm exterior.

She remembered the sensations of his mouth upon her. His breathing ragged, the insistent, assured way he'd made his way over her skin with his lips. She gulped. 'What if we do, you know... and it's... moreish?'

The burst of laughter from Harri drew out her own, and they both folded over and cackled, letting the tension lift.

'You know what I mean,' she said, swinging her elbow towards his arm but making sure to miss. 'What if we really... clicked. What then?'

'Annie Luna, are you asking me what if we had amazing sex and we both properly liked it?'

This version of Harri, forthright and bold and rosy-cheeked, was all new to her. Her brain lit upon an image of him laying his weight down upon her in her big white bed, his eyes alight like they were now. She whipped her

269

gaze away from his, scuffing her boots on the gravel, taking a breath.

'When you put it like that it sounds stupid,' she told the ground. 'But you know what I'm getting at. I have to leave in…' She didn't want him to know she'd calculated their remaining time, or that she was counting it down in secret. '…a day or two, and I don't want to fly home feeling sad.'

'Because you can't have any more of this?' Harri grinned, sweeping his hands down his cardigan. He'd done it to make her laugh, but it was also kind of hot. 'If it'd help at all,' he was saying, 'I could always try to be less good. Don't know if I can, but I'd give it a go.'

She slapped his arm and they both laughed, but the tension was hard to deal with. 'This is ridiculous,' she told him.

'No, you're right, it is ridiculous.' He said this so primly, and in the strongest Welsh accent, like he was telling himself off, it made her laugh again.

'*Argh!* And it's infuriating!' she said, pulling her body tight. 'We can't just… do it.' The space between them felt suddenly wider. How had it been so easy in the library?

'In the library, we'd been drinking,' she told herself aloud. 'And on empty stomachs too, like total amateurs. And it was after dark and there were candles and a roaring fire and… it was a big old gothic castle for Christ's sakes.'

'And now it's a Wednesday lunchtime and we've got book inventory to be getting on with back at the shop?' Harri added, not without a sorry frown.

'Exactly. The moment has passed.' Yet, as the words left her lips she knew that if he just reached for her and kissed her, right that second, with no time for thinking or words or awkwardness, she'd kiss him right back.

But she was stuck fast. Nothing could induce her to lean closer or meet his eyes in the lustful way she had by the glowing hearth of the castle library.

She could feel his eyes on the side of her face.

'You're probably right,' he said. 'It'd be weirdly... planned? Right?'

'Exactly. It would be artificial.' She glimpsed at him long enough to catch his face fall like he knew it'd be absolutely real and not one bit artificial.

'Artificial's not what I meant,' she corrected herself. 'I mean it would be too forced. Too premeditated and too much like an experiment. It should be easier than this, without all the toing and froing and *should we, shouldn't we*? And it'd have happened already, years ago, if it was meant to happen.'

'I hear you.' Harri was making to move now, brushing away cookie crumbs. 'We're probably way too sober anyway.'

'Yep,' she said, half-heartedly.

'Yep,' he echoed.

He picked up the basket with an exaggerated sigh. 'Pity, though.'

'I'll live with it,' Annie said dryly, smiling, trying to convince herself she'd said all the right things to protect their friendship, to protect herself. It made her sad though, but what exactly had he just offered her? A night of 'getting it out of our systems'? That wasn't what she wanted.

'So... now what?' he said, the very last whisper of any possibility of them spending the evening with their skin touching skin, mouth upon mouth, hidden away under white bedsheets upstairs in the bookshop, sharing something experimental, just to see if there was magic there, dissolved away in the air like the smoke from an extinguished candle.

Annie shrugged. 'There's a drinks kiosk at the convenience store. Cup of tea?'

'All right.' He got to his feet, looking down at her with quirking lips. 'So… just to clarify…' he pulled her to her feet, quickly dropping her hands once they were eye to eye, '…it's two cups of hot tea and *not* passionate sex? I forget what we decided?'

She dug at him with her elbow, laughing once more. 'Milk, no sugar.'

'All right, all right,' he said, as they made for the glasshouse door, carrying their two tiny seeds in their pots. 'Just making sure.'

Chapter Twenty-Five

Valentine's Eve

Thursday was supposed to be a normal day. Harri had promised himself it would be. It had started that way, with him brewing vanilla iced lattes, a nod to the sunnier weather that was settling in over the village. He'd been sure to make it the Italian way with equal proportions of espresso, milk and light foam. Annie wasn't going to drink any washed-out insipid, milk-drowned latte on his watch.

Annie had floated into the cafe in a long white dress and her white cowgirl boots and carried the glass away to the bookshop where she switched everything on like it was second nature now.

'You look like a swan,' Harri said as she glided away sipping her coffee. She'd shaken her tail feathers as she left in acknowledgement.

She lit the fire and opened the door, just as William arrived, dropped off by Bella on foot from the Siren. He had a mind to sort through the shop's Shakespeare titles and since neither Harri nor Annie had any strong feelings about it, that's exactly what he did.

Harri emerged from the cafe having served his first few customers and wiped down their tables after they left, carrying with him a chalkboard and a thick white marker he'd found while organising the pantry.

'Hey,' he said, ease in his voice and everything simple, even when his emotions after yesterday's holiday-sexual-tension-truce were far from simple. 'I found this. I was going to write my *coffee of the day* on it, but we could also have a special book quote? It's big enough.'

'There's a bookshop I follow on Instagram does that,' said Annie, keeping an eye on the couple browsing the stacks. 'They post a bookish quote of the day.'

'What would we write on ours? Something Valentine's themed?' suggested Harri. 'To go with the Valentine's book display.' He looked at it now. Many of the books were gone, and all but two of the Valentine's cards. They'd have to set up their own display to leave in place for the next holidaymaker-booksellers. That would be a job for tomorrow, their last full day here.

William, who usually ignored the goings-on in the shop, preferring to shuffle around doing his own thing, immersed in his own thoughts, spoke up. The idea of the board had caught his attention.

'I have many a pertinent line in mind,' he said, grandly.

Harri surrendered the liquid chalk marker to him, and in moments, and without having to check it, William had written in the most lavish script the line:

> *Tomorrow is Saint Valentine's Day, all in the morning betime, and I a maid at your window, to be your Valentine.*

William held the sign to his chest for Annie to see.

She pulled an impressed face. 'That's very romantic, William.'

'*Hamlet*,' he said. 'Act four, scene five, when poor Ophelia loses her wits to love.'

Annie nodded. 'Course she does. Well, let's put it at the door, since it's not raining. Folks can see what you're serving up today.' She directed this to Harri, who quickly took the marker and board, adding:

Single origin Brazilian espresso dark chococcino,
£4

As Annie carried it approvingly outside, she remarked how if Ophelia had stuck to artisan coffee and steered clear of troubled princes she'd never have ended up in that brook. William had agreed sagely that this was too true.

The morning would have continued in this peaceful vein, and Harri and William may well have set about emptying out the last box from Castle Lore, if there hadn't arisen an alarm across the village, with voices raised from door to door, and notifications and alerts pinging, all carrying the news that a search was underway to find Mrs Crocombe who hadn't returned to her home above the ice cream shop for another night. It was Jude – accompanied by three greyhounds on a single tether – who brought word to the bookshop.

'Those of us with cars are setting off down the country lanes looking for them,' she said. 'The Big House people are combing the woodland and the fields. I'm heading down the cliff path with the dogs.'

'Are the police involved?' Harri asked, already looking for his coat.

'Mrs Crocombe's daughter reported her missing but since Mr Bovis hasn't been seen either, and his Land Rover's not in his driveway, they said they wouldn't investigate yet, not unless anyone had suspicions.'

'About Bovis?' Annie asked, looking for the shop keys.

'You just never know with people, do you? And Mrs Crocombe has been known for her flighty behaviour, what with her and that sea captain. She's not the best judge of character. But still, I don't think our Bovis is capable of kidnap, or anything else for that matter. He's the most devoted lapdog to Mrs Crocombe, and has been for some time.'

Harri was at the door, joining Annie. 'Somebody will have to stay here,' he said, turning to Annie. He nodded silently in William's direction. 'Look after the shop?'

She seemed deflated, to be denied the opportunity of dashing around the countryside like this was a BBC police drama but she agreed; someone had to stay behind.

Harri bounded out the door with Jude and the dogs, saying he'd help in the search along the cliff path, and looking not a little relieved to get out of the strange atmosphere in the shop since yesterday. Strange, not because things were tense or awkward, but because they were so laid-back, at least, on Annie's part they seemed to be, and he had to keep up his side of the agreement.

Annie had busied herself all afternoon in the shop yesterday and in the evening she'd kept her eyes on the laptop screen, reading up on individual cases of book banning and library protests. There were so many they'd kept her silent, taking notes and yawning, late into the night. Harri had served up beans on toast and, later, headed to bed, but stayed awake until he heard her climb the staircase.

He was cross with himself for not being able to keep the promise he'd made Annie the day she arrived here, of keeping her safe and secure in their friendship. He'd risked it all. He'd lapsed into lust and selfishness. He'd wanted her so badly. Now the need was burning in his stomach, but he was doing a good job, he thought, of being a friend. Everything, as far as Annie was concerned, was chill. As it should be. He wasn't going to be the creepy, disrespectful male friend who wouldn't let a tiny transgression between them lie. Annie had forgotten it, dismissed it out of hand as a mistake, and he had agreed, like a good friend should. She was happy now, and thinking more and more about what awaited her back home. His job was to support her in that.

As he listened to Jude reeling off details of all the places Mrs Crocombe might have gone to with Bovis, favourite walks and scenic spots, and she told him about the dangers of rockfalls and floods around here, he listened hard. As they made their way further from the bookshop, he told himself this search party was the ideal opportunity to rehearse what it felt like to be out of Annie Luna's presence. He'd have to get used to it soon enough.

–

Annie closed the door to the cafe, and swiped the white pen through Harri's coffee special. She couldn't run the bookshop, look after William – not that he knew he was being looked after – *and* make fancy drinks.

She swept the floors, rang up sales, and generally – to all observers – had a calm day in her bookshop.

Harri had told her she looked like a swan, and that's exactly how she felt. All grace and elegance above the surface, with two furiously paddling, frantic feet unseen underwater.

The effort of staying emotionally afloat was exhausting. It was made all the worse by Harri's absence all day. She was worried about Mrs Crocombe and Bovis, of course, hoping they'd turn up soon, but secretly admitted to herself it was a shame to lose a day with her friend, no matter how important the reason that had taken him from her. She didn't want to think too hard about how hers were not simple friendly feelings, but something much more pressing and jagged, so to distract herself, she told William all about her school library and he listened placidly as he pottered in the stacks, and the day passed far too quickly.

At four, when Annie was talking with William about closing up, Jowan appeared. He came alone and with a grave face. At first, Annie felt panicked to see him.

'Something happened?' she said, unsure if she was thinking of the safety of the missing pensioners, or of Harri.

Jowan asked her to join him outside.

The courtyard lights swayed on their criss-cross strands overhead as Jowan bid her step away from the shop door entirely.

'What's going on?' she said, concern seeping deeper. 'Have they been found?'

'No, not a dickie bird,' said Jowan. 'That's not why I came. I haven't the heart to tell him yet, but Minty's heard from Social Services. A flat is being made ready for William, sheltered accommodation. In Yelverton.'

'Ah! Good! Is that close?'

Jowan shook his head. 'Hour and a half drive, I'd say.'

'Oh.'

'But without any independent means, no savings, no home, no record of national insurance contributions, not even a pension, he's considered homeless. He's lucky to get this place, honestly, way this country's been going.'

'And nobody's told him yet?' Annie said, her heart sinking.

Another shake of Jowan's head.

'He'll never see Clove Lore Castle again, will he?' Annie said, before trying to find a bright side. 'Maybe there'll be a library there, or a bookshop. In Yelverton?'

'Maybe. An' who'll take him there, I don't know.'

Annie knew how these things went. She wrapped her arms around herself. 'Only, Mr Sabine's already become a part of bookshop life. He seems happy, which, you know, given what he's gone through, is miraculous.'

Jowan agreed.

'When does he have to leave?' she asked.

'Dunno yet. Social Services will send a car, take him and his belongings down-country. They'll let us know when it's time.'

'Okay,' she said, letting Jowan leave.

When she returned to the shop, William was settled in the armchair enjoying the fire.

'Mr Sabine?' she said, and he turned his head, a picture of placidity. She thought of him arriving that day last week, hungry and disorientated and, as it turned out, grieving.

'Yes, Annwyl?'

'I uh…' She couldn't tell him. William leaving Clove Lore was inevitable. Why hasten his sadness? 'Would you care to join me for dinner? I'll have something sent up from the Siren's Tail? I'll order for Harri too.'

'That would be a very great pleasure.'

The search for Mrs Crocombe ended as the dark closed in. Harri arrived through the door moments before their meals arrived. He was chilled to the bone and glad of the fire, and the bottle of Madeira that Bella had sneaked in with their order. William's day closed sitting by the fire with a full belly, surrounded by books, a blanket over his knees, and in undemanding, youthful company.

After Harri returned from walking him back to his rooms at the pub, Annie had turned in, taking with her to bed the copy of *Hamlet* William had read aloud to them over dessert, when the old man was at his most contented, utterly unsuspecting how soon his sense of having found another place in which to nest was going to come to an end.

Chapter Twenty-Six

Valentine's Day

Annie lingered by the door, and not because the postman usually called in at this time.

Harri had decided to start packing his cases first thing, even before he'd brewed the morning coffees, so she concluded he was truly set on getting out of here. She didn't know what was worse, the countdown running in her head (*twenty-four hours exactly*), or the methodical calm with which Harri was treating the approaching end of their time together.

'Guessing the cinema thing will be called off?' he shouted from his room, out of sight as Annie peered once again into the courtyard.

This drew her up. 'Why? I thought it was a sell-out, and the weather report says it's gonna stay dry all day.' In fact, it had said it was going to be a 'perfect Valentine's Day', but she didn't tell him that now. He seemed to have forgotten it was the fourteenth of February.

Harri popped his head around the doorframe of his room. 'We'll be looking for Mrs C., I guess?' He disappeared again. Annie heard a case drag across the floor.

Of course they would. A woman was missing and here she was waiting for a Valentine she had no idea Harri had even written, let alone mailed, and certainly not addressed

to her. If anything, it had gone to Paisley, or it was somewhere in one of those cases of his, forgotten.

None of this prevented her from swooping upon the
mail as it fluttered onto the mat. The postman gave a
cheery wave through the glass as he went, like this was his
favourite day of the year, when he was at his most appre-
ciated. She tried to smile back in a dignified, unbothered
way, before diving for the red envelope as soon as his back
was turned. She pulled it to her chest. It had her name on
it. She glanced back at Harri's door. He was singing, badly,
to one of his playlists. He must have headphones on, she
thought, about to rip into the envelope when she saw the
US frank, the airmail sticker. It wasn't from Harri.

She toed at the pizza menu still on the mat. Would it
reveal another card beneath?

'Nope,' she muttered under her breath. Opening the
card, it read 'Happy Galentine's Day'. Of course, it was
Cassidy returning the favour of her letter.

Inside she'd written:

> *See you in Arrivals. I'm bringing you to the*
> *Old Santa Fe for Galentine's cocktails and we're*
> *working on our battle plan for Principal Johnson.*
> *I've got your back this time, Cass, x*

'What you got there?' came Harri's voice and she swung
around too quickly to think of hiding the card. Harri
stared at it, then at her face. She felt frozen. Could he
tell she was disappointed it was a card from her girlfriend?
Did he know she'd been wishing for one from him?

He broke the silence first. 'Of course, of course,' he
said as if to himself, before brightening. 'So, uh… coffee?'
And he was gone, and he stayed gone, clattering around

in the cafe, cleaning down the machine, making great jets of steam fill the serving area, baking one last batch of hangover buns, the original recipe, which seemed more than appropriate given the vacation hangover that was going to hit them both around about the time Annie was at thirty-thousand feet tomorrow.

Eventually Harri carried through two mugs.

'Ooh, what did you make for me this morning? Colombian single-shot, extra froth, extra-rare…' She was wittering, she knew it.

'Just tea,' he said.

'Oh.' She schooled her features. She'd got hooked on his coffees and wondered how she'd do without them. 'Perfect,' she said, and Harri was off again, working hard in the cafe, serving the early customers, all couples in the village on Valentine's breaks.

Shortly before ten, Kit and Anjali arrived, bringing two scruffy dogs in matching harnesses.

'Oh wow, hi! You've adopted some pooches, then, Kit?' Annie was genuinely pleased to see them both, and they were holding hands too. At least some good had come out of their excruciating double date.

'We thought we'd better pop by,' Anjali said sweetly. 'To say, thank you.'

'Thank you?' Annie echoed.

Harri stepped into the bookshop too, swinging a tea towel over his shoulder. He looked different today, Annie registered. Like a weight was off. He was dressed for spring too. Grey t-shirt, eyeglasses, dark pants.

'Thanks for not fancying us, I guess?' Anjali said to them both, accompanied by a nervy flutter of laughter. Kit grinned shyly by her side.

Harri looked like he wished he hadn't come through, but Annie didn't mind the weirdness. 'Are you kidding me? You two are so cute; but you're cuter together. And who's this?'

There followed a long, involved discussion on the adoption of Danny and Sandy (not names Kit would have chosen, but what can you do?). All Annie had to do was listen and nod and pet the happy dogs. The whole time they spoke, Kit's tattooed fingers clasped Anjali's and they shared soppy smiles.

'Are you helping with the search for Mrs Crocombe and Bovis today?' Harri asked when they stopped for air.

'We're on our way to the Big House now. Minty's co-ordinating efforts,' said Kit.

'I'll join you up there in a bit,' said Harri.

'Anyway,' said Anjali, 'we just wanted to wish you a happy Valentine's Day.'

'And we hope you both get home safe,' Kit said, already finishing their girlfriend's sentences.

'It was great meeting you,' Annie said, her cheeks hurting from smiling, and they were gone.

Harri fled back to the cafe in an instant.

William hadn't come up to the shop today, Annie mused. Not that he had to. It's not like it was his job or anything, but he did seem to like it here, and where else was he going to spend his days? She shuddered at what his absence might signify. Had Jowan told him the news about his new place? Was he sad? Was he sulking? She hoped he hadn't gone stalking off across the cliff paths like he had when he'd been lost and wandering. The last thing Clove Lore needed was another misplaced senior.

She pictured herself alone and shutting up the shop later today for the last time, when there'd be nothing left to do but pack her things, if she and Harri were going to pull their books for the display table sometime after dinner. She didn't relish the thought of doing any of that but still, she checked in to her flight using her phone, hoping somehow it would be cancelled due to bad weather, but no such luck. It was showing as departing on time. In fact, the plane that would carry her home was already on its inward journey to England. She rubbed at her stomach to stop the queasiness.

'Hey, Harri,' she called. 'Got any of those hangover buns?'

His answer, however, never met her ears. Instead, a great commotion in the courtyard drew her attention, and Patti, Austen's girlfriend, appeared. She shoved the door open, her face a picture of delight and urgency.

'Here,' she shouted, out of breath, throwing something to Annie behind the counter. She caught the box out of the air, and Patti threw a second. 'No time to explain. Just be waiting out on the slope in a few minutes. They're on their way down. I still have half the doors to bang on...' Leaving a cackling trail of laughter behind her, she was gone.

'What the heck was that about?' Harri said from the cafe doorway.

Uncomprehending, Annie looked down at the boxes of confetti in her hands.

–

The noise came Down-along first, before the sight of children picking their way quickly downhill surefooted on the cobbles like mountain goats. Then came the adults, all in their winter coats, unbuttoned in the mild morning air, scarves flapping, and in the middle of them all, being bumped and jostled on one of the sleds usually reserved for transporting laundry or groceries, sat the happy couple, Mr and Mrs Bovis-Crocombe, if the snatches of shouted gossip passing from open door to window were to be believed.

'They eloped!' Austen told Annie as she passed by, making her way a few cottages further down from the bookshop turning, to where the Ice Cream Cottage waited for the newlyweds.

Harri could only gape and shake his head. He glanced at Annie. She was tearing into her box of confetti, a huge grin on her face.

The couple drew nearer, and the crowd progressed alongside them, a great billowing cloud of confetti already in the air above their heads.

Mrs Bovis-Crocombe wore a lilac skirt suit and a boxy hat with a spray of white netting over her eyes. Bovis looked odd in a corduroy suit. They both looked very sheepish.

'Three cheers for the return of the happy couple!' someone was shouting, and the *hip hip hoorays* rang between the cottages.

Harri spotted Bella and Finan making their way up from the pub to meet the din, and between them, William Sabine, each of them supporting his arm. He looked out of breath and fed up with making the journey Up- and Down-along.

As the couple drew nearer, Jowan emerged from the crowd. 'Here's a turn-up for the books, eh? Been to bloody Gretna Green, they have!'

'No way!' Annie thought it was fabulous.

Harri took a dimmer view. 'The whole village was out looking for them!' he said, surprised by how annoyed he was. Maybe it wasn't entirely the newlyweds to blame for his mood, but it was as good an excuse as any to vent some of the frustration he'd been saddled with for the last couple of days.

'Apparently, they wanted a quiet ceremony,' Jowan said, his eyebrows raised.

The younger Mrs Crocombe appeared now, her arms folded across her chest. Laura didn't seem to be in the same celebratory mood as her mother, who was blushingly responding to the building chant of '*kiss him, kiss him, kiss him,*' with a slow lean towards her husband on the juddering sled, her eyes twinkling in the low winter sun.

Annie had her confetti poised for their passing and emptied the whole box over them, cheering and hollering as loud as she could. Harri held his confetti firm in his hand, unimpressed.

'Why didn't you tell us?' he caught Laura shouting to her mother as they drew alongside them.

'We wanted to keep it private, just us!' the bride shouted back.

This raised a great roar of approval and laughter from the locals. It almost drowned out her daughter's observation. 'That's rich!'

Annie was pulling at Harri's t-shirt sleeve, making for him to move down the slope in the wake of the wedding sled. Reluctantly, he walked with her.

When they reached the Ice Cream Cottage, Mr Bovis helped his wife roll off the sled in a slightly ungainly way.

'We'd no idea you'd all be so worried!' the bride called out, standing at her gate, addressing the crowd.

It was Jowan who called back over the heads now. 'Why wouldn't we be? We're all one family 'ere in Clove Lore!'

Bovis said a few apologetic, shamefaced words, and his wife wiped a tear from her eye. People snapped pictures on their phones and Izaak asked if Bovis planned on carrying his wife over the threshold.

Minty hung back, not saying anything, but Harri noted she wasn't quite so unsmiling about the eyes as she might be, in spite of all the anxiety their disappearance had caused.

Mrs Bovis-Crocombe caused a little more furore by asking that everyone respect their newlywed privacy, and all the couples she'd brought together over the years shouted back indignant things without a hint of malice in them.

She banished the last of the grumbles by pulling a key from her lilac handbag and announcing, 'Before this afternoon's Valentine's Day movie, my husband and I would be honoured if you would all join us for… free ice cream!'

The noise that went up made Harri stagger a little, and he slowly pressed his way back through the villagers, surprised to note Annie following behind him.

When they got to the turning for the bookshop, William was there waiting for them.

'Are you coming in?' Harri said, gesturing down the passageway.

'I won't, thank you. I've come to take my leave,' he said, cleaning his tiny gold specs on a freshly pressed handkerchief, just another sign of how well looked after he'd been down at the Siren.

'Ah!' said Annie. 'I see. What about the movie night? Are you coming to that? Whole village will be there, by all accounts.'

'No, I'll turn in early. Long journey on Saturday morning,' he said stoically. 'So…' He put out a hand. 'Good luck, Annwyl.'

Harri watched as they shook hands. Annie's eyes were wet with tears. Now William was offering a hand to him. 'I'm grateful to you for your hospitality,' he said, his voice wavering. 'And your friendship.'

It was Harri's turn to well up. 'You've got a place to go?' Harri asked.

William only bowed his head, drawing his hands behind his back. Harri spotted that his pockets were stuffed, just as they had been when he arrived, with all manner of paraphernalia, tiny treasures saved from the castle. The edge of the photograph he'd taken from one of the boxes was just visible in his breast pocket with his handkerchief. A picture of him and Sir Nicholas kept close to his heart.

Annie had stepped forward, hugging William. Even though he was surprised, he chuckled and patted her shoulder. 'There, there,' he said.

After they left William with Bella, Harri knew Annie was crying all the way along the passage to the bookshop, but the lump in his throat stopped him saying anything. It wouldn't help anyway. They were both solemn and silent, and Annie was already mentally on her way home, if her preparations were anything to go by. Not to mention the Valentine's card she'd been holding this morning, not that he'd said anything about it. Who had sent it? Were they a part of her steadfast focus on getting home? There couldn't be someone at home intent on dating her? Someone she'd not spoken of?

Annie said she didn't feel much like bookselling and went for a lie-down upstairs.

Similarly deflated, Harri didn't feel like making coffee. In fact, he didn't feel like doing anything. So he shut the shop and made himself wipe down the syrup bottles and arrange them neatly on the shelves for the next Borrower-barista, his heart sinking low like the winter sun on the horizon.

So it was all over? Paisley had moved on, William had a place to stay, the castle was being sold, Mrs Crocombe and her new husband were safely home, Kit and Anjali were set to adopt every dog in the South West for the rest of their shared lives together, and he had backed himself firmly into his corner of the friend zone with Annie. That was it. Everyone else had taken great big leaps forward except for him.

Two weeks had passed in a blink. Two weeks of not knowing how to act around Annie, and in the morning she'd be hugging him goodbye like she'd hugged William, and that would be that.

What would become of them now? Was Jowan right? Had the wanting her ruined things anyway, just like he'd warned against? Had trying to preserve their friendship only thrown up his selfish, grasping, lustful feelings and repelled Annie so much that she didn't even want to spend her last afternoon in the shop with him?

An awful desperation hit him and it wouldn't let him go. He needed a do-over. Like when he failed his summer exams because he'd gone off to see that band with Annie. He'd been given a second chance then, a whole summer of making things right, and it had worked. That's what he needed now.

He looked at the time on his phone. Two hours until the outdoor cinema showing. Without even knowing what he was going to do, he ran, all the way up the slope and into the Big House garden, not stopping until he found Jasper Gold amongst the deckchairs.

'I'm going to need your help,' Harri told him, breathlessly.

Chapter Twenty-Seven

Movie Night

'It's too long since I saw this movie,' Annie was saying as she made her way with an unusually quiet Harri past the Big House and into the parterre gardens where they'd been only two days before, only now the place was transformed.

Fairy lights led the way towards paired deckchairs, each headed with a low parasol also twined in twinkling lights. Every chair had a blanket folded neatly on the seat. The gardens were abuzz with activity. Hot-dog smells wafted in the cool afternoon air.

'Only the English would think it was a good idea, sitting outside on Valentine's Day after dark,' Annie continued, but she drew her lips closed when Jasper Gold presented himself.

'Tickets, please?' he said. Annie set about rifling amongst her layers to find the pocket where they were stashed. 'Only kidding, I sold them to you guys, remember? Step this way.'

Annie didn't notice the glance the two men shared, and if she'd been paying better attention she'd have seen Harri growing conspicuously paler but with a look of determination in his eyes.

Jasper led them through the seating area and up the stone steps that had taken them onto the lawns on Wednesday. Only now the steps led to a little tepee, a pink tepee in fact, and the entire thing was bedecked in yellow roses.

'What's all this?' said Annie, watching as Jasper drew apart the folds, tying them in place, to reveal a glowing pink interior of artfully arranged cushions on a softly carpeted ground sheet. Gold tealight lamps with holey cutouts cast mottled light across the fabric walls, and these hung amid silver stars and crystals, all shifting with the movement of the tent and casting shimmering sparkles everywhere.

'VIP area, I guess,' Harri said, not needing to take credit for this. It had been a group effort, after all. He had begged and borrowed and run around for two hours straight, rummaging through Big House Wedding Inc.'s storeroom of props and decorations. Patti and Samantha had helped too.

Jasper hung around long enough to exchange knowing nods with Harri and to wish Annie a nice evening.

'Shall we?' Harri put out a hand to walk Annie inside.

Stooping, she made her way into the cosy tent and sat on a squashy round cushion. Harri settled himself beside her, crossing his legs.

'Why do I get the feeling this isn't just Clove Lore busybodies mixing in?' Annie asked, her nose wrinkled with suspicion.

'Hah!' Harri was glad she was looking around admiringly. He reached for the contents of the ice bucket at the back of the tent. 'Champagne?'

She laughed in surprise as Harri loosened the cork and let it fly out of the tent onto the dark lawn with a pop.

Her eyes sparkled as much as the liquid in their tall glasses as he proposed a toast.

'To...' he did the maths, 'twelve years of friendship?'

She only hesitated a little before bringing her glass to his with a soft chime. 'To friendship,' she repeated.

As they took their first delicious, crisp sips, Harri arranged the blankets over their legs. Fuzzy, soft and new, he'd been delighted when he found them left over from a Big House wedding at Christmas.

The other movie-goers were noisily arriving and finding their seats. Harri watched them, returning their greetings, but each one of them was conspicuously not coming over to interrogate them.

'That's weird,' Annie remarked. 'They aren't sticking their noses in?'

'Very weird,' Harri said, smiling, trying to ignore Jowan's conspiratorial wink from over by the daffodil beds where he was helping Minty (wrapped from head to boot in vintage furs like she was in *Dr Zhivago*) into her deck-chair. They gripped mugs of steaming, spiced Shiraz.

The aroma from the drinks stall – hot chocolates with marshmallows and a great big pot of mulled wine – wafted in the air.

More and more people arrived. Patti and Austen, the heavily pregnant Joy and Monty, and little Radia in a Paddington Bear duffel coat sat together as one family.

Joy was asking Radia what she wanted to drink. 'Hot chocolate or a babycino?'

'Ugh, babycino!' Radia sulked. 'I'm not a baby.'

Joy, now settled in her deckchair, hauled her big girl up onto her lap and rocked her. Harri just made out the words. 'Radia Pearl, you will always be Mummy's baby, even when you're a little old lady, okay?' And the pair hugged and giggled, and Radia conceded that a babycino with extra marshmallows, 'might be all right, actually'.

Their attention was drawn by the arrival of Estée Gold who was having something of a one-woman red carpet moment as she steamed into the garden in a great glittering gold frock and acres of bunched tulle wrapped around her arms. There was a smattering of confused applause from some of the tourists, and a loud whooping and appreciative catcalling from Leonid and Izaak, who were snuggled together under a duvet in their bobble hats. There were a few eye rolls and tuts as well, but it was all the same to Estée who was having the time of her life at her first launch night in many years.

'Thank you, thank you,' she said graciously as she lowered herself into a deckchair, only struggling a little with her massive gown. Finding herself stuck, she snapped her fingers for a drink and three village husbands jumped to their feet to assist. 'How kind!' she cooed.

Annie was finding all of this delightfully bonkers, of course.

'I'm gonna miss these crackpots,' she said laughing. Harri felt the joy blazing from her body, even through all their layers.

'Rose for the lady, sir?' came an irreverent Scottish voice.

Peeping their head around the flap of the tent they saw Jude Crawley in neck to toe hiking gear and an usherette's headdress on top of her beanie.

'Hey!' Annie welcomed her. 'You're helping here too?'

'That's what we do,' Jude replied, with a knowing stare aimed at Harri. She held out the bucket of single roses, each one wrapped in a brown paper cone.

Annie looked them over.

'Go on, pick one,' said Harri.

Annie was hesitant, her fingers passing over the deep velvet-red blooms, then over the soft pinks, landing on one of the yellow roses. 'I'll take this one, I think? Yellow, for friendship,' she said, falteringly, and making to pull it free.

Harri stopped her with his fingers on the back of her hand. 'How about… this one,' he said, lifting out a lush red bloom. Jude discreetly made herself scarce as soon as he was done.

Annie was watching him, her lips parted, unsure what was going on.

He handed her the flower. 'A long time ago, on our first Valentine's Day, I gave you a bunch of yellow roses, and clearly, you remember.'

Annie screwed her mouth to show she did remember. 'I wish I'd given you red roses then,' he said. 'I wish I'd given you red roses every Valentine's Day.'

She held the flower to her, wordlessly. She seemed to be thinking hard.

Beneath them in the knot garden, the deckchairs were almost filled. The whole village was here, it seemed, and arriving just in time was a fish-out-of-water William Sabine, between Bella and Finan.

So they'd talked him into coming out on his last night in Clove Lore after all? Harri waved to him over all the heads, but William didn't see him. He was clutching a vast box of popcorn and greeting the people around him as Bella wrapped him in blankets and tucked him into his chair with a hot water bottle.

Arriving late, and still looking contrite, having heard more details about the worry they'd caused, were the newlyweds, Bovis and his wife. Their arrival prompted a burst of applause.

'Here,' Jowan made a point of calling over the garden. 'Izaak? I believe I owe you this?' He held a ten-pound note in the air. 'Now these two are officially wed!'

This prompted a lot of standing and rummaging in pockets and exchanging of notes amongst the village gossips.

'What's all this?' Mrs Bovis-Crocombe wanted to know, watching the cash changing hands.

'You thought you were the only one placing bets on love?' said Leonid, pocketing his winnings.

'We've had money on you pair for years,' joined Jude, presenting Bovis with a rose to give to his new wife. 'You made us wait, but I just earned a tenner off you!'

Mrs Crocombe-Bovis made to tut and protest but evidently thought better of it and sat, chuckling, at her husband's side.

The movie was about to begin. Jasper was nervously scanning the crowd. Samantha watched him from the projection tent. She gave him an emphatic double thumbs up.

'Friends and neighbours, welcome,' he shouted, and the garden murmur dropped away. 'This is the first Clove Lore Outdoor Film Society screening. I hope you enjoy tonight's feature, *When Harri Met Annie*, I mean…' he made a show of correcting his mistake, '…*When Harry Met Sally*.' This engendered a lot of laughter and eyes turning towards the little pink tent where Harri's cheeks glowed as pink as the tepee itself. 'Enjoy the film, and Happy Valentine's Day!'

Applause followed him to the booth and in moments the windowless grey wall at the side of Clove Lore Big

House burst into silver light. Speakers around the gardens buzzed awake and the opening titles rolled.

'I, eh, wanted to give you this earlier, but I chickened out,' Harri said to Annie, pulling an envelope from his coat pocket in the comfy enclosure of their tent.

Annie didn't say anything. She exchanged the envelope for her glass, her eyes wide.

'Open it,' he urged.

Annie freed the card from its envelope, the same card she'd seen him picking out late at night in the bookshop when he thought he was unobserved.

She opened it up.

Annwyl, be my Valentine and I'll be yours.

When she lifted her eyes to his, she was brimming with questions, but her words seemed stoppered.

'I wrote this a week ago, and kept it hidden, not knowing what to do,' he said. 'I've kept it all hidden, for years, how I've liked you.'

Annie looked from his face to the card to the rose. 'I thought you were decided on us being just friends, after we talked in the glasshouse.'

'I know, but we talked about it all the wrong way. The other day when I said we should get it out of our systems, I was totally wrong. I don't want to get you out of my system, not ever.'

'What do you want?' Annie said, her face serious.

He turned his body to face her, drawing his knees beneath him, new urgency growing within him. 'I want to ruin our friendship. I want to be your boyfriend. I want to help you with your job and taking on the book-ban people. I want to be there for you every day, making your

298

morning coffee. I want you *in* my system, and me in yours, for keeps. If that's something you want?'

'How would that work, exactly?' she said, still thinking hard, her eyes dancing across his face.

'I don't know,' he said, catching her eyes as they fell. '*But!*' He could not lose her now, not when he was finally making sense. 'But, I was thinking I could come to Texas for a holiday?'

'We've just had a holiday.'

'And we both used this time to get our heads on straight, but I think we need more time together, without all the doubt and wondering. What do you say?'

'You want to come to Amarillo?'

'Definitely. Think how pleased your dad will be!'

This brought a laugh from her lips. Her eyes were sparkling again.

'I need to fix this library stuff. It could get wild. It could be a long fight. Lifelong maybe?'

'I've got the time,' he said.

'You can't just follow me around helping me with my stuff. What about your own dreams? The things you need?'

This stopped him.

'Be serious now,' she told him, looking for all the world like everything depended on whatever he said next.

'I have my barista wages saved up. I want to spend them doing something amazing.' The words spilled out. It was his heart talking. 'I'm going to have my own coffee shop. Like, the *best* coffee shop one day soon. You make me feel like I can achieve that. I swear I'm going to do it.'

Annie laughed in delight. 'Yes you are!'

'And I want you. That's plenty for one man, I'd say.'

She drew her knees to her chest. 'Can you get a plane ticket?'

His hand found his phone, all the while keeping his eyes fixed on her. 'I already made my reservation.'

'What the…?'

'A couple of hours ago, when I realised I'd been thinking and talking but never *doing* anything. Same flight as you. See?' He showed her his e-ticket.

Annie was on the move, casting aside the blankets. For a horrible second he wondered if she was making a run for it, but instead she pulled at the ribbons holding the tent flaps open. In seconds they were enclosed in soft pink light and she'd clambered across his lap with a leg on each side.

Harri blinked up at her. She was smiling wickedly, like all those times she'd hatched a plan and inveigled him into helping her execute it. She was pulling something from her coat pocket, handing it to him. A pink envelope.

He opened it in the small space between them. She watched him, smiling as he found her own Valentine's card.

Inside it read:

If you're sure; I'm sure.

He stared up at her in wonder. 'When did you write this?'

'I got up in the night to do it. I couldn't risk not having a Valentine for you, not if you were going to give me one, and I'd hoped… I'd hoped very much you would.'

Nothing but warmth bloomed between them. Harri spread his hands across her back, pulling her nearer, lifting his mouth to hers.

'Just a kiss,' she said. 'Because we have all the time in the world, right?'

He nodded, feeling every atom in his body responding to her with love.

She lowered her mouth to his in a soft, slow coming together. It only lasted a second and she pulled back to watch his response.

He didn't care that he'd glazed over, that his lips were parted and he was stunned and silent. He let her warmth bloom right out of her body and into his, her fingertips at his cheekbones and in his hair, her eyes drifting over his face. He suddenly had no idea how to breathe. He didn't mind suffocating one bit.

She kissed him again, slower this time, letting her eyes close, everything unhurried and exquisite.

He'd kissed her in the castle library but it hadn't felt like this. This was how two people kissed when they were set on leaving 'friends' behind and searching for deeper feelings, closer connection.

He brought his hands to her face too and they held each other smilingly.

'Is it sunny in Amarillo this time of year?' he said, his voice barely there. She kissed him. 'I'll need some factor fifty, right?' Another slow kiss, languorous. He moaned, but pulled a millimetre away. 'Are there really snakes in Texas?'

She nodded and smiled and opened his mouth with the tip of her tongue. Another slow, aching kiss.

Still, after a moment, he pulled away. 'Is your dad going to murder me?'

They both laughed, already near to forgetting what they were laughing about, then they were kissing again until the formation of actual words and coherent thoughts was a thing beyond their abilities, missing every second of the movie, stopping only when best friends Harry Burns and Sally Albright were finally happily in love, all of their reservations obliterated and their old pain forgotten.

Chapter Twenty-Eight

Moving Day

Seven twenty-six in the morning and they stumbled out of the stacks in the Borrow-A-Bookshop, hair tousled, lips bee stung, eyes sleepy, and both smiling dopily having kissed the whole night away.

While the movie credits rolled, they'd sneaked away from the gardens, beating the crowds and the gossips, running laughing and stumbling all the way down the dark slope, stopping under the Victorian lamps and kissing hard, drinking straight from the Champagne bottle, then slipping and sliding further Down-along, pulling one another into doorways and turnings to kiss some more until they arrived back at the door of the bookshop where they couldn't pull themselves apart to retrieve the keycard from Annie's bag, only stopping when they were both shivering with cold and excitement, when they'd at last fallen in through the door.

Annie had lured a helpless Harri with a crooked finger into the stacks where they'd stayed all night, hands roving over clothes, outer layers dropped to the floor, breathing raggedly, kissing for hours.

The winter dawn's light bled into the shop now.

They stood side by side in the middle of the bookshop, looking around them.

'Did it always look like this?' Annie said. 'Everything seems different.'

'It's like I have new eyes,' Harri said. He laughed and shook his head at how silly it sounded, but everything was new this morning. 'I know what we need,' he said.

'Coffee,' Annie said, 'and hangover buns.'

'Coming right up.' He walked away, only dropping her hand when their arms were fully extended.

Annie stayed where she was. Her eyes fell over their suitcases and bags, which they'd left by the shop counter yesterday before setting off for the movie. She shook her head at the thought of how she'd felt then, bent out of shape and regretful.

Now here she was at dawn with Harri ready to fly all the way to Texas so he could see more of her. Everything had worked out in ways she couldn't have imagined. Her eyes fell on the last box from the castle. It was already opened but only half unpacked. *Almost* everything had worked out. She'd made lots of new friends in Clove Lore, and all of them were happy, except one.

'We should finish that box, before we get our cab to the airport,' she said, just as Harri reappeared with the mugs on a tray and with a glass of water for the red rose that had laid on the counter all night.

He glanced at the shop clock. 'We have time.'

Together they sat on the floor, nothing hurried, everything calm. They tasted their coffees, cortados to wake them up. Annie told him this was her favourite so far and delighted, he'd noted that down in his app.

They lifted books and papers from the box and spread them on the floor. There were some old architectural sketches in faded ink, an engraved stamp which, on closer inspection, they found bore the Courtenay coat of arms, mirror-reversed for sealing letters in wax. There were some receipts for books, yellowed and useless, an expired TV licence, a *Yellow Pages* dated 1983, its dog-eared pages stuffed with pencilled quotes for restoration works on the stable block, which presumably never happened. Harri handed Annie the book that had languished at the bottom of the box.

'*In Memoriam,*' she read from the inside leaf. 'Published in eighteen-fifty.'

'Looks important,' said Harri.

Annie turned the pages and just inside was a hand-written pencilled note in a lovely sloping script which read, 'First edition Tennyson. His poetry grieving the loss of his beloved friend, A. H. Hallam'.

'One of Sir Nicholas's treasures?' said Harri. 'Slipped through the auctioneer's net, this one. We studied Tennyson in first year, remember?'

Annie held the book all the more carefully. 'I bet this is worth something. We'd better make sure William gets it before he goes.'

The mention of their friend brought some quiet pondering. Annie opened the book again, finding a random page, and read.

> '*I hold it true, whate'er befall; I feel it when I sorrow most; Tis better to have loved and lost, Than never to have loved at all.*'

She looked to Harri. 'We definitely need to get this to William. This is a book about grieving your best friend. It might bring him some comfort when he's living who knows where.'

'And we need to get his address so we can keep in touch,' said Harri, standing now. 'I'll ring down to the Siren, make sure he doesn't leave before we see him.'

'I'll grab a shower and get dressed.'

As Annie stood, the leaves of the book opened and from them fell a folded piece of paper. She stooped to lift it. 'More receipts,' she guessed. This paper felt different than the others in the box, thicker, and it was folded in such a curious way, like a flat knot, that it took her a moment to open it out. What she read inside made her throw a hand to her mouth, and before she'd got to the end, tears were stinging her eyes.

'Harri! Look!'

He read the paper in her hands.

'I, Sir Nicholas Courtenay of Clove Lore Castle, appoint as the Executor and Trustee and soul Benefactor of this my last will and testament, Mr William Sabine, my friend these fifty years.'

He stopped, aghast. 'No! I thought he died intestate!'

'Everyone thought so,' Annie said.

Harri read on in snatches. 'Being of sound mind… leaving all that I own to Mr William Sabine… no living relatives… contents to be auctioned off insofar as they cover estate debts and funerary costs… the entirety of Clove Lore Castle and estate grounds to be transferred in right and deed to Mr William Sabine for him to do with as he pleases.'

'It's signed as well, look. And there's the Courtenay crest stamped on it!' Annie pointed to the scratchy signature of Sir Nicholas. 'And it was witnessed.'

Harri peered at the name. 'Dr Mateeva, General Practitioner! That wasn't the doctor who called here, was it? What's the date on this?'

Annie pointed at the page, and Harri stifled what threatened to be a great big sob. 'Last Valentine's Day.'

'The doctor must remember witnessing this?' said Annie, her brain racing ahead.

'But that doctor had no idea who William was when they called here last week to examine him,' said Harri, wiping his eyes, piecing it all together. 'William said they took Nicholas to the hospital to die, and he was already unconscious by then. Doctor Mateeva probably didn't even hear about Sir Nicholas's death, or didn't think to put two and two together when examining William?'

'That makes me think Sir Nicholas did this in secret, without William ever knowing?' said Annie. 'William did tell us his old friend had many doctors call on him at the castle when he was ill.'

Harri let that sink in. 'I bet you're right.'

'Does this mean William owns the castle? Is this even legal?' Annie was growing frantic.

'I've no idea.' Harri was searching the floor for where he'd cast off his coat last night. 'But we need to get this to William before they come for him this morning.'

Chapter Twenty-Nine

Flying

Annie stretched out her legs and snuggled into Harri's side. The seatbelt sign had gone off and the cabin crew was just about to make the rounds with the first coffees after take-off.

Harri was going to accept a cup and even though he knew it would be a crappy cup of airplane instant, he was going to write in his notes app that it was the best damn coffee he'd tasted in his life, he was so profoundly happy.

Annie was already reading, engrossed in her novel. Harri held her close and placed a kiss on the top of her head, watching the white fluffy clouds as they sped by.

He smiled to himself at the memory of that last two hours in Clove Lore this morning; the way they'd run and skidded and screeched all the way down to the Siren, scaring the living daylights out of Kit who was cooking the breakfasts for the Valentine weekenders staying over at the pub.

They'd found William awake and in his overcoat waiting solemnly for the local authority car coming to take him to the flat in Yelverton, miles from Castle Lore and all of his treasured memories.

There'd been a lot of excitement, so much so William had to comfort Annie as she cried. It had taken a while for the discovery to sink in. William's old friend had wanted to reward his years of devotion and companionship. Even when Sir Nicholas, had been wracked with pain and growing thinner and weaker by the day, he'd made sure there was something in writing to protect his friend.

'But why didn't he tell anyone? Why didn't he tell you?' Harri wanted to know, returning the Tennyson to its rightful owner at the same time.

William had only smiled tearfully. The truth was William would have refused his friend's gift, telling him his friendship had been enough for him, that knowing him and being known was worth the pain of losing him in the end, of losing everything; something that their favourite poet knew more than a little about himself.

Bella had rung for a solicitor friend to come down to the pub, and she made sure to tell Social Services when the car came that Mr Sabine found he no longer required the flat in Yelverton, that he was, in fact, staying right here with his friends until this was all sorted out.

Minty had turned up – as though somehow she'd felt a disturbance in the Clove Lore air and been supernaturally summoned – and once she was availed of all the facts, took it upon herself to ring the Clove Lore Holiday Park to let them know there was a spanner in the works with their purchase of the castle.

William, however, had been clear. If he was to inherit the crumbling old place, he'd be glad to sell it so that the grounds might be filled for once with families and children and noise and laughter, all of the things he would have wished for his beloved friend Nicholas, had he been able to stand the clamour and chaos of other people and the wider world.

William had pulled the heavy old key from his breast pocket and asked Minty for yet one more favour. He would like to visit his old home, just for a short while.

She had set about activating the Clove Lore phone network, telling the whole village that today was the day they would get a look at the castle while it remained the way William would always remember it.

They'd had to leave at that point, Harri and Annie, knowing their cab was on its way. They had just enough time to get up the slope and pull books from the shelves to replace the Valentine's titles, books to reflect their particular interests.

It hadn't taken long to make their display, given that there were so many books that fit their chosen criteria.

Lady Chatterley's Lover, *The Bluest Eye*, *Ulysses*, *The Well of Loneliness*, *Annie on My Mind*, and in case their theme wasn't clear to everyone, right in the middle of the table on a Perspex riser, a copy of a charming children's story about a secret society of kids who set out to read books rendered tantalising and intriguing by the disapproval of the grown-ups, *Ban This Book* by Alan Gratz, which, perhaps predictably, had also found itself banned.

Harri left his cases (and his tomato seedlings) up at the Big House, knowing any homeward journey would have to include coming back here to check up on William and all of his new friends. He'd set off for the airport with only a backpack.

He couldn't know if Annie – his Annwyl – would accompany him on that return trip, but he was certain that any separation would be temporary. They had their whole lives together to work out the where and the how of it all. For now, he had her in his arms and that was what mattered.

As the plane circled over the South West, making its way out over the wide expanse of sparkling ocean, the late winter sun shone low in the sky.

Down below, unbeknown to Harri and Annie, the next Borrower was making their way down the slope, enjoying the mid-February sunshine, thinking of getting an ice cream perhaps, and planning on a quiet fortnight of untroubled bookselling.

Meanwhile, on the tallest tower of Clove Lore Castle, observed by a gathered crowd of newly forged friends, all busybodies and matchmakers and book-lovers and the kindest of neighbours, William Sabine smiled at the sight of the Courtenay flag being hoisted into the air. It unfurled against the blue sky: an ancient crest depicting an open book and above its elegant curling pages, two hearts forever entwined.

A letter from Kiley

Hello, lovely readers!

Here we are, back in Clove Lore for book number five in the Borrow-A-Bookshop series! You can read this story as a standalone book, but if you want to go right back to where it all started then you need *The Borrow a Bookshop Holiday* (2021).

This time we're meeting old uni pals, **Annie and Harri**. She's a Texan librarian and he's a bookish Welsh barista and they're reuniting for a fortnight's bookselling by the English seaside having not seen each other for the best part of a decade. The trouble is Harri's having a hard time ignoring his old feelings for Annie, and Annie's got too much on her mind to even consider a holiday romance; that is, until Clove Lore begins to work its magic.

This story is about the wonder of that rare and precious thing, lifelong friendship. I have been beyond fortunate to have in my life my best friends **Mouse and Nic** and their combined fifty-three years of love and companionship. I bless the days I met you both.

This story also features the themes **of reading for wellness** and **the vital importance of being able to read freely for education and for pleasure** and the insidious dangers of book banning. All of my books contain some kind of protest, it's in my nature, and if you thought romance novels aren't (or shouldn't be) political, well, that in itself is political. I hope this book does good and most importantly makes you feel good.

Thank you to **Hera Books** for letting me write all the things I want to write about. We've made eleven books together so far and I've loved every second. Thank you so very much for everything, Keshini Naidoo and Lindsey Mooney. Thank you also to everyone at Hera and Canelo, and to Diane Meacham for her beautiful cover art all these years.

Thank you also to Liz, MJ, Vicky, Gaynor and Stephanie for answering all of my questions about topics in this story and generally being sweethearts.

I owe a big thank you to **Foster's Little Bookshop** (The Victorian Arcade, Barnsley) for introducing me to the idea of a silent book club. I've loved following their cosy group reading sessions on Instagram. Since I can't get to Foster's to take part, I made up my own silent reading event right here in the Borrow-A-Bookshop on a wintry, firelit night (and it proves to be a *very* tense evening for poor Harri, who is forced to read in silence when he'd rather be letting Annie know exactly how he feels about her). Don't you just love that angsty tension when one of the pair is unaware of the other's feelings? Although, Annie may not be quite so oblivious as Harri thinks!

I sincerely hope you enjoy your return visit to Clove Lore, or if this is your first visit, I hope it was love at first sight and you'll return again very soon.

If you enjoyed *A New Chapter at the Borrow a Bookshop* please consider leaving a review and some stars on your favourite reviewing platform. It seriously does mean the world to me when you do.

You can keep up to date with everything going on at the Borrow-A-Bookshop by signing up to my quarterly subscribers' newsletter found here on my website: http://www.kileydunbar.co.uk/ or come and say 'hello' on my Facebook page: https://www.facebook.com/KileyDunbarAuthor/ or my Instagram: https://www.instagram.com/kileydunbarauthor/

Until we meet again, I wish you many happy hours of freely reading whichever fabulous books take your fancy.

Love,

Kiley, x